THE DARK WEB OF THE BROTHERHOOD
|————— 1882 —————|

The Dark Web of the Brotherhood
1882

Helen Walsh Folsom

Published by
Montlake Romance

The characters and events portrayed in this book are fictitious. Any similarity to real persons, living or dead, is coincidental and not intended by the author.

Text copyright © 2012 Helen Walsh Folsom

All rights reserved.
Printed in the United States of America.

No part of this book may be reproduced, or stored in a retrieval system, or transmitted in any form or by any means, electronic, mechanical, photocopying, recording, or otherwise, without express written permission of the publisher.

Published by Montlake Romance
P.O. Box 400818
Las Vegas, NV 89140

ISBN-13: 9781612186580
ISBN-10: 1612186580

To Anthony,
TO A family member by marriage, but a tremendous addition to my family! GOD brought you into our lives, and our hearts, son! Butch

This book is dedicated to the Author of Language: a porpoise may whistle a call of warning to his fellows, and an elephant's earthshaking nasal roar will declare his kingship of the jungle, but only the words of a human being can describe the flaming burst of a volcano's scattered shower of blazing crystalline rocks...or the delicate, frail pink center of a yellow tea rose.

Chapter 1

"Dear saints, will you be looking at those long knives!" Fianna leaned forward in the seat of the covered carriage and stared at the Royal Irish Constabulary in dark-green uniforms lined up along the train track.

"Hush, lass! Those knives are called bayonets, and they're razor-sharp. And those guns, they are fixed too—they're filled with buckshot." Sean Rooney turned a bit on the driver's seat and frowned back at Fianna. "Don't be talking so loud. Many are the women that have been arrested and thrown into jail for saying only a word against the RIC. Even children too. Believe that, lass! D'ye see now why Marcus Maher and your cousin, Brandeen, didn't want you to be traveling across Ireland on the train alone?"

The stocky, broad-faced stable master pulled the horse to a stop on the cobbled street. Townspeople of Castlebar and all the townland around were hurrying past the carriage to join the crowd already milling about the railway station. Uniformed RIC police stood in formation, rifles at the ready, waiting for the least sign of rebellion in the excited mob.

Farmers in coarse brawn trousers and threadbare sweaters stood with their hands in their pockets, careful not to make any move that could be interpreted as hostile toward the officers. Their silent wives huddled in thick woolen shawls against the soft, misty rain. Voices were muted, bodies massed together a safe distance from the gleaming bayonets. But their eyes under battered hats and heavy cotton kerchiefs spoke volumes of outrage, hate, and fury.

Sean Rooney stopped a rosy-faced boy trotting to catch up with the rest of his family. "Here now, lad. What would all the fuss be about today?"

"And don't you know? Himself is coming on the train from Mayo. 'Tis the grand Charles Stewart Parnell, it is, coming to make a speech for his man of choice in the election—Captain O'Shea!"

"That's grand, for sure. But why are the police standing guard? The great man is no troublemaker, sure."

The boy stopped still. He frowned and leaned close to Sean to whisper, "The Peelers are always about, everywhere. Arrested my little cousin, Mary O'Sullivan, just for grinning at one of them—and she, only twelve years old. Said she was disrespectful of the law."

Alarm came into the boy's blue eyes then. Abruptly, he turned and ran on toward the assembly, obviously afraid that he had said too much.

"Why, that little lad is scared to death!" Fianna observed. She couldn't help feeling sorry for the young fellow.

Sean turned full around on the seat. "And well he might be! It's dangerous just to say a word in Ireland in these times." His voice was low. "The Parliament's not caring about justice— only keeping us from making trouble against them. You've been out there at Leaghanor in County Clare, not even seeing Dublin for a year now, while Parnell has been stirring things up, talking about Ireland having Home Rule. England's new chief secretary of Ireland is a fellow named William Forster, who hates us and fears us at the same time. You're not knowing how he has come down on the people."

"I do know." Her dark eyes were angry. "Marcus brings home *United Ireland* newspapers."

"Quiet now, lass. You don't know how close it strikes. Why did you not go with Marcus and Brandeen on one of your Fitzmichael ships around the coast to Dublin instead of demanding to ride the train?"

Fianna lifted that stubborn chin in the attitude Sean Rooney knew so well. "You'd be knowing why I did not go with them. I'm waiting—sure that Jamie will be coming back soon. It takes a week longer by ship to go to Dublin, a week that I would not be there if he comes. I'm not wanting to take this fool trip to England anyway. I hardly know my sister, Alice. I haven't seen her for nine years—not since she married into that pompous Nugent family and went to live in England. I will hate having to be among them."

Sean Rooney's expression changed from scolding to deep sadness. "Sure. I'm missing my boy too. Jamie's my son, and I'm bound that I love him more than you do. I watch for him day and night, hoping to see him come walking up the drive to the Big House of Leaghanor, or see him standing in the open doors to the stable. I've heard little from him since he left, and it's hard not knowing what he is doing—only that he still hopes to start himself a horse breeding farm in spite of the Ascendancy's objections to the Irish owning land. But your family is right, Fianna Fitzmichael. It's not good for you to spend months of your young

3

life out there in the lonely hills of Connaught just waiting for Jamie to come back home."

With youthful certainty, Fianna shook her head so hard that the big black bow holding back her rich red-brown hair nearly came loose. "I'm sure I love him more than you, Sean Rooney. I want to marry him and spend my life with him."

"So you're thinking." He studied the girl in her expensive fawn-colored travel suit and saucy straw boater. "I'm wondering how you would match up—you, the daughter of a fine, wealthy family with a shipping company, and him, the son of a stableman. Sure, I can see now that it was a mistake for them to ask Jamie to be your playmate while you were growing up. But you were so lonely, what with your folks dead and your sister married and gone. He's a good boy and was glad to do it. Took a real liking to you, he did."

"It's more than just a liking. You'll see when he comes back to me."

Fianna barely had the words out of her mouth before a shout went up from the crowd near the station. Smoke from the engine of the train appeared around a stony curve of the hillside. The police lowered their weapons forward, eyes glaring from under their black leather helmets, menacing the people with their gleaming bayonets. The crowd hung back, but their excited voices still rose in welcome to the famous Parnell, the "Uncrowned King of Ireland," as the black engine roared to a stop alongside of the stone depot building.

"Plain it is that we'll not be able to get near the railway here," Sean said. "I'm getting you out of here before trouble starts."

"But Parnell? And the train—"

Sean whipped the horse into a full turn and headed fast onto the road that led away from Castlebar.

"It's not safe for you here," he called to her over his shoulder. "Even Parnell can't stop it if trouble starts. It could get fair bloody, and I'd not want to be to blame if you were hurt. Marcus and Mrs. Brandeen will be watching for you in Dublin. It will take the train a while in Castlebar, with the crowd and himself speeching and all. We'll make it to the stop at Balle to put you on that same train in good time."

Rocking in the carriage over rough country roads, Fianna thought about Sean Rooney's words. Crossing stone bridges over rushing streams, breathing the scent of wet green leaves and hay, watching the soft ridges of blue-green mountains not far away, she found it hard to imagine the seething fury building ever higher in the hearts of the Irish. She leaned forward under the carriage hood to see out across the meadows. Sometimes she glimpsed a sleek horse or a flock of black-faced white sheep ignoring the steady, soft rain as they grazed on the green between weatherworn limestones.

Jamie loved horses. His dream was to own a small farm and produce grand mounts fit for the races at Kildare and the Dublin Horse Show. *It might be possible,* she thought, with the help of the Land League. With pressure put on the British by Parnell in the Parliament, and Captain Moonlight raids out in the fields, new laws were being passed. Those laws allowed some farmers to sell their rights to their plots. With a decent bit of money, Jamie might be able to pay down on a small farm and buy a good stud and a couple of mares.

He taught Fianna to love horses too. When she had learned to ride, she was still a little girl, so Jamie had put her astride a saddle and she had never changed to sidesaddle. It made it easier for the two young people to go racing up into the mountains together, rejoicing in the wind on the powerful animals. Sure, they could go on like that through life! She had told him that.

It happened one day a year ago. There they were, knee-deep in Lough Sheeaun, Fianna's skirts caught up in her apron, the delicious cold water washing around her bare feet on the smooth rocks below. They were fishing in the sparkling lake in the meadow below the Fitzmichaels' house at Leaghanor. Fianna thought she felt a tug on her pole and started to yank on it. She lost her balance and would have fallen if Jamie had not caught her.

His sturdy arms were around her, holding her tight against him to keep her from sliding down into the water. Suddenly, she realized how firm and strong they were, how protective. Something strange went through her, a tingling excitement. He held her up, his merry blue eyes only inches from hers. It was then she knew that she loved him, and she said it. He grinned, and his ruddy, round Irish face turned the color of his brick-red curly hair.

"Shame on you, Fianna Fitzmichael," he scolded, teasing. "Such talk from a lady of the Big House. Put such ideas out of yer head."

"I will not! Jamie Rooney, you love me too, now don't you? Say it!"

She stood nose to nose with him, demanding an answer—the *right* answer! He still held her, that embarrassed grin across his face. A lovely man he was, and he was the man for Fianna!

Then he sobered. "Sure, and who wouldn't love you, girl? You're a beauty, you are. It's grand to see you riding on that chestnut mare and the sun shining copper on your dark hair. We've had grand times."

It wasn't the right kind of answer.

"Then shall we be married, Jamie boy?"

Carefully, he loosed his hold and steadied her on her feet in the water. Then he laid his hand against her cheek, studying the glow of rose on her skin, the fine arch of her brows above the wide brown eyes.

"You honor me, Fianna girl. But it won't do. I have nothing to offer you. So let's be talking no more of this."

Impulsively, so his refusal should not bruise her pride, he kissed her cheek. Immediately her arms encircled his neck, and she drew him into an embrace that he could not resist. There was an electric vibrance between them.

Jamie drew away and set her on her feet. His usually merry eyes became dark and intense, gazing at her.

"Fianna Fitzmichael, don't you feel the spell that's been put on us? It's a bad thing, it is."

"It's a wonderful, thrilling spell, Jamie boy," she murmured.

"I should not be talking to you this way. We should not be talking love, not us two. I'm thinking we'd best be putting a stop to our constant company. And, sure, I'd best be getting about making a man's life for myself."

"Jamie—" She started to lean toward him but he pushed her away.

"Think clear about it, Fianna. You're seventeen and ripe and ready for a good husband—some fine man who can make a living for you and the children you'll have. I'm not that man."

Suddenly taking her shoulders, he shook her.

"Now stop it! You are like family to me. You don't know what you are doing. I do!"

Fianna leaned against him again. "I've loved you for years but never put a name to it until now."

He smiled sadly. "There you are, ever the strongheaded, stubborn little lass. Well then, it's up to me. Pick up your fishing pole and get yourself up to the house! Your supper will be waiting!"

And that was it. He acted angry, and Fianna couldn't change his mind. Excited about her new emotions and certain that she would make him see her way eventually, Fianna laughed and carried her pole and bucket happily up the meadow to the house.

He was gone by the next morning.

A full year had gone by. At first she stormed about the place, commanding Marcus to send messages out and find him. Where had he gone? Dublin? Jamie liked Dublin because of the Phoenix Park races and the annual horse show. Marcus sent messages, but no one had seen him there.

They inquired at Kildare and the pony farms in Connemara, but the trainers and stable hands said he was not there.

Could he have taken ship and gone to America, as so many were doing? *Oh, dear Saint Brigid, no! They never come back from America!*

It was against her nature to be patient, and she was not, but she decided to wait. Surely he loved her too much to stay away. Day after day she went through the motions of living, but it was obvious to the household that she was agonizing after Jamie Rooney.

Finally, Marcus and Brandeen decided she must get away from the boredom and loneliness of the west of Ireland. It would be good for her to go to London, where there were young people and music and lively activity. Alice lived there with her kindly, good-humored husband. They told her at supper one evening.

"So, you'd be packing me off to London now?" Glaring around the table at the family, she burst out, "And why would you be wanting me to go there? Sister or not, Alice and I hardly know each other, and, sure, I'd not be wanting to visit that snobbish Nugent family!"

"You will go." Brandeen calmly buttered a scone and continued. "You're needing perspective, that's what it is." Brandeen Fitzmichael Maher accepted the tea that the housekeeper poured for her. She was dressed in one of her favorite light cotton gowns. Dappled sunlight filtered through the lace curtains of the dining room at Leaghanor and gave flame to her red-gold hair. Fianna had never really liked her, even though the older cousin had brought some stability to the household after all the troubles. Fianna did not like her now.

"Well now, it's true, pet," Marcus Maher spoke gently. He leaned over the wooden high chair where his five-year-old son sat waiting for his supper. Marcus spooned a bite of cornmeal stirabout from the bowl for him. "There you are, Kells Fitzmichael Maher. It's a fine man you'll grow up to be if you eat it all. Now, Fianna, we have all been troubled about you. A fortnight holiday in London will be good for you. Parties, no doubt, and young people about. Not like being buried out here in the west of Mayo with nought but farmers and sheep."

Marcus handed little Kells the spoon and pushed back his own curly black hair, which was ever determined to be unruly. Then he looked at Fianna with those familiar blue eyes and made a tender smile for his favorite young friend.

"And it's a good time for you to be going." Brandeen added honey to her tea and stirred it briskly. "Marcus and I are going to Dublin. The family needs to concentrate our efforts to expand Fitzmichael Freighting Company. We'll be leaving by ship from the bay three days from now and sail around the southern coast, stopping off at Kinsale and Queenstown harbors. You will come with us until we reach Dublin. Then we will put you on the ferryboat for Liverpool while we go on to France. Alice's husband, Rodney Nugent, will meet you in Liverpool and take you to the Nugent house just outside of London. Rodney and Alice are looking forward to having you."

"And what of that pompous Horace Nugent?" Fianna asked acidly. "That grand old member of Parliament likely won't welcome one of us barbaric Irish into his home."

Brandeen smiled in agreement. "Quite true—but it seems from Alice's letters that she and her odd little Rodney have living quarters in the great mansion far apart from his people. The twins annoy their grandparents."

"And how would you be making me go?" Fianna asked smugly. *Will they drag me away bodily?*

Fianna pressed her full pink lips together in a firm line, but it was plain to see that she knew it was hopeless. Tears of frustration might have welled up in her eyes, if ever she allowed them to—which she did not.

She set forth her final demand. "Well then, I'll not be piddling around the coast with you. That I will not! If you are determined that I must go on this jaunt, then I'll be taking the train and meet you in Dublin."

Their arguments and warnings did no good. She had her way in this at least. Now the carriage had arrived at Balle, and Fianna paced the platform, anxious to get on the way and get this two-week ordeal over with. She had her parasol open, but the rain had almost stopped. That was a relief. It had rained more than usual since late winter, and the ground was saturated. Even Fianna's crisp little suit felt damp, and she could smell the moist wool mixed with silk in the poplin cloth. Expensive narrow brown-velvet piping edged the high mandarin collar and the cuffs of the sleeves. The skirt had just the hint of a fashionable bustle in the back. Her little straw boater was decorated with two or three silk flowers.

Fianna's big trunk was on its way to England by ship. Sean Rooney took her carpetbag, and a basket of biscuits and scones prepared by the cook at Leaghanor, out of the carriage and put it beside the track. He sat down on a bench beside the little depot's stone wall and watched Fianna pacing back and forth on the platform.

The skirt of her crisp fawn-colored suit swished at every impatient step of her high-buttoned black boots. She was a beauty. Sure, she had grown to become a pretty lass, not much like the sallow-skinned, unhappy little girl she used to be.

Born just five years after Sean's own boy, Fianna seemed to be unwanted by her mother. Priscilla Fitzmichael already had a lovely pair of eight-year-old twins, a lass named Alice to groom to marry well and bring higher social standing to the family, and a son who sadly died before he could inherit the family fortunes.

So Fianna grew up generally ignored, except for the children's tutor, Marcus Maher, himself a motherless foundling adopted and educated by Fianna's grandmother. Ah, indeed, Marcus was a kind fellow and took the place of a doting uncle to little Fiona, whom he insisted upon calling "Fianna."

A big change had come into Fianna's life, Sean remembered, the year that her cousin, Brandeen, arrived at the Big House of Leaghanor. Fianna's brother drowned in Lough Sheeaun. The girl's mother became wild and strange and was killed in a fall from the upper floor of the Big House.

Sean shook his head. Without a father, himself killed years before in the races at Kildare, Fianna was left lost and confused and fearful.

Sure then, as might be expected, Fianna became grandly spoiled. As long as it didn't place her life in danger, Brandeen

11

and Marcus—even the house servants—gave in to Fianna's every wish.

Now Sean could see the lass getting more and more agitated, waiting for the train to come clanging and hissing into Balle. He grinned when she turned her back to him to stare down the track, gloved hands on her hips in that impatient manner—just as she always did when she was a frustrated little girl. At eighteen she was still the same impetuous, stubborn lass.

She marched to the end of the flagstone platform and stated, "The stupid train is not coming. We will wait no longer, Sean Rooney. You will take me back home."

Slowly, deliberately, Sean shook his head. "No, lass. Likely it is held up at Castlebar, what with Parnell's speeching and all. We will not be going back to the Big House. We will wait."

Fianna stamped her foot and scolded, "You know quite well that I don't want to go on this ridiculous trip! And you know why. Take me home now!"

Sean studied his rough, work-worn hands as he responded, "That I will not do. Your family has decided you should go and visit your sister in Londontown, and you will."

The girl was angry at the stable master's unbelievable refusal to obey her order. But she had known Sean Rooney all her life, and it was plain he was not going to budge. She stomped off down the platform again, waiting.

"Ye'll be careful on the trip now, child, d'ye hear me?" Sean called to her. She turned and walked back toward him. His ruddy face and sturdy body, so much like Jamie's, was dear to her. His red curly hair was now mostly gray. Fianna always knew she could depend on his good old heart.

"I will be careful," she replied. "I'm prepared for trouble," she added, patting her soft leather reticule.

Sean squinted at the purse, at the place where it sagged heavy at the bottom.

"Why, it's yer pepperbox, you're taking! Will that suit the English society folk?"

"I care not what suits them! My pistol will ward off any troublemakers on the way. And you're knowing I can use it. Jamie taught me well."

Worry wrinkled Sean's brow. "Listen now, Fianna lass, if the RIC find that gun on you, you'll be arrested sure."

"Arrested? I hope they will. My family has influence—"

"That they do. But it's Irish you are. And if the Peelers could clap the great Charles Stewart Parnell in Kilmainham Gaol, and himself a member of Parliament, they wouldn't think twice to lock away an Irish girl on suspicion of treason. For that matter, they could hang you on the spot and never be called to account for it. It's happened! Sure, I'm going with you. I can't be letting you go all the way to Dublin alone in these terrible times!"

"You will not, Sean Rooney! By this very evening I will be in Dublin with Marcus and Brandeen. But perhaps I should take Marcus's advice then and go by my legal name while I'm away. He says that 'Fianna' is not only the name of the ancient Finn MacCool's army; it is now used as another name for the Fenians of the Irish Republican Brotherhood. The very sound of it could set off the Royal Irish Constabulary, the British army, and the prime minister himself, he says. So, Sean Rooney, just go to church and ask Father Tobin to pray for *Fiona* Fitzmichael."

It wasn't long before they heard the raspy toot of the train whistle up the track.

Chapter 2

The last of the three wooden coaches would wag like a dog's tail as it followed along the narrow-gauge track. The first coach was too near the locomotive and the baggage car in the front of the train, and nothing could keep the black smoke from seeping through the windows, choking the passengers, and sifting soot over their clothes and luggage. Sean Rooney settled Fianna in the second coach of the train.

Fianna found one of the woven straw double seats that was not too worn. Ragged edges of the coarse webbing could scratch and drag the threads of her nice suit. The stable master lifted her carpetbag and slid it onto the wooden shelf above her that ran the length of the car. With the basket of barmbrack and scones on the seat next to her and her heavy purse on her lap, Fianna was ready for the journey across Ireland to Dublin.

As Sean patted her shoulder and started to leave, she stood up and impulsively gave him a soft kiss on his leathery cheek.

"I'll be coming back soon, Sean Rooney," she said. "All of Leaghanor's children will come back, especially your Jamie."

He grinned, a bit embarrassed but appreciative. "That you will, lass. And, sure, me boy will too." Then he shuffled through the aisle to the fore of the car and swung himself down off the steps of the train.

The only other passengers were three young fellows clustered in the front of the car. As she had boarded the train, Fianna had noticed just a few people in the car ahead. Not too many people rode the train from Connaught eastward, and those who may have been on earlier likely got off in Castlebar to hear Parnell speak.

From their style of clothes, Fianna assumed that the young men in her car were college students on holiday from school. Their hats were wide-brimmed and flat. Short tweed jackets were worn over stiff-collared white shirts. They lounged on the seats, laughing and comparing notes on the hurling game they had watched in Mayo. As Sean Rooney ambled off the train, one of the boys turned around and tilted the brim of his hat, boldly allowing his dark eyes to roam over Fianna's pretty face and figure. Then he gave her a curious wink, and an invitational smile spread below what appeared to be a futile effort to grow a thin black mustache.

Fianna's chin went up, and she deliberately turned her eyes to the sooty window, where she could see Sean Rooney waiting on the platform for the train to pull out. Possibly the young man thought she was "easy," riding alone on the train. She knew it was not often seen—a lady traveling on the train unescorted. So be it. She would let him know right quick that she was not looking for good-time company.

She caught his offended glare before he turned back to his fellows, and she saw little more than the back of his straight black hair thereafter. A second boy sat against the window, and she could see very little of him. But the third, who actually sat in a seat five rows up and directly in front of her, took off his hat and dropped it on his seat in order to stand up and adjust his fishing rods and tackle basket on the overhead rack.

He had flaming-red hair, rather curly but trimmed short. In the tweed jacket, he seemed to be well built, although the narrow stripes of his trousers accentuated tall, slim legs. As he started to sit down, he glanced at Fianna and gave a quick nod and smile before he turned back to rejoin his friends' animated conversation.

Except for a couple of short stops for the post, no more passengers came on the wobbling, bumpy train until they arrived at Ballyhaunis. Then two young ladies in ruffle-collared waists with perky bustles on their skirts came aboard, followed by a single tall man. Apparently the girls knew one of the fellows—the one with the attempt at a mustache. Introductions were made, and soon the five young people were making a merry group. The boy who sat on the front seat by the window left his place so that one girl could sit beside the dark-haired fellow. Then he politely joined the girl who had settled herself on the second seat. The red-haired fellow sat across the aisle but turned comfortably to take part in the jovial company.

As the lone tall man passed Fianna on his way to a seat in the back, he politely touched the brim of his old tweed flat cap and looked her over, swiftly but thoroughly.

He wore a rough brown woolen coat and trousers, with no waistcoat over his frayed muslin shirt. A well-trimmed light-brown Prince Albert beard covered the lower half of his face. Fianna couldn't help but notice that his boots made almost no sound on the wooden floor of the car as he walked between the line of seats. He was wearing pampootie boots, the soft leather kind that men wore on the seacoast.

Something about him nudged Fianna. He seemed polite enough, but his bright-blue eyes were too forward, almost rude. Although the man—slightly paunchy, with a short beard and tacky clothing—appeared to be a simple country farmer, something gave her a feeling of arrogance, something familiar. She didn't like him.

Her instincts were right. At the very next stop, he came forward in the car and sat down across the aisle from her. Fianna was glad that her food basket took up the rest of her double seat.

"Traveling alone, my lass?" His voice was smooth, almost oily, and had no accent of the western counties of Ireland.

I'm not your lass! she thought.

"I'm quite accustomed to it. I've been to Dublin many times."

"Ah, Dublin is it? Grand town. I know it well. Where will you be staying?"

Fianna turned away as if to study the scenes passing the smoky window. "With my family."

"Indeed?"

No answer. The man sat for a while, appraising her suit, her figure, her dark, wavy hair caught in the big bow below her little straw hat, even her soft black boots. Fianna could feel his brazen stare. Her cheeks began to redden. She sat stiffly, holding her reticule tight and her chin high.

"These Irish trains aren't fit for people. They should be carrying cattle, don't you agree?" he asked confidently, in a stiff Irish accent that she couldn't quite identify.

Why would Irish trains be different from any other? Fianna kept silent.

With no answer from her, the man's attitude did a swift change. Apparently he was annoyed that she would not make encouraging conversation with him. After all, surely a young woman alone on the train was an obvious invitation to become familiar. He sat in the seat, glaring first across the aisle at Fianna and then at the noisy young people five rows in front of him and then at Fianna again. At the next stop, he rose up and went to a seat two rows behind and opposite from her.

She saw the red-haired boy glance her way, listening to the older man's fruitless but embarrassing attempts to get familiar with Fianna. A few minutes after the man moved away, the boy made his way through the wobbling train to her. He leaned close, comprehension of her awkward situation in his dark-hazel eyes. Casting a slight, knowing nod toward the older man, he spoke in a low, slightly husky voice covered by the racket of the clacketing wheels of the train.

"My name is Neill McBride, miss. We'd be pleased if you'd be joining us up front. You might be more comfortable."

Fianna smiled. The young man's hazel eyes were thoughtfully sincere without a hint of flirtation, clearly concerned only for her discretion. At her smile, he smiled back, a disarming grin in a slightly freckled face, eyes crinkling up in mutual understanding.

"I thank you, sure, for the offer, but I'm fine here with my basket and things. I'll do for now."

"So be it, but we have hours before we reach Dublin. If you feel the need for company, you are welcome to come along, and I'll help you with your basket."

Fianna settled back into her seat. There was something she liked about the young fellow. He was not handsome as masculine attraction went, but there was an easy friendliness in his manner that revealed confidence in himself—a sort of assurance that he could approach other people and have never a care if he was rebuffed. Perhaps it had to do with that red-gold question mark of a cowlick in the front of his thick, wavy carrot-red hair. She watched him go forward in the aisle to his friends, holding on to the upper corners of the seats to steady his steps, his boots clicking on the bare floorboards.

After a while there was a stop at a small village. Fianna could see country people standing in clusters on the single winding street of the town, watching dark-green-coated police on the platform, bayoneted shotguns in hand. An older woman climbed the steps into the car, her eyes red with tears, her shoulders slumped with grief under her rough woolen shawl. She stumbled blindly between the seats, avoiding the well-dressed, merry young group in the front, and, weeping, dropped heavily onto the seat across the aisle from Fianna, her belongings in a sort of kerchief knapsack on her lap.

At the same stop, a thin fellow with a concertina got onto the train. He wore the coarse muslin shirt and dark vest of a farmer and a shabby tam-o'-shanter on his head. Seeing the young folks in a cluster, he found a stool and sat down in the corner facing them, unbuckling his instrument. As the train shook itself into motion again, a lively jig filled the car. The group of students sang along, enjoying the music and laughing.

The tall man in the back glowered and seemed to bristle at the noise. He crossed his arms and sat stiffly, glaring at the fellow passengers.

Fianna opened her basket, and the woman accepted a scone gratefully. The red-haired boy named Neill brought a jar of cold tea, pouring some into a tin cup so that she could wash down the roll. He leaned over the old lady, a freckled hand on her shoulder while she tried to gain control of herself. Finally, she was able to thank Fianna and the young fellow, and he went back to his friends. Fianna questioned her gently.

"What is your name, mistress, and what would you be doing on this train and so upset as you are?"

"Me name is Eileen McCrory. My good man is long since dead of the coughing disease. It's me boy, my Tommy, that's got me on this train," the woman hiccuped. "There's been a deal of trouble in our townland. The Peelers have got him in Richmond Gaol in Dublin. They'll be sending him to prison in England tomorrow. I barely got permission from the police to go see him, if he's still alive, and I have to get there tonight, don't ye see?"

"Sure, and you'll be doing that," Fianna murmured as soothingly as she could. Perhaps Sean Rooney was right. Things might be much worse across Ireland than she knew. First the terrified little boy on the street in Castlebar. Now this poor old woman driven to desperation just to get a glimpse of her son before he disappears for life. "What did he do to go to jail?"

"The process man was going to serve papers on the McGees, their farm being just down the road from ours. They had a sick old woman in there, McGee's mam, and his wife is going to be birthing a baby any time now. They crashed in the walls of the house with a battering ram and dragged the family out onto the road with nowhere to go. I know our place will be next, for sure. A clutch of our boys tried to stand in the way, and the police, they shot at them. Old Forster's buckshot killed two and wounded more. Then the Peelers, they just waded into the crowd with those knives on their guns, swinging them this way and that. They stabbed Corlie Mahaney to death. Me boy Tommy was cut on the arm pretty bad, but they arrested him and took him away. When he is gone to England or beyond, I know I will never see him again!"

Her last words were a wail and brought a scowl from the man in the back.

Fianna tried to comfort the woman, but words were hard to come by. She knew that every word that Eileen McCrory said was true. If the boy was not hanged or shot in jail in Dublin, he would be lucky. Then again, the sadistic guards in British prisons were legendary. The boy might be better off in heaven.

The train vibrated and rocked as it gathered speed on the narrow-gauge tracks. A drumlin loomed ahead, and the train wobbled around the hillock. In Ireland it was too costly to move stony hills to cut the railbed through. Like the people, the railroad resigned itself to tolerate inconveniences. It circumvented bogs, passed through old streambeds, and chugged over and down inclines.

Overhead, the sky was thick with curds of gray clouds. Rain fell hard outside the coach, darkening the fields and glens they passed. By leaning close to the window, Fianna could see ahead eastward, where light shone pale yellow and azure beyond the dark edge of clouds. Likely they would pull out from under the clouds soon, and she would be in Dublin before the rain caught up with them again.

They crossed the River Shannon where the ruins of an ancient castle stood on the western bank. It had always intrigued Fianna as she traveled to Dublin with Marcus. Someday she would visit a castle, if she could wangle an invitation from an English landlord.

Long since, the countryside had changed as the train traveled through. Deep-green mountains were left behind, along with the white, stony hills of Connaught. The patchwork of the fields of Roscommon became the farming midlands of Westmeath.

Fianna shook her head at the sights. The insanity of it all! Where verdant, rich lands should have been thick with late summer crops, some lay fallow. Farmhouses stood with their roofs torn off, the stones of the walls crumbling into decay. Where others had once stood were only piles of rocks knocked apart by the RIC so no farmer's family could sneak back in for shelter.

The people had been evicted—literally thrown out of their homesteads to wander the roads without food or shelter. Fianna had heard that some of the English landlords had turned to raising cattle. There was more profit in cattle, and emptying the small farmstead spaces made more grazing land.

The afternoon was waning. Ahead of the train, the Wicklow Mountains began to grow on the horizon. With the help of the long summer evening, there should still be daylight when they reached Kingsbridge Station in Dublin. That was the station nearest to the Clarence Hotel, where Marcus always kept a suite. At a steady thirty-five miles an hour, they would be in Dublin in two hours.

The merry group of young people in the front of the coach had grown quieter. Even the concertina was groaning out softer tunes. The thin musician leaned his tam-covered head against the vibrating wall, his eyes half-closed. From his vantage point, he surely could see everyone in the car. Then his instrument began to moan the sad strains of "The Wearing of the Green."

Most of the group ignored the music and continued their chatter. Fianna saw the red-haired boy suddenly sit up straight. A look passed between himself and the musician. Then he glanced quickly away.

The melody rolled on. In her mind, the words echoed, raising fiery-red anger.

Oh, Paddy dear, and did ye hear the news that's goin' round?

The shamrock is by law forbid to grow on Irish ground.
No more Saint Patrick's Day we'll keep, his color can't be seen,
For there's a cruel law agin the wearin' o' the green...
She's the most distressful country that ever yet was seen,
For they're hangin' men and women there for wearin' o' the green.

The hundred-year-old ballad was still able to set aflame the fighting spirit in Ireland, no matter how the British tried to crush it. Fianna glanced back at the tall man to see if the song had affected him. It had an effect alright. His blue eyes were blazing anger, his face was red, and he stared at the skinny musician as if memorizing his features.

At the next stop, the musician collected a bit of gratuity from the boys and let himself off the train. Fianna thought she saw the angry man in back writing something on a scrap of paper.

Fianna mused on the spirit of her country. Pride welled up in her Irish soul when she thought of the grand Hill of Tara some thirty miles north where the High Kings of Ireland administered realistic, fair Brehon laws centuries ago. And she was on her way to England!

Her sister was married to Rodney Nugent, the son of one of the most arrogant British members of Parliament and an absentee landlord of an estate near Leaghanor. Somehow Fianna would have to control her caustic loyal Irish tongue and her temper while she spent two miserable weeks among the British. She would be staying in a nest of them!

Fianna would also have to take care if she was asked about her family. To begin with, she had to circumvent questions about the prosperity of Fitzmichael Freighting Company. Money bespoke power, and the British might not like to hear that the Irish family was doing well. And, sure, they couldn't hear that the Brotherhood was flourishing in Ireland or that Fitzmichael ships were smuggling Irish wool and animal skins out of the country against the English trade laws.

Brandeen had given her to understand that Alice and her chubby, beloved Rodney kept themselves and their lively six-year-old twins in separate rooms from the elder Nugents. Apparently not so with Rodney's sister, Emily. She raised her eight-year-old son, sired by the detestable Major Spencer George, at the haughty table of his grandfather. Her husband had left the British army and had transferred to the Special Branch of the Royal Irish Constabulary, the group whose purpose was to flush out members of the Irish Republican Brotherhood, the Fenians. He was pursuing his career in Ireland while they lived in England.

Fianna couldn't remember Major George too well—just a sharp red uniform and the toothy smile of a shark. She did remember that he caused the family a great deal of trouble. She hoped not to meet him at the Nugent mansion.

Suddenly the train's steady rocking motion became a bone-rattling shudder, and it lurched to a hard, jolting stop. Fianna's bag tumbled off the overhead rack, and the fishing rods of the red-haired boy rolled and fell to the floor. Fianna was thrown forward so quickly that she nearly hit her head on the back of the seat in front of her, and her little boater flipped down over her forehead. She pushed it back and saw Eileen McCrory pulling herself back up onto her seat from the floor where she had been thrown, shock silencing her constant cries.

The passengers looked at each other, questioning. They opened windows, leaning out to see what happened. Passengers in the other cars hung out the windows also, exclaiming in alarm. Nothing could be seen near the train but a narrow, muddy road trailing between the pale lavender of heather-covered bogland and a barley field beginning to turn a soggy green-gold.

Then, through the fading light under the darkening sky, Fianna saw the problem. The heavy iron engine and the wooden coaches stood in a riverbed where the tracks were laid. It was no longer dry. Loose, silty black mud oozed over the rails and around the wheels.

The engineer and fireman eased themselves down out of the cab and slid into the slimy dark water. Slipping and sliding, they managed to crawl up onto the bank, wet to the hips.

Walking along the muddy bank, the engineer, trailed by the sooty fireman, called up to the passengers, "It's a washout, that's what it is! Sure, it was a gully washer of a rain that must have broken the old river's fountainhead and filled her up again. The crossties are holding the rails together, but we're sunk in mud and dead stopped, that we are!"

The two pretty girls in Fianna's car began frantic histrionics, as if terrified that they would never get out of the train and die there. They were calculated to bring the young men hovering over them in grand solicitude. They did. The gentlemen soothed the girls' fears and smothered the frail little things with comforting and redundant phrases.

The red-haired boy came to Fianna, getting there at the same time as the man in the old brown suit from the back of the train.

"Sure now, the engineer will be sending word ahead," the young fellow said confidently. "Our only problem will be getting ourselves out of this bog and onto the road."

"Indeed, yes," the older man said, smiling under his beard, obviously quite sure that Fianna would warm up to him under

25

the circumstances. "I'd be happy to be of service if you need help, miss."

He removed his cap and leaned toward Fianna, revealing ash-blond hair neatly parted in the middle, strangely well groomed for a farmer. Once again, Fianna had an odd sense that she had seen him before, had heard that overly polite, clipped accent some other time. And the feeling she got was not pleasant.

"I'll be fine," she said crisply, looking with disdain past him to the hysterical females ahead.

A smile spread over the boy's lightly freckled face. "I believe you will."

The tall man was affronted at her rebuff of his offer and left her to go to his window again, frowning.

By then the red-haired boy was attending to Eileen McCrory, who clenched her shawl around her in distress. Tears welled up out of her pale-gray eyes again as she told him, "I must get to Dublin tonight to see my Tommy before they haul him away to prison."

He went forward and explained the lady's quandary to the other fellows, and they listened without argument.

"I don't know what we can do, Neill," the dark-haired boy said. "We can't get out of this swamp. My parents' house is only two miles from here—the Whyte mansion. I was going to get off at Ballymoyne and visit them before going back to school. But we can't even get ourselves out of this mess, much less be bothered with some old Irishwoman."

Neill studied the situation, staring first out of the windows and then around inside the car. "I've got an idea, Robert. If we can get off this train, we may be able to go for help."

The three young men began pulling luggage off the overhead rack and pounding upward under the long boards. Fianna realized what they were doing and rose up to get out of their way. As soon as the boards were loosed completely from their braces, the fellows maneuvered them out the door of the coach. Neill got down into the water and carried the ends of the two long boards to the riverbank. The engineer and the fireman stood in the rain, watching.

"There you are, ladies," Robert Whyte announced proudly. "A gangplank!"

The young heroes and the man in brown all walked precariously down the plank to the bank of the stream. It worked fine. The ladies would be free to leave the shelter of the coach when the rain stopped.

Standing under an umbrella, all the men discussed the next step. Finally, it was decided.

The engineer, a wizened little fellow, called to the passengers, "Now then, me and Collie here—" He indicated the fireman with his thumb. "We'll be going on foot to Ballymoyne ahead. I'll send a telegram to the railhead for help, and I'll be trying to find transportation for you all!"

"Wait for me then," Neill said. "I'll be getting my fishing tackle and come along. I was hoping to do some fishing in the Royal Canal before being cooped up in the grand halls of Trinity College for the next months. This may be my opportunity."

Fianna was sorry to see that bright-red head disappearing into the mist and rain. He seemed to be the only one aboard the train with good sense and a spark of kindness.

The men climbed back on board the coach and settled in for the wait. The poor old lady began loud keening in despair. How would she ever get to Dublin in time now? Her wailing was barely tolerated by the young people in front, and they gave her looks of aggravation. The man in brown was not tolerant at all.

27

"Woman!" His voice was loud and harsh. "You will have to stop that noise or be ejected from this train. I will not bear such racket any longer!"

She tried, she truly tried, to muffle her sobs in the tails of her shawl, but her heart was breaking, and it was impossible for her to keep silent. The man became furious!

"It matters not why you howl like that. You must keep quiet!"

That did it. Fianna stood up and took her basket.

"Mrs. McCrory, we'll be getting off this train. Mr. Whyte, is that your name?"

She spoke to the dark-haired boy. "I'll be taking that umbrella of yours so the lady and I can wait outside in the rain. Sure, you'll all be happier then!"

Her voice was acid with anger at their lack of understanding. The young people were somewhat abashed, although they looked relieved. Robert Whyte helped Fianna get the lady and umbrella down the gangplank and then went back inside to his friends. Fianna gave one last glare at the train windows, where she could see the tall man in brown sitting in his seat, arms folded, looking smugly satisfied.

Once they were on the bank, Fianna led Eileen McCrory to a large flat stone and seated her there. Sitting with the rain falling around her, the fresh cold air chilling the tears on her cheeks, Eileen calmed down a bit. Perhaps being out of the train gave her less sense of being trapped without any hope at all of seeing her boy.

"I'm that sorry to be causing you so much trouble, lass," she said, sniffling. "There's no need for you to be standing out here in the weather with me."

"There is that," Fianna said. "I'm sick to death of those high and mighty ones in there. We'll do fine here, that we will. I'm thinking the engineer should be coming soon with help."

"Too late!" Eileen started to wail again. "It's forty miles to Dublin from here. I'll never reach the jail in time to say goodbye to me boy!"

Fianna paced, holding her useless little parasol over her head. The rain was not falling heavily. It had become a soft mist. The thick clouds were bringing twilight on early. She searched the road where the engineer and fireman had gone, hoping for sight of their return with a conveyance of some sort.

It was virtually impossible, she was sure. Robert Whyte said his family home was two miles away. Surely the nearest town was at least that far. The train would have made short work of that distance, but the little engineer slogging along the muddy road would take many times as long.

"Something is coming!" Fianna could see through the mist a dark shape moving over the rise in the road out there.

"Oh, praise the saints, they are coming with a wagon. Maybe I will make it to Dublin after all!" Eileen rejoiced as they strained their eyes to make out what kind of vehicle the engineer had found for them.

It came closer. They could tell that it was pulled by only one horse. Not many of the stranded passengers might be able to get into it. Then they saw that it was roofed.

A strange outline was taking shape.

"Ho, there!" a voice called out from the vehicle. "Met your engineer and fireman a ways down the road! He said you were needing help. It will take him a long time to find a wagon for you all. Is anyone needing a ride?"

They saw it now. It was a covered wooden box on wagon wheels, painted bright colors, rattling with pans and kegs attached to the sides. It was a Gypsy vardo.

Tinkers!

Chapter 3

"It's tinkers!" Eileen muttered. "Keep away from them, lass. Don't let them near you. They'll steal your purse!"

Tinkers. Irish Gypsies. A clan of travelers who lived in covered vehicles and roamed the roads. Long ago they had actually been tinsmiths, who repaired pots and pans, or they were peddlers, carrying thread and tin cups and healing ointments to outlying farms. Not anymore. Their clever swindles and outright thievery were well known. Any place they found people gathered, at fairs or races, they would camp and offer trinkets for sale; all the while their tricksters told fortunes, picked pockets, and took advantage of gullible folks. They lived in poverty, but it seemed that they thrived on it, depending on the pity of ordinary folk to clothe their children and provide food if needed.

Fianna hadn't had much experience with them. They were rebuffed at the little town of Cullymor near the Fitzmichael estate, and, sure, Sean Rooney and his men sent them packing whenever they appeared at Leaghanor. At this time, she speculated that they just might be the solution to her problem.

The trainmen were nowhere in sight, likely still trudging the road looking for help. The man sitting on the tongue of the odd-looking wagon said he had seen them a way back. They might not be back until full dark. It would take hours to get to Dublin after that. At least the tinkers' wagon had wheels and a horse. And she had her pepperbox.

Fianna studied the contraption and the pair on the seat. It was an odd rig, wider on top than below. A hood of sorts projected forward over the wagon seat. The wooden cabin of the wagon was painted garish red, with yellow shutters on the side windows. Yellow paint was also on the trim around a miniature Dutch door behind the driver's seat. A cluster of pails dangled and rattled on the back corner.

The couple needed washing, that was true. Grubby white muslin grown threadbare was the husky tinker's shirt. His greasy brawn trousers hung loose, obviously having belonged to someone more stout before he acquired them. He had shaggy dark hair and a beard obviously clipped with dull shears. The woman sat silent, dark eyes lowered, staring angrily at the scruffy old cob that pulled the wagon. A dark-red shawl was wrapped tightly over her head and around her shoulders.

"They're not frightening me." Fianna spoke low to Eileen. "I have means to take care of myself. If you are going to see your boy tonight, we may have to take advantage of this chance. We can make them drive us to a farm or clachan where we can hire a proper carriage. Here, fellow!" Fianna hailed the driver. "Do you have room for two?"

"Sure, and we do!" His voice was hearty, and he smiled amiably. "Come along then."

"Don't do this." Eileen's voice was desperate. She reached out and clung to Fianna's skirt. "Child, don't be foolhardy for my sake! It's sorry I am that I've made such a fuss. Better to be late than to be robbed and killed! Send them away. We'll wait for the trainmen to come back!"

Fianna looked over the couple on the wagon more carefully. Dirty they were, and poor, but they did not look dangerous to her. And what could they do when she had her pistol to protect her? But the old woman seemed so positive that they were criminals. Fianna hesitated.

"You'll not go?" she asked Eileen. "At least we would be moving and trying to do something instead of sitting here all night, waiting. I promise you will not come to harm. We'll find a house and hire someone to take us on toward Dublin, d'you see? By the time the engineer gets all the way to Ballymoyne and back, we can be halfway there. Come now and don't worry."

Suddenly another voice broke into the talk. The man in brown came marching down the gangplank toward them, shouting orders.

"Neither of you will be going with that rabble! You will stay right here with the rest of us on the train until proper help comes. I will not let you go off with that trash!"

Fianna looked at the couple on the wagon. The woman still looked angry, eyes fixed on the horse in front of her. The man's head hung low, eyes downcast, as though shamed at the man's words.

Will you then? Red-hot fury shot through Fianna. How dare he speak to her in such a manner, giving her orders, insulting the poor tinkers. She wondered just how safe she would be in the dark of night enclosed with *him*, with his lecherous looks at her and arrogant demands. She would trust the unknown more than she would place her trust in that egotistic, domineering tyrant! If she had any misgivings about going with the Gypsies, his words totally dispelled them.

She turned to the tinker. "I'll be going with you. Wait for me!"

Robert Whyte and the rest of the young people were hanging out the windows of the train watching the scene, amused. Fianna called, "Mr. Whyte, would you bring my bag down here, *right now*?"

He laughed and drew back inside the coach. In seconds he came down the gangplank carrying her carpetbag to the riverbank.

The tall man's face was flaming with fury. How dare she refuse to obey his orders! Apparently, he was accustomed to being obeyed. His scowl was dark as thunder and his voice was loud and harsh. "I will not allow you to go off with these tinkers!"

How will you stop me? She knew he would not dare to put his hands on her. Aside from bodily holding her back, the man could not keep her from going with them.

Leaning down and comforting Eileen McCrory, Fianna said, "Don't you be worrying, now. These folks will take me to the nearest farmhouse. They will know where to find one in this part of the country, and I will come back with a wagon and we'll be hurrying off to Dublin right away, you'll see."

She told Robert Whyte to hand up her bag to the wagon driver. It was tossed into the cabin of the wagon. The Gypsy woman crawled through the Dutch door behind the tinker man. She shut the bottom so that only her head and shoulders could be seen. Fianna lifted herself up onto the wooden seat and settled beside the tinker.

"Young woman, I will not be responsible for anything that happens to you!" came a shout from the furious man standing on the riverbank.

"And who asked you to do that!" she called back. "Certainly, I have not! I can take care of myself!"

The tinker slapped his reins, and the shabby old horse moved off, turning around to head toward the direction that the engineer had taken. They left the red-faced man on the bank, and poor Eileen weeping hysterically for having brought the girl into danger.

Apprehension nudged Fianna when she glanced back at the woman riding behind her. The tinker's wife looked hostile. The dark, narrow eyes in her unwashed face seemed to dare Fianna to say anything to her.

"Your wife does not seem pleased with my company," Fianna remarked.

"Och, it's angry she is to be married to a rover like me." The man pushed back his tattered black hat. "She was raised in a fine little farmhouse with a straw roof over her head every night, until the eviction of her Da from his farm and the family turned out into the road. That was years ago and, sure, she's not over it yet. As to me, I was born to the roads, generations back. Give me the free air and no chores to bind me." He made a bit of a laugh. "We do alright, don't we, old woman? I know how to get a shilling now and then."

The road trailed along beside the tracks before it wound up over a small hill and out of sight of the train. The curious passengers watched the wagon go, with Fianna clinging to the wooden seat. Fianna studied the countryside, looking for a sign of a plantation or cottage where she could find acceptable help.

As soon as they had trundled over the hill, the tinker man spoke, "Happen you have the price of hiring a carriage if we find one, young ma'am?"

A cold feeling prickled down her back, and she grasped her purse firmly. "I have."

"That's good. We're poor folk," he said casually. "Our old vardo here is all we've got. And with evictions all over the land, there's none that will give us work."

"Not that we'd be wanting any," came a voice from behind her. Fianna turned. The Gypsy woman was gone, and in her place was a young man with tan skin and thick, curly black hair. A wide-brimmed hat sat jauntily on the back of his head, and a red kerchief was tied at his neck. He flashed a broad, smug grin.

"Look here now, what a pretty lass my good Da has found for me. Sure, we'll be wanting your company for a long while. We've had no time at all to get acquainted, Caileen." He reached out a hand and let a curl of her dark hair twine around his finger.

The back of Fianna's neck tingled. Clearly there was danger close at hand. Instead of a man and wife who simply offered a ride for help, she was going to have to deal with a feisty young man with evil ideas. Certainly, the tinkers had purposely kept him out of sight. Now she found herself out on the road alone in what had become a trap. Perhaps she should have stayed with the train. *If that bully of a man hadn't tried to order her about...*

She looked around the fields and wooded areas to see if there was possibly any house nearby. All she saw was the crumbled remains of a vacated cottage—broken roof beams, scattered and rotting thatch, stones tumbled into heaps. No other dwellings were in sight.

"Where will we find an occupied house out here?" she asked.

"You won't," the young fellow said with a laugh. "What is your hurry, lass? Let's get to know each other."

It was time to make a move and get control of things. Swiftly she slipped her hand into her purse and took out the pistol. Pressing the barrel into the driver's rough muslin shirt, she said, "I think we'll be going right along to the next town without delay. If you're thinking of overpowering me, you're feeling the barrel of a Mariette Brevete twenty-eight-caliber pepperbox against your side. It takes less than a second to send a bullet into your body!"

The driver's eyes got wide with surprise. "Here now, Rony. Don't you be making a move. I'm not wishing to have a hole in me belly!"

"Sure then, Da. I'll not touch the lady. Too bad. We could be having a grand time of it, if only she was agreeable."

"Agreeable, is it?" Fianna's eyes blazed. "What would I be wanting with the likes of you, you lazy hoodlum. It's not much of a man you are, to be trying to take advantage of a decent woman who finds herself in a bad situation. One more move from you and it's a bullet in your Da and four more for yourself!"

The young man's face darkened red with anger, and his happy-go-lucky grin turned into an ugly sneer. He said no more but watched her, his eyes narrowing like a cat prepared to spring at the first chance.

Suddenly the tinker turned the horse into a narrow bohreen with stone walls along the sides.

"Where is this going?" Fianna demanded. "No foolishness now. I've shot many a rabbit and fox. The sight of blood doesn't bother me. In fact, I have decided to leave your company right now. Stop here," Fianna ordered.

"No need," the man said pleasantly. "I'm taking you to a kindly old lady who will keep you warm in her home and in out of the rain. It will be better than sitting out here on the wagon for miles to get to the town."

Fianna didn't move the pistol. "Why here then? Why not find a place along the road?"

"This be the nearest, lass, and the sooner that gun comes out of me ribs, the happier I'll be, sure."

It wasn't a good reason to leave the main road and likely a lie. Fianna made a quick decision to go along with it for now. She wanted to be rid of these tinkers as swiftly as possible, but the twilight in the mist was dimming. If she left the wagon, she would be out in the countryside completely alone. If indeed they were taking her to a house, any house, it would be better than the jeopardy she had gotten herself into.

Clinging to the edge of the wagon seat with her left hand, she carefully kept the pistol in place, directed at the tinker.

"How far is it to the woman's house?" The question was brisk, calculated to make the Gypsies feel that she would tolerate no tricks.

"Just ahead, just ahead." The driver shook the reins a bit, and the horse plodded on.

After several minutes, while she could feel the threatening eyes of Rony on her back, Fianna said, "We'd best be seeing the house soon, or you'll turn this wagon around and go back to the road."

"It isn't far now," he mused with good humor. "Just around this little rise."

A few more minutes and Fianna said, "Far enough. Turn the wagon around and go back to the main road."

"Hist now, lass! It's here we are! You'll be taken in and warmed like a queen, that you will."

He pulled the horse to a stop. Fianna looked around. Rony popped out of the back of the wagon and came around, sturdy arms raised to help her down. He wasn't very tall in his blue shirt and snug brawn pants, but he was muscularly built and obviously proud of it.

"Step back. Don't touch me," Fianna warned. She lifted her skirts, and, pepperbox still gripped in her hand, she slipped nimbly to the ground.

"It's a sad tale, it is," the tinker father said. "Thrown out of her cottage, the poor old soul was, when her husband was shot by the Peelers. See here, now, where the hill hangs over the edge of the bog? She's got herself a hovel under there. She's a good, kind old woman."

Rony lifted his eyebrows, staring at Fianna's skirts as he leered. "That's quite an ankle you turn there, Caileen."

"Never you mind my ankles! You can be getting my carpetbag out of that cabin."

She held the gun steadily on the men and took note of the tinker woman's angry face when it appeared again behind the seat.

Suddenly a bloodcurdling screech came from behind her. She whirled around and saw a hag come howling out from under the hill, waving a broom and shrieking at the top of her voice!

The reins snapped, and the Gypsy wagon went tearing off down the bohreen with her bag still inside. Shrill, hysterical laughter sounded from the bouncing, lurching vehicle. She was left standing alone beside the road, openmouthed, with a madwoman running toward her, flailing a broom.

Chapter 4

The old woman shouted, her voice so shrill it cut the ears, "Get out of here! Begone with you!"

It took Fianna some seconds to realize what had happened. The tinkers surely knew that a madwoman lived here. Fianna had not been abused, but she was in trouble, sure! They stole her bag with a few clothes. She was stranded in Westmeath with no one knowing where she was. Not an occupied house anywhere. The Gypsy driver had kept mollifying her until here she was, at least half a mile from the main road, where the trainmen would have come across her. And a crazy old woman wanted to take her head off with a broom!

Sudden silence from the screaming hag made Fianna look away from the tinkers' retreating wagon. The woman stood, broom held high and snaggletoothed mouth open, her white hair streaked with red trailing wildly in the wind, her strange yellow-green eyes fixed on the pistol in the girl's hand.

Fianna gave a big sigh. Here she was, and there was nothing she could do about it. She decided to try to calm the madwoman.

"The gun is not for you, old mother." Fianna moved her hands slowly so that the hag would see her carefully slipping the pistol into her purse. "I had the pistol out because those rascal tinkers tried to rob me. I believed them when they said they would take me to find help, but they carried me here, far from the main road. It could have been much worse if I had not had my pepperbox."

Instantly, the woman began to shriek curses again. "Get yourself away from here, you faerie spawn!"

"It's not a faerie I am! I am lost and in trouble!"

The old woman began to back away, still waving her broom. "You want to rob me, I know you do! The tinkers brought you here to take all my treasures. Go away, go away!"

"No, no!" Fianna called out. It did no good. The old woman turned and ran into an opening under the straggly grass and weeds of the edge of the hillside.

A good, kindly old woman, the tinker had said.

What ridiculous lies, and she had almost believed them! He knew exactly what she would find, and he tricked her with delight. Now the tinkers were gone with her carpetbag, and she had not even a change of clothes in order to get out of her damp suit.

She tried to see exactly where the witchwoman had gone to. A cut about thirty feet long had been dug into the side of a low hill. Along the front of the opening, sapling trees had been woven together and plastered over with mud. Wattle and daub, it was called—an ancient means to build walls of huts. The hillside itself had been made into the ragged roof of some kind of shelter.

The light was fading quickly. Soft rain became large, serious drops. The umbrella had been left at the train for Eileen McCrory. Fianna could hear her own voice mocking her now, shouting at that hateful man in the brown suit, *I can take care of myself!*

Although it had taken only minutes for the Gypsy wagon to go from the road to this place, it was too far to walk back to it. She was starting to get really cold.

Looking around for cover of any kind, she saw several young trees standing at one end of the crude wattle wall. She walked to them, her boots digging into the soft black mud. Under the low branches of the little trees, she curled down on the grass and drew up her knees, wrapping her arms around them to concentrate her body warmth. The leaves of the elm trees protected her from the worst of the rain. Her buttoned shoes were stiff and uncomfortable. She removed the pins in her little straw hat and set it forward to help shield her eyes and face from the drops, leaning her head back against the twisted bark. Fianna was miserable.

With thick clouds covering the sky, dark was settling in fast now. After a bit, Fianna caught sight of movement in front of the shelter. The old woman was outside, broom in hand, looking around. With her shawl wrapped over her head and shoulders, the woman stepped cautiously around the mucky yard, obviously looking for the girl. She did not see Fianna huddled under the bushy trees.

The light was almost altogether gone by this time. Carefully the woman edged along close to the wall, moving toward the end of it. Then she leaned down and peered under the trees and gasped. There was Fianna sitting on the grass, watching her.

"Will you be driving me out into the rain again, old mother?" Fianna asked sarcastically. The hag gained her composure and wrinkled up her face in thought.

At last, the woman spoke, her voice raspy as a raven. "You may come in to the fire. But be warned, I've a pail of holy water from Saint Brigid's well yonder and I'll throw it on you if you threaten me! If you are a faerie, it will turn you into a weasel! I know how to take care of myself, I do!"

The last words rang familiar in Fianna's ears. Only a little while ago she used those same words as she confidently drove off with a pack of thieves. Now she was at the mercy of a madwoman who thought Fianna was a *púca*.

"I'll come." Fianna pulled herself to her feet and followed the hag through a makeshift door and into the darkness of the hovel. The only light was from the hearth, where a turf fire lay smoldering.

The fire felt so good. Fianna sat herself down on a three-legged stool and reached her hands toward the fierce glow of burning peat. It was a pitiful fireplace, just stones stacked on each side to make space for the fire on the floor and a graceless chimney drawing the smoke up through the earthen roof.

From across the dark room, the old woman looked at her suspiciously. Her shawl hung limply over her shoulders, and her apron was soiled. Fianna saw that the earth in the back wall of the cave had been somewhat shored up with dry-set stones. What had once been a good oaken table and a decent dresser were split and swollen from the musty dampness. They were piled with an old potato, shriveled apples, tin cups, and a few cracked delft dishes. A large cupboard bed was meeting with the same unpleasant decadence. The floor had been strewn with some loose river gravel stones, now mashed into the damp floor.

"Why would you be riding with the Gypsies if you are not a thief?" the old woman challenged Fianna.

"I was on the train to Dublin, and it bogged down in a flooded riverbed. I thought the Gypsies would take me to find a carriage or wagon, especially for a passenger who had to get to Dublin to see her son off to prison in England."

"Ah, I know about the train."

"How could you know?" *Was she a real witch then?*

Surprise showed in Fianna's eyes, and the old woman's face almost crinkled in a smile.

"Never mind." Clearly the question was not going to be answered.

Fianna, shivering, looked around the dark room, the furnishings and black, root-streaked walls.

"You have made a home here," she commented.

"I have."

"Why here in this dark, damp cave?"

"Why indeed—and my good man shot down by the Peelers at Mitchelstown."

"I understand. The massacre. The RIC."

"They did. They battered down the door. I was ready. The first ones that came running in got a pot full of boiling water in their faces. But they threw me out in the road. All I could do was sit in the ditch and cry and watch them while they had men on the roof ripping away the thatch and knocking down the same stone walls that kept me and mine warm and safe for many years. They ordered me begone, and when I wouldn't go off down the empty road, they took a whip to me."

"By all the saints…" Fianna was stunned. Many were the times she had heard of these things happening. It didn't happen around Cullymor. Old John Fitzmichael, her grandfather, had made it possible for the farmers to buy and own their little farms. He wanted only the lands around the Big House and access to the coast with his ships.

"Your furniture?" she questioned.

"There are men about, good men, that the landlords and Peelers never see. They came in the night and brought me here and dug out this place for me. I care nothing about the cooking and the cleaning." Her yellow-green eyes indicated the rotting fruit and the soiled table.

Then, carefully watching her unwelcome guest, the woman came and hung the black iron kettle over the fire.

"It's for the tea," she said.

"I am Fianna Fitzmichael," Fianna said softly, shivering in her damp clothes and hoping the crone would not start raving again. "What would your name be?"

"I'm Nan. Crazy Nan, they call me."

"I'm sorry."

"I am not. Keeps them away." Her voice went high and shrill with emphasis. "You too. I'm wanting you out of here!"

"I'll be leaving as soon as ever I can. Have you a cart or a wagon then?"

Nan looked at her, outraged. "Where would I be having such? They took away everything. If the Anglos find out I'm living here, they'll drive me out into the bog where others are trying to live. It's lucky I am to have this cave. I'm not afraid of your gun!"

"I come from County Mayo."

"Are ye now?" Crazy Nan's yellow eyes took on a tinge of curiosity.

"I'll be leaving as soon as it's light. Where is the nearest town?"

"No town between here and Ballymoyne now. Used to be farms and cabins and people. All driven out by the landlords so they can raise cattle on the lands. Too far to walk in them tight boots of yours."

"So be it." Fianna rested her head on her hand and resigned herself to the facts. Somehow she would get away from here and back to towns and relatives and Dublin. Right now, she didn't know how, and she was too cold and tired to try to think it out. It had been such a long, strange day. If her family wanted her to get away from Leaghanor and meet different people and have new experiences, they certainly should be gratified.

When Nan made the tea, she poured it into fat pottery cups at the table. Fianna thought she saw the old woman stir something into a cup before bringing it to her.

"What was that you put into the tea?" she asked.

"Only a bit of honey to make it sweet."

"Indeed. Thank you." Fianna accepted the cup gratefully. She took a tiny sip. There was no honey in the tea. Something else was there that left a bitter taste. Fianna drank no more of it, and, as soon as Nan's back was turned, she emptied it into the cold ashes next to the fire. If indeed the old woman was some sort of sorcerer or just plain insane, Fianna was taking no chances of being poisoned or drugged.

She watched Nan pour herself a cup from the battered old teapot and drink deeply. Fianna sat, holding the empty cup and watching the fire.

Nan saw that her cup was empty and brought the pot over to pour another for her. "It's tired you are. When you are ready, there's the cupboard bed where you can sleep the night." She indicated the large chest standing in the shadows along the back wall.

"I am that tired," Fianna said. "But where will you be sleeping?"

"I'll not be sleeping tonight. Go on with it then and sleep there."

Fianna took a long draught of the tea that came straight from the pot. It tasted like tea and nothing else. Then she peeled out of her damp suit jacket, revealing a soft, white pleated blouse with long sleeves. "I'll be glad to lie down, thank you, ma'am."

Fianna was indeed weary and cold and craved lying down. However, she had no intention to sleep. She would rest in that cupboard bed while she gathered her thoughts and decided what the next step would be to get herself out of this predicament. But she would stay alert and be certain that Crazy Nan did not do anything to harm her.

She walked across the room under the low, slanted ceiling and opened wide the cupboard doors. The bed was narrow, but there was a coarse woolen pad stuffed with hay. Tossing her jacket along with her purse holding the pepperbox into the back of the bed, she unbuttoned her boots and pulled them off, giving a sigh of relief. Then she climbed up into the confined space, tucked her boots to the back with her jacket and purse, and lay down. A roll of dingy sheep's wool served to pillow her head. She hoped it harbored no fleas. The smell of musty cloth and molding wood was choking, but she was too cold and tired to care.

Crazy Nan sat down on a stool by the table, the pail of water beside her on the floor.

"I'll be right here through the night, watching you," she warned. "My bucket of holy water from Brigid's well is here. Don't you bring out that gun or I'll be ready for you!"

"I'm not of a mind to change into a weasel tonight," Fianna murmured. "And you won't have to sit up all night. I will get up soon so you can have your bed."

It was late in the night when Fianna woke to the sound of voices, men's voices. It took several minutes to remember where she was. Then a sickening feeling came over her. She was in a horrible dark cave house with an insane old woman and no apparent way to get back to her own people waiting for her in Dublin. She was lying in a narrow cupboard made into a rough bed, and she had been asleep. It was pitch-dark. Someone had closed the cupboard doors. She might be locked in!

Fianna reached behind her. Her purse was gone. The *pepperbox* was gone! A thrill of fear shot through her. Men's voices. *Who would be visiting the crazy old woman in the night? Didn't she say something about men coming to her in the night, men that landlords and police never see?*

Fianna dared not move much. The rustle of the crisp, dry hay in the coarse mattress would be heard.

"Don't you be worrying about her," Nan said, with a shrill, discordant voice. "I couldn't let the fool girl sit out there in the dark soaking wet. But I put enough laudanum in her tea to sleep a cow. She won't hear a thing until morning."

"Are you sure? We don't know anything about this girl. She could be a spy for the RIC."

"She said she was on the train that bogged down. Himself came by and told me about it before ever the tinkers left her here. Spy or not, she is no trouble tonight, Eamon. I took her gun away as soon as she fell asleep, and I closed the doors on her. Get on with your business."

"*Himself* came by, did he? Well then," the man said in a quiet, confident voice, "is everyone here?"

"Indeed," a rather gruff voice responded. "All but the Cobbler. He had to go to Mayo to see after his family and do some making of pampooties to earn a bit of money for them. He will be back in time for the raid."

"Brought you a bit of brown flour and lard, Nan, for you to make yourself some bread. Sorry it couldn't be more," came Eamon's voice.

"You've all been good to me, fixing up this place for me to live and bringing me food."

"It's us that's thankful to you, old girl. No one will bother a madwoman, and we can meet here without fear of being caught."

Nan's raspy voice came low and full of hate. "I'd be out there with the Fenians meself if I could. I'd be killing every landlord and Peeler I met!"

"We'll be doing our best to take your place out there," Eamon said, and the voices of several men stumbled over each other in agreement.

Several men. Fenians. Fianna took that opportunity to raise up so that she could see through a crack between the cupboard doors. In the light from the hearth and a single candle, she could make out several men seated around the oak table. None of them looked prosperous. They wore old hats, muslin shirts and vests, and tattered sweaters.

"Now then, lads," Eamon said. "Has anyone heard from Larkin or O'Dwyer? It's been at least a fortnight since they left to meet that ammunition ship in Kerry."

A negative murmur went up around the table. A graybearded fellow growled, "Not likely we will be hearing from them. The word is that the ship sailed all the way down the West Coast trying to get rid of that load of rifles and ammunition, and no one appeared to receive it. Then, at Kerry, the RIC tried to arrest them at the dock, and they took off out into the Atlantic. We've lost those rifles we're going to be needing when the time comes for the big rising someday soon."

"Are you sure that is so, John Conor? How did the Peelers find out about the ship, and where are our boys? If the ship was turned away and they didn't get the guns, they should have been back by now to report."

"It's informers, it is." Conor's coarse voice was tight with hate. "Some dirty spy for the English must have found out about the ship, and, when Larkin and O'Dwyer showed up, they could have got them."

"Is it a spy we've got in our bunch?"

"Sure, someone is tipping off the police about everything we're doing!"

"Doesn't have to be right here in our troop. Could be anywhere in the network."

Troubled words rose from all corners of the room, cautious and not a little afraid of the truth of their suspicions.

Conor's voice rose again. "That ship spent two weeks cruising the West Coast, all the time keeping it secret about their cargo. It was only when our group found out about it and sent men to bring back guns—then the ship was targeted. Our men haven't come back."

"I'm not believing that one of our men is an informer, Conor," Eamon puzzled. "Who would it be? We all know each other well."

There was a general stirring among the men, some rising to emphasize their innocence. Suddenly the hay under one of Fianna's knees gave way with a slight crackle. Quickly she adjusted her weight. It seemed that no one in the room heard the sound, but she caught her breath.

Spies they were talking about! Informers. The most hated persons of all. Sometimes they were Irish. Fianna had often heard Marcus referring to them as despised turncoats, worthy of death at the hands of their fellow Irishmen.

As the voices quieted, Eamon said, "Keep your eyes open, boys. It could be someone else that we know."

Fianna could hear someone moving about at the hearth, out of her sight through the crack. Probably Crazy Nan. She didn't blame them for their hate of informers, but she was a stranger to them. Crazy Nan had been smart enough to take away her pistol. Fianna felt helpless fear. Somehow she must stay quiet until the meeting broke up and then slip away at the first chance.

Slowly she started to ease away from the crack. Just then the doors flew open! She found herself falling out of the cupboard bed and being caught by one of the conspirators!

Fianna fought! She scratched and pushed at the viselike grip of the man, tearing at the rough shirt with her nails, pounding on the man's chest. It wasn't until she started to reach for his face that she saw the astonished blue eyes of her captor.

"*Jamie!*"

"Fianna, what are you doing here?"

Before she could speak, Crazy Nan came charging across the room, broom held high, shrieking, "You tricked me!"

"Whoa, there now, Nan!" Jamie laughed, that wonderful, good-natured chuckle that Fianna loved to hear. Still holding onto her, he said, "This girl's no spy. I've known her all me life, I have. What she's doing here in Westmeath, miles away from Connaught, I don't know. Have you got an answer for me, Fianna Fitzmichael?"

Fianna was so full of mixed-up emotions and thoughts that she could hardly answer. Words came pouring out. "I was on the train...Brandeen and Marcus are making me go to visit Alice in England...The train bogged down and I took a ride with some tinkers...They tried to rob me, but I had my pepperbox..."

She looked around at the scowling faces of the Fenian outlaws around the table. "Och, Jamie, I waited so long for you."

She turned into the safety of the curve of his arm, dropping her face onto his shoulder. Jamie's freckles disappeared in the blush on his face, looking ruefully at the slightly amused but suspicious faces of his cohorts. "Fianna lass, now don't be fussing like that. Now set yerself down here on the bed a minute."

"The question is, what will we do with this lass?" Eamon's voice was stern. He was white-haired, somewhat older than the other farmers in the room. It was clear that he also was a laboring man, but there was a quiet dignity and common sense about him that made Fianna feel safer. He sat at the table in his ragged white shirt and sleeveless sweater and weighed the situation.

"I'm as Irish as you." Fianna sat on the bed and backed into its depths a bit as if to protect herself, but she spoke up in her defense with spirit. "My grandfather left all in Dublin to start over in Mayo and help the people survive the Famine."

"Indeed?" the bearded man muttered. "And we're supposed to believe that you, a rich woman, are on the side of the patriots? I doubt it. You're a Unionist, sure."

"She's telling you true, John Conor," Jamie's voice was low, warning. "The Fitzmichaels are for the people. Like me own sister, she is. This lass has kept many a Captain Moonlight secret in her time. No one in this room will touch her. D'ye hear me, now?"

"I'll not be putting my life and the outcome of the war against the Anglos into the hands of a fool girl who, if she is not a spy, had no better sense than to ride with tinkers! Jamie Rooney, you know the oath. She must disappear, that's all, and no one knowing the difference. The Gypsies will be blamed," Conor growled.

Quickly, Jamie stepped in front of Fianna, returning Conor's glare and ready to fight.

"Fitzmichael, is it? I know that legendary name," Eamon commented. "Well then, we'll have to go along with you now, Jamie boy. But what we will do with her has to be decided by us all. Remember that."

"I remember."

Fianna looked at Jamie's face. His jaw was set, grim, resigned. He stood beside her, leaning against the cupboard, watching the men. Around them, the faces of the Fenian men revealed anger at the foolish lass who had brought them confusion. What to do with her? It would not be the first time they had had to perform a duty that was abhorrent to the tender Irishmen.

What have I done? Fianna berated herself. *Jamie is in trouble because of me. They want to silence me, that Conor does, sure! And I'm not blaming them. I know how it goes—Marcus told me often enough. One outsider who knows too much can send them all to the hangman, even Jamie. Sure, I've muddled it this time!*

She knew that Eamon likely knew his superior in the IRB but no other. And his superior did not know these men, and they didn't know him. It was their protection in the three levels of the secret society so that, no matter what the RIC did, they could never completely destroy the furtive army of the Irish Republican Brotherhood.

"Well now," Eamon picked up the discussion. "As long as the lass has heard the gist of it, let's get on with it. How are we going to find out what happened to our boys, Larkin and O'Dwyer? Jamie, what are you hearing from the Big House of Whyte?"

Jamie frowned in consternation. "Not a thing, and it's got me worried. I have had no word from my partner there for a fortnight. It seems that the mansion is locked up tight. Not a servant or groom has been in or out. It's not natural. Something must be going on with that old Anglo devil."

"Whyte is a sharp one and merciless," Conor said. "But this is strange."

"Strange, indeed," Eamon said. "I'm wondering, could there be a connection? Our boys gone and out of sight for two weeks and Whyte shutting off his house for that same two weeks."

Several of the men around the table began to discuss the odd happenings, throwing out ideas and conjectures.

Whyte?

"Is it Whyte, then?" Fianna spoke low so that Jamie alone was expected to hear. "I saw a Robert Whyte on the train. He said his family lives near here."

Conor heard. "So you know the son of the Whyte house? She's a spy for landlord Whyte!"

"I only saw the boy on the train. He was making merry with his friends. There was a man with a concertina playing music for them. I was not part of it all."

"Likely." Conor's voice was acid with disbelief.

Jamie's face went red with anger. "Conor, I'm weary of hearing your way of calling Fianna Fitzmichael a liar. I'll hear no more of it or I'll be meeting you outside!"

"Enough!" Eamon broke in. "We've no time for trouble between us. Let's get on with it. And, lass—" He turned to look at Fianna. His face was kindly but stern. "Best you keep your comments to yourself for your own sake."

The men continued to ruminate on reasons why no activity had been seen outside the Whyte mansion and where their two scouts had disappeared to in the past couple of weeks.

Fianna held tight to the large, square hand of her protector. Jamie Rooney had been her hero and her shield forever. His muscled shoulders were round and solid like his arms. Pity Conor if he met Jamie in a fair fight. But it would not be fair.

The conflict would be about her, and all of the fellows would be obliged to side with Conor. If there was trouble, it would become an execution!

As she listened to the men talk, an idea began to grow in her mind. She glanced down at her bedraggled, damp clothes. Her hair must be a sight too. Was it only yesterday that Robert Whyte saw her leave the train with tinkers? Now she looked as though she could have been mistreated and robbed by them. Wouldn't the Whytes take pity on her and welcome the daughter of the wealthy Fitzmichaels into their home to recover from her ordeal? Excitement overcame fear and sent a surge of spirit through her! She spoke up loud and announced:

"I can get into that house!"

Chapter 5

The men looked at her, startled.

"Sure, I can do it! I'll get into the Whyte Big House and find out what you want to know. I'll prove to all of you that I'm loyal Irish and not a Unionist!"

"What are you thinking?" Jamie demanded.

"Look at me. Robert Whyte knows that I left with the tinkers. If I appeared on the Whyte doorstep looking like this and with my sad tale, they would have to take me in, wouldn't they now? And me the niece of the wealthy Fitzmichaels and Marcus Maher, who is known as the shipping genius. I will tell them that the tinkers robbed me and dropped me along a road and I've been wandering all night. I can do it!"

"Fianna Fitzmichael, don't be getting wild ideas!" Jamie stood in front of her, his hands gripping her shoulders. "I'm finding myself responsible for you, since you popped up out here alone. Marcus will have my head if I let you get into the middle of this. You are already in trouble enough. You will not go pushing yourself into a hangman's noose!"

Fianna slipped off the edge of the bed and stood barefoot before him, her color high and her large brown eyes flashing anger.

"You'll not be telling me what I cannot do, Jamie Rooney. You lost the chance to have that right!" *You did that when you kissed me and then went off without a word*, she amended silently. She turned to the older man at the table. "Eamon—that's your name? I will do it and gladly! You're needing to find out what goes on in the Whyte place. I can get in there in the blink of an eye, you'll see."

"Just a minute, lass. For all we know, you will turn us in, and we'll all be kicking at the end of a rope. How would you find out anything? Old Whyte is not likely to confide his evildoings to you."

"I'll find a way—you'll see."

"Here now, I'm not liking the sound of that, girl!" Jamie protested. "And don't forget that I already have a contact in that house."

"Your contact may be eliminated by now," Fianna argued.

Jamie's face went white. "Don't say that! Don't ever say that!"

John Conor spoke up, "She's a spy, sure."

Jamie turned on him, odd desperation in his eyes. "For that, John Conor, I'm saying she can go. It's stubborn and willful she's always been, but I would trust her with me life. May be that she can find out if everyone in that Big House is alright. I just pray that she doesn't get shot or hung."

Eamon looked her over thoughtfully. "What she said is true. The Whytes would have to take her in. If she can just hear a word that would give us a clue to any of the strange happenings that are going on, it would help. She need not stay there long— perhaps over one night only, because she has family looking for her. What we might be needing is a plan to get the information from her, if indeed she has any."

The men clustered around the table once more to put together a scheme to reach her after she left the Whyte house, without casting suspicion on her as an informant.

Fianna looked at Jamie, relieved, proud that she had talked them into trusting her.

There was no relief in Jamie's appearance. His lips were pressed together in a line of distress, his face was only barely beginning to get its color back, and his eyes stared straight ahead intensely.

"I wish I had not said that, Fianna lass. I am putting you in terrible danger. I was just hoping that you might be able to learn something of what is going on there. I need to know."

"Don't you worry, my Jamie boy." She tried to reassure him. "The worst that can happen is that I will not be able to learn anything useful, but I will be on my way to Dublin and Marcus and Brandeen and not be troubling you."

"Be careful, Fianna. Remember, family or no, you are still Irish and can be suspected, even arrested, by the RIC. They can hang you without trial if they think you are working with the Fenians. They put Parnell in jail just for making a speech, and himself a member of Parliament. They wouldn't stop for you. I am desperate for word from the Whyte house, but I don't want you in danger either."

"Why then, Jamie, you have to trust my judgment. Put your mind at ease. I am the one who made this decision, and you cannot stop me. How many times did I see Marcus slip out of the house of Leaghanor riding off on his black horse and myself frantic to go with him? And one day soon, we'll both go back home. Didn't I promise that to your Da when he left me on the train?"

Jamie looked at the muddy floor, thoughtful. "It's ashamed I am for leaving the grand old fellow to worry. But things were getting out of hand between you and me, lass. When you get back to Leaghanor, tell him that I am working with horses. He will understand that. I make a few shillings working the mounts at the races and sometimes at the big horse shows at Dublin. I'll be coming back home as soon as ever I can, but I want to come home proud, don't y'see? Will you tell him that, Fianna my little friend?"

"We're more than friends, Jamie. You know we are. Sure then, I'll be glad to set his mind at rest as soon as I can, Jamie love."

At those last words, Jamie turned to look fully into her eyes, his own blue eyes dark with distress. "You've got to stop talking that way, lass! There's nothing for us two together. Believe it now."

"I'll never believe that." Fianna leaned close to him and took his hand. "I love you, Jamie, and I know you love me."

Their talk was interrupted by a call from Eamon at the table.

"I believe we've worked out a plan, girl. You'll go to the Big House of Whyte before morning light comes."

Just before dawn they left the hovel of Crazy Nan, riding three horses. Jamie rode the first one with Fianna up behind him. Farther back, watching, were two more riders, Eamon and Conor the Suspicious.

Through streambeds and fields, around groups of trees, and following hedgerows, they traveled as the darkness turned to pale light. In the east a salmon-pink glow tried to force its way through the cover of clouds. They dared not use the bohreens bordered by stone fences, for fear of meeting a farmer taking his cow to pasture. But they need not have worried. Every farmstead they saw was broken or burned.

They began to come upon barley fields. Even in the dim light, Fianna could tell that the grain was tall and almost ready to harvest. It smelled green, though. A few more weeks and it could be brought in, if the rains dried up a bit. It would be harvested and shipped to the distilleries in England, filling Whyte's pockets with money.

At last the tall brick Georgian mansion of the Whytes could be seen beyond a small knoll. Carefully, Fianna and Jamie approached the house a bit closer while the other riders hung back, shielded by the hillside. Then, behind a cluster of hawthorns, Jamie reined in the horse and lifted Fianna down.

He stood there a long minute, holding her at arm's length, gazing at her soberly.

"What am I to do with you, Fianna Fitzmichael? You're so headstrong. Sure, you've done it this time."

"Have I now? And what would you be doing, joining up with the Fenians and putting your own head in a noose? Don't you think it tears my heart knowing the danger you're in?"

"Does it, Fianna? Does it mean so much to you?"

She raised her hands to touch the sides of his dear, familiar face. "It means my life, Jamie Rooney. I love you."

"It's sorry I am for that, lass." He drew her closer and kissed her forehead. "Now go along with you. I'll be praying to all the saints that you come out alive and bring me good news."

"I will then. I can take care of myself!"

She walked away, stumbling over the rough ground in her high-buttoned boots. She heard Jamie leading the horse back along a drystone fence beside the barley field, slow and quiet so that no noise would be heard over the terrain to the house.

After she made her way around the hawthorns, she had a long way to walk to the house—all open ground. By the time

Fianna waded through tall, wet grasses over a rise in the meadow and followed the other side of the bohreen to the drive that led to the Big House, she surely did look lost and ragged. Her feet hurt in the fancy little boots, her hair was loose and windblown, and her suit was more soiled and soaked with muddy dew around the skirt bottom. Jamie had relieved her of her purse and its precious contents.

"Sure now, if the tinkers robbed you, they would have taken your purse. You're not wanting to go into the fine house of an English landlord armed with your pepperbox. I'll give it back to you, I promise, when I meet you at Ballymoyne. Try to make it quick."

Remembering those words made her more determined than ever to get the job done, and done well. At the tall front doors, she rapped the brass knocker urgently. A butler in black livery opened the door and stood openmouthed, staring at her.

"Please," she begged frantically. "Please, is the family home? Robert Whyte, doesn't he live here? I must see someone!"

Chapter 6

"Your name, miss?" the butler stammered.

"I'm Fiona Fitzmichael. My uncle is Marcus Maher of the Fitzmichael Freighting Company. I met Mr. Whyte on the train. Oh please, call someone to help me!"

Fianna's act was beginning to affect her. Something like panic actually began to grow inside her. She began to feel the exhaustion of the last day and night in her arms and legs. She really needed to sit down! And recognizing the cold efficiency of the British butler struck her vulnerability. Fianna was totally helpless in this nest of Anglos who, she knew quite well, would despise an Irish lass for her bedraggled appearance and her story.

She had the good sense to use her given name instead of Fianna. She tried to gain control of herself, but real fatigue and jeopardy were scratching at her nerves. She had no trouble pretending to be desperate. She was frantic.

"Williams, who is there?" A female voice came from the open doors to the left of the entry hall.

Williams marched stiffly to the open doorway. "A young woman, madam. I believe she wants to see Mr. Robert."

Quickly, the young man from the train appeared in the hall, breakfast napkin in his hand. Behind him came a superior-looking woman in a rose-colored day dress with a crisp white collar. Next appeared a short, stocky, red-faced gentleman in a tweed hunting jacket and jodhpurs. They observed Fianna's disheveled appearance with alarm.

"Robert, who is this person?" the lady demanded.

"Why...I don't know," he stumbled. "I believe...Oh, dear God, it's the girl from the train!"

"Yes, it's me." Fianna really felt close to tears. "I'm sorry to be troubling you like this. I should never have gone with those tinkers! They robbed me and left me on the road. I've been walking so far!" She reached for the edge of the hall table and clung to it. "I heard your name on the train—you said you lived near, and I thought this must be the house. I am so desperate!"

"Did they—?" the woman demanded.

Reading her thoughts, Fianna protested. "No, no! It was just an old man and his wife. They took my bag and my purse and threatened me, and I ran off from them, I did!"

"What is your name, girl? Where did you come from?" the portly man asked suspiciously.

"Connaught. I come from County Mayo. My uncle is Marcus Maher of the Fitzmichael Freighting Company. I have to meet him and my cousin in Dublin. I am Fiona Fitzmichael."

"Indeed?" He was curiously impressed. "Well then, I believe we can give you sanctuary. Interesting..." He looked her over with amused curiosity and a gleam of avarice in his small gray eyes.

"Williams, call Annie to help the young lady clean up," Mrs. Whyte ordered briskly, then studied Fianna. "After you have made improvements to your appearance, young woman, we will discuss your problems." She scowled at Robert. "You must be more discreet about making acquaintances on the train."

He followed his mother back into the dining room. "But I didn't! I hardly spoke to her. It was the other girls—"

The red-faced man, Mr. Whyte, remained standing in the entry hall while Williams left to get the maid. His graying brown mustache twitched as he appraised Fianna's condition. He had long sideburns that hung on thick, florid cheeks.

"So you went off with a pack of Gypsies? Fool girl! You could have been murdered. Or worse. Anything can happen in this mad country. Disgusting, bestial people! What possessed you?"

Fianna was hard put to keep her pitiable attitude at his words. Repressing a retort that would have burned his Anglo-Saxon ears, she forced her eyes to go wide with what she hoped was a look of innocence.

"The train was bogged down, and I knew my Uncle Marcus and cousin would be worried, waiting for me in Dublin. The tinkers offered a ride to anyone who wanted to go on instead of waiting for the engineer to come back with help. My uncle must be out of his mind with worry by now."

"Ah…" He nodded, his mind calculating behind the heavy-lidded gray eyes. "I know of Maher. Good man with a pound. Annie," he addressed the maid who arrived in the hall. "Help the young lady—Miss Maher, is it? Fitzmichael, of course. Make Miss Fitzmichael comfortable and get her some tea. I will send a telegram to Maher in Dublin and let him know you are safe with me. Where will I find him?"

"He keeps a suite at the Clarence."

As Fianna followed the little housemaid in her gray uniform and white cap up the stairs, she wondered just how safe she would be in this house with such a bigoted, mercenary Englishman. Better she get this errand over with as soon as possible.

The house was larger than the Big House of Leaghanor where the Fitzmichaels lived. Huge brass and crystal chandeliers hung over the grand entry hall. The floors were made of decorative stone tiles, and the ceilings were covered with elaborate painted relief carvings of flowers and ferns. Fianna couldn't help but compare the mansion to the muddy, moldy cave of Crazy Nan. True, Nan would not want to live in this cavernous monument, but, sure, she deserved to have her own tiny cottage with her bits of household things around her.

Annie was a sturdy Irish girl with thick dark-blond hair trying to force its wispy, tight curls out from under her cap. She looked to be about Fianna's age. Fianna could barely keep up with her on the broad, carpeted staircase. Now her legs felt like rubber and her body ached with exhaustion.

Annie helped her get out of the damp, soiled suit and into a warm linen nightgown.

"We'll be seeing what to do about your poor rumpled hair when you feel like it," the maid said cheerily. "Right now I'm thinking you want sleep—your eyes are that sunk in."

"Do I look that bad, Annie?" Fianna let the girl settle her onto a large comfortable chaise lounge.

"You do. But you'll be better after you're done sleeping, and we'll fix you up nice. Where did you come from? London?"

"London, indeed! Sure not! I'm from Mayo and of good Irish stock, I am."

Annie smiled, such a pretty, merry smile on her rosy face. "Well then, I'm glad the tinkers didn't hurt you more. What's yer name?"

Fianna lowered her voice. "It's Fianna Fitzmichael, but you must call me Fiona. The Whytes likely wouldn't like to hear me called after the rebels."

Annie's face revealed surprise and interest in Fianna. "Fitzmichaels from County Mayo? Would that be at Cullymor now? I've heard of that family from a friend."

"And who would that be?"

Annie blushed. "No one you'd be knowing, I'm sure. Well then, Miss Fiona, I'll be bringing you up some tea and scones right away."

When she left for the tea, Fianna began to silently berate herself. *There I go, trusting someone just because she is Irish. Fool that I am, she could tell the other servants, and then the Whytes would hear that I am a patriot and turn against me, sure. They would have me out of here before I could find out a thing. Or worse! And who would the girl be knowing in Cullymor? Not much of a spy I am.*

But she felt better when Annie came bustling in with the tray. Something so likeable, so natural, about the girl put Fianna at ease.

"Mr. Whyte, he told the mistress to treat you like a lady," the maid said as she set the tray on a small table beside Fianna. "He said you would make a good 'connection.'"

"Oh, that I will. I will indeed." Fianna cast a significant smile at the maid. "Annie, I want you and only you to wake me when I have slept awhile. Wake me at two o'clock this afternoon."

Surprised at her emphasis, Annie nodded and tucked Fianna into the deep, soft bed in the room. It felt so good after the scratchy wool-and-hay mattress at Nan's. Fianna was glad she had thought of asking Annie to wake her. She could be caught off guard on waking, perhaps disoriented and not aware of her precarious situation. If she said something that revealed her mission when she came out of the stupor of sleep, she would have to trust Annie to keep it to herself.

It turned out well. Annie woke her promptly at two. She had with her a nice blue gown which, she said, Mrs. Whyte had sent up. Fianna's travel suit was being cleaned and freshened.

The afternoon went by without incident. Annie brushed and dressed Fianna's hair and tied it back with a new black ribbon. The blue gown was a bit too large but comfortable. They tucked it in at the waist with a wide white sash. Instead of her boots, which were being cleaned up also, Fianna was provided with a pair of velvet slippers.

Robert Whyte was obviously instructed to escort her about with great deference, and he did. Fianna had some difficulty wandering about the house and gardens on his arm while listening to his boasting about all the young ladies who were hopelessly charmed by him. His principal interest in life seemed to be parties and balls. He never mentioned plans for a vocation or his classes at college. She tried to make the proper comments at the proper times, hoping that her boredom didn't show.

Clearly he remembered Fianna's aloofness on the train, so he made no effort to attract her, only to impress her with his grand popularity. She was utterly grateful when it was time for dinner.

At the table, Mrs. Whyte was condescendingly polite, no doubt directed by her husband. Mr. Whyte must have realized that Fitzmichael and Maher were definitely Irish names, so his tirade against the race was guarded and somewhat subdued.

"I sent a wire to your uncle," he said over a plate of beef and Yorkshire pudding. "You are welcome to stay as long as you like, Miss Fitzmichael. May we call you Fiona?"

"Sure and you may. I'll be going as soon as I can get my strength, thank you, sir," Fianna responded. *As soon as I find out what I need to know.* "My Uncle Marcus and his wife—my cousin she is too—need to be off to Brest on company matters, and I don't want to be holding them up."

"Company matters, indeed?" Mr. Whyte murmured thoughtfully into his teacup. "No hurry for you to leave," he said almost jovially. He seemed to want to secure his "connection."

Mrs. Whyte gave her husband an angry, suspicious look before she asked politely, "What is your errand in Dublin, Fiona?"

"I'm on my way to visit my sister near London," Fianna answered casually. *Might as well play it to the hilt if they want connections.* "Alice is married to Rodney Nugent. Rodney's father is Horace Nugent, a member of Parliament. Do you know of the Nugents?"

"The Nugents! And London! Oh, my dear, I wish you could tuck me in your pocket and take me with you! The parties and balls and calling. It's been years—!"

"Of course, I know the Nugents," Mr. Whyte interjected. "Good connections. They have a daughter married to a certain Spencer George, an officer in the RIC. I hear he is operating in the Special Branch now. He will round up those barbaric Fenians! He did it years ago in Connaught, and he will do it again."

"I doubt it."

The words were out before Fianna knew it. After all, she *knew* that he really did not crush the Fenian movement in the west of Ireland.

A sudden ominous silence filled the room. She looked up to see the Whytes staring at her, outraged.

"And why would you say that?" Mr. Whyte asked, a mixture of fury and suspicion in his small gray eyes.

Fianna grabbed at her senses and quickly answered, "Because they are so devious and cruel. Our plantation has been in danger of being raided many times. Marcus Maher keeps a watch every night around Leaghanor. I've heard they will murder anyone who finds out who they are. Isn't that true?"

She gazed at the man and woman and Robert with wide eyes, as if conceding to their greater knowledge of the subject.

Mr. Whyte appeared to be not completely convinced that Fianna was talking purely out of innocence, but he responded with as much politeness as he could muster, considering her family "connections."

"Major Spencer George can and will break them again. Devious is a better word for him than for those pigheaded, bumbling Irish. Mark my words, young lady."

"I will that, sir," she said, and seeming embarrassed by her ignorance and lack of faith in the Royal Irish Constabulary, she concentrated on buttering her bread roll.

After an evening of cooing over Mrs. Whyte's antimacassars and hoop embroidery and discussing the pros and cons of sailing ships versus steamers with the gentlemen, Fianna excused herself and went up to bed.

Just outside the drawing room, she overheard Mr. Whyte tell Robert, "That's a strange one, she is. Seems sweet as honey, but there is a barb there somewhere."

Fool! Fianna scolded herself as she lay on the fine linen sheets of the bed. *How could I spout words like that when I can see what a passionate Englishman and Irish hater he is! Marcus was able to deceive the English for years, and still does, gentle schoolmaster that he was* supposed to be, but he had better control, and no temper like mine. It will be my neck in a noose, sure, if Whyte even thinks I am a spy! My only hope is that he will be so afraid to offend the Nugents that he won't suggest such a thing. How can I get in his good graces again? I must get my job done and get out of here!*

If she slept at all, it was light and fitful. Just before dawn she was wide-awake and heard Whyte's boots on the staircase as he went downstairs.

She slid out of bed and reached for a red satin dressing robe that Annie had left on a chair. On bare feet, she stepped out of the room and onto the upper balcony just far enough to see him enter the dining room, closing the doors behind him. Holding the robe tightly around her to keep from the least rustle of cloth, she slipped down the stairs. Near the closed dining room doors, she stopped. Fianna turned to see if anyone appeared on the balcony upstairs. Then she listened.

"Well, my man, how is it going down in the hold?" It was Whyte's voice, low and secretive, but audible.

Another voice, just as quiet. "Not well. Never seen any so stubborn. Before long, I will have to take them on to Richmond Gaol. Can't have them starve to death before I turn them over to the courts. But, if possible, I want to get the information out of them myself. We must find out who their contacts were in Kerry when they went after those guns, and where the information about the ship came from in the first place. With that information we can scoop up a whole network along the Atlantic coast. If they go to Richmond, the whole RIC will be in on it. I have worked too hard to infiltrate the Brotherhood to let prison torture get the credit for breaking this society."

Whyte's voice again said, "I wish you would get on with it. I can't keep my house servants cooped up forever. We need supplies and services, and soon I will have to hire harvesters. I don't think any of my servants have heard or seen anything about the goings-on down there in the cellar, but I have kept them on the estate just in case. And to top it off, I have an unwelcome guest in the house."

"A guest? Who is he?" The man's voice sounded alarmed.

"Just a fool girl, got mixed up with Gypsies after the train bogged down. They robbed her, of course, and she came begging to my door. Couldn't stop her, but I'm watching her close."

"A girl off the train, is she? Lost and begging? Good enough for her, trusting Gypsies." Fianna thought she heard a chuckle. "Get her out of here *now*!"

"She will likely be leaving today. Her family is waiting for her in Dublin. And I have my own reasons for wanting to get her back to them all safe and in good order."

"Then do it!" the other voice almost hissed. "I will finish my business as quickly as I can, but it looks like I may have to send them to Dublin no more than two days hence, or I will lose them. Pain seems to have little effect, no matter how severe. I have kept their mouths gagged to keep your people from hearing, but it doesn't matter. All they have to do is nod and I will stop the procedures, and they know it, but they refuse to tell me what I want."

"How are you going to transport them to Dublin? You will need guards."

"If it comes to transporting them, I promise you, they will surely be in no condition to fight. However, I will call for a couple of guards from the garrison at Mullingar. If I get what I want, there will be no need to transport what is left of them."

"Then get yourself back down there in the cellar and get it over with."

The last voice was Whyte's, and Fianna heard the door latch click behind her. She darted across the hall, where the drawing room doors stood wide open. When Whyte came out of the dining room he saw her, the red satin dressing gown wrapped tightly around her slim figure, standing at the windows and staring out at the dawning light.

He stopped in his tracks and glared at her, anger and suspicion flaring from his narrowed eyes.

"What in blazes are you doing down here and in that costume?"

Chapter 7

Fianna turned and blinked her large brown eyes as though startled. She was trembling, and it was real. What she heard had left her horrified and almost sick.

"I couldn't sleep. I am truly worried that I may have caused Uncle Marcus to lose a valuable contract he was supposed to seal in Brest. I must go to Dublin today."

Eyeing her figure, every youthful curve outlined in shimmering red satin, her rich dark hair falling around her shoulders, and her bare feet standing on the cold parquet floor, Whyte spoke a bit too quietly.

"Why, my lovely girl, you are pale and shaking. Of course, you may go to Dublin today."

"How kind of you to understand." Fianna's soft pink lips parted in a nervous smile. "I hope you are not too angry with me for disturbing your family."

"Not at all, not at all." The man moved closer to her. "It is so early—the rest of the house is not up yet. You are trembling. You must lie down, but I don't believe you should try to make it back upstairs in your condition. Let me show you a comfortable couch in the library right over there."

What to do? Of course, she was not going to lie down on the couch in his library! The look on his face was so lascivious, so disgustingly lewd, that it added to the nausea she already felt hearing about the dreadful torture going on in the cavern below the house. Yet, if she didn't handle it carefully, if she offended him outright, he could become furious and accuse her of enticing him. Here she stood downstairs, dressed only in her nightclothes. In his present mood, he wasn't thinking about informers. His hate was directed to the men who suffered at the hands of his cohort, but his body at present could only crave one thing, and that seemed to be delightfully accessible to him. She wanted to slip away casually, but he stood between her and the door.

Perspiration stood out on his face as he reached out and stroked her arm in the silky robe. "Come along, dear girl, and rest on the couch."

Crash! The sudden sound of shattered dishes broke the quiet!

Shocked and angry, Whyte marched into the hall and shouted into the dining room, "What is this noise about? Who is it? Annie! What are you up to? You are supposed to be in the kitchen helping Williams prepare breakfast!"

"I'm that sorry, sir," the maid's voice came back, contrite. "Just trying to clear away things from your morning tea, I was, and the cups slipped."

"Then clean it up and get back to the scullery!"

By the time Whyte had finished berating the housemaid, Fianna was on her way up the stairs.

"I thank you, sir, for your kind concern, I do," she called down to him. "But I'm thinking I'd best be getting dressed to go to Dublin. Uncle Marcus will be angry if I impose upon your family too long. Is the train running yet, or must I be hiring a carriage for the whole long way?"

Frustrated, his face almost purple with anger, Whyte answered in a tight voice, "The train runs from Ballymoyne to the Pale now, not westerly, until the tracks are cleared. Your uncle, of course. Marcus Maher. Glad to be of help to him," he muttered, calming a bit as he reminded himself that her relative now owed him a favor. "That girl is going to suffer for those broken dishes."

Entering her bedchamber, Fianna slipped out of the glorious red robe and dropped it on the chair. Worry for Annie was now added to the whirling trauma of shock and fear that she felt. What kind of punishment would the evil old lecher dole out for interrupting his nasty little game?

Annie appeared carrying Fianna's suit, clean and pressed.

"It was no accident that you dropped those cups, was it now, lass?"

Annie grinned. "Sure, don't you know I wouldn't be about breaking the mistress's china dishes, would I?"

"God bless you! I didn't know what to do. He's so set against Irish, he could get angry and accuse me of anything, get me hanged! But what will he do to you, Annie?"

"I've been slapped before, by both of them. I can take that. But the man's fat hands on me behind, I don't take kindly to. I've learned how to slip away from him or catch the missus's eye. Sure, I'm planning to leave here someday soon. Me and my dearie have plans. We want to have some land."

"It will be hard work, Annie. Is your dearie good for that?"

"He is. We're not minding the work. It will be grand working together to build a home and get a family."

Wistfully, Fianna nodded. "I'm sure it will be. Hear me now, Annie. If you have to leave this place, you must come to me."

"Why, Miss Fiona, I could not trouble you with meself. Sure, we would never take from you."

"I owe you, that I do, for this morning's rescue. You will come to me if you need to. And there's the end of it."

Annie helped Fianna into her suit and dressed her hair. They decided to pull back the front of her hair to the crown of her head and let all the rich red-brown waves lay down to her shoulders. The maid produced a little toque hat and a basic leather reticule, donated, she said, by Mrs. Whyte, who seemed to be keen to help Fianna out of her house and on her way.

Leaving the hat and purse on a table in the hall, Fianna entered the dining room for breakfast. Then she stopped. Beside the sideboard, helping himself to ham and boxty, stood the red-haired boy, Neill. He turned and his hazel eyes crinkled up in a smile at her on his way to the table with his plate.

Fianna did some swift calculations. He knew no more about her whereabouts after the train than Robert Whyte—in fact, not as much. He had gone off with his fishing poles before the tinkers arrived. Very well.

"There she is, Neill McBride." Robert's voice was acid with sarcasm. "The girl who rode off with a pack of Gypsies and came begging to our door, looking like the last rose of summer."

"Well then, you're not looking the worse for wear now, miss." Neill pulled out a chair at the table for her. "Let me get you something from the breakfast buffet, may I?"

"Just a scone and tea," she said. Truthfully, she could not eat, knowing that somewhere under this building were men being starved. "Sure, I did look bad when I got here. The Whytes have been so kind."

Mr. Whyte shoveled a spoon of eggs and potatoes into his mouth, keeping his eyes on his plate, his cheeks still a dull red. His wife only nodded, accepting Fianna's words of appreciation as very much deserved.

Fianna thanked Neill for bringing her plate and then asked, "Robert, I have been so upset, I forgot to ask you. What happened to Eileen McCrory at the train?"

"It took a while for the engineer and fireman to get back with a wagon and a jaunting car to take everyone off the train. I assume she went on to Dublin. I got off to come here to the house before the rest of them."

Neill said, "I saw them when I was fishing. It seems that a carriage picked up the ladies that were on the train and went off on a fast trot toward the city. There is a good chance that she saw her son before they transported him to Van Diemen's Land."

"Poor thing. That boy of hers should behave himself and stop causing her heartache." Fianna hoped that she sounded to the Whytes as if the boy was deserving of imprisonment. She tasted her scone and barely sipped her tea. She was anxious to get out of there, to get to the train station at Ballymoyne and tell what she learned. It was possible that Eamon and the Fenian group could rescue those who were being held here and stop the torture.

After breakfast Robert sent to the stable for the surrey to take Fianna to the train. Apparently, Neill McBride was going to take the train too. He had only stopped at the Whytes after two days' fishing on his way back to Dublin and school.

Leaving the family, Fianna reiterated her extreme gratitude to Mrs. Whyte for her hospitality and to Robert for his attentions. She assured Mr. Whyte that she would tell Marcus Maher of his kindnesses and that Marcus would be everlastingly grateful. *In fact, she would be glad to tell Marcus everything!*

Whyte only grunted and barely looked at her as she prepared to go through the front doors and out to the waiting surrey. However, he called to her just before the carriage pulled away,

"Tell your uncle I'll be calling him about transporting my grain to England. Good business for both of us!"

"Oh, I will!"

At Ballymoyne, Robert let them off at the steps to the small stone station house. Neill helped her down and gathered his poles and tackle.

"Will you be waiting with us, Robert?"

"Not if you think you can keep the lady from wandering off again. She might go breezing off with a herd of Fenians next time. I must be going back home to get ready for a ball at the next plantation tonight. Lots of girls, Neill. Don't you want to come with me?"

"Got to be getting to Trinity. It's my thesis I'd best be working on, good as a party sounds to me."

"You're as big a fool as Fiona," Robert derided. "You've got months yet until your final papers are due."

Neill grinned easily. "I'm slow," he said, and slapped the rump of the surrey's horse, sending it trotting off down the road.

They stood together on the wooden platform beside the station. Fianna frowned, wondering just how she was going to maneuver her next move. Having Neill with her complicated her instructions. Finally, she decided to speak, no matter how ridiculous it sounded.

"I'm needing to go across the tracks there to the blacksmith shop. The smithy there is a friend of my uncle, and I should be giving him his regards."

"Your uncle is a friend of a smithy? I understand your family is rather wealthy. Shipping, isn't it? And you take time to discourse with a blacksmith? How democratic."

Fianna looked at him sharply. What was he getting at? Did he suspect more than she told? But the young man leaned on his fishing poles and smiled engagingly, as if amused at her lack of snobbery.

"Shall I go with you then?"

"No!" The word popped out before she knew it. She had to cover it quickly with polite solicitude. "You'll not be wanting to go in there. That light-colored suit of yours would show the least bit of black soot."

"And your lovely tan costume would not?"

That did it. People always trying to tell her what she should do!

"I'll be going to visit the smithy," she said in a no-nonsense tone as she turned to the steps leading down to the loosely cobbled road. "I'll be back before the train leaves."

"So be it." He pushed his wide-brimmed hat back, revealing that gleaming golden cowlick that curled up from his forehead and blended into his carrot-colored hair.

She glanced back at him as she started across the road. He still stood in the same place on the platform, leaning on those fishing poles and grinning good-naturedly.

What kind of fool is he, letting me go without a real argument like a gentleman should? Whatever he is, it's glad I am that he is so.

Ballymoyne was a fair-size town. There were hardly any people around the long strip of tall, colorfully plastered buildings. A few shops on both sides of the street and a pub, of course, were almost empty. No one had money to spend in the evicted community.

The blacksmith shop was set apart from the rest on the opposite side of the railroad track, due to the smoke and noise—and possibly for convenience, since he often would have to make small repairs to the trains. There it was, a few yards from the rails, a squat stone building with a yawning opening on the front.

Inside the building there was the hot smell of burning iron. The inner walls were dark from years of smoke. Not far inside, close to the entrance, a hulk of a man leaned over a blazing fire, tongs in hand, beating on a red-hot, glowing horseshoe. Sparks flew as the hammer rang against the anvil. While Fianna watched, he let the horseshoe down into a tub of water. It hissed viciously, and steam billowed up, adding to the glisten of wetness on the big man's already sweat- and soot-covered face.

When Fianna approached, he looked up from his work. "Well then, lass. I wasn't expecting you so soon."

"You were expecting me?"

He grinned, a yellow-white swath in his darkened face. "Aye, and give me your name."

"Fianna Fitzmichael."

"That's not the name I'm wanting to hear. Give me your true name, which you should be telling to all on this trip of yours."

"Ah, indeed. It's right you are. My name is Fiona."

"And your uncle?"

"Marcus Maher."

"Marcus, indeed. And how is the man? I've heard no word from him for years."

Realization flowed over Fianna. Apparently the shop had been one of Marcus's contacts with the Brotherhood.

"He is well. He has a son, Kells."

"Grand name for the son of that man. Now, child, state your business."

"I'm here to meet a friend. That's all."

"Jamie Rooney, is it?"

"Sure and it is." Fianna was puzzled. "Now then, why would you be asking so many questions?"

The big man turned to face her. "May be that you don't understand what goes on. May be that you lack the cold feeling on your back of a firing squad or a hangman's noose. You'd best be getting that feel, if you are going to be part of this and you want to survive it."

"I don't intend to do more than I am doing now. As soon as I give my report, it's off I have to go to England, hateful as that is."

"So you say, lass. So you say now."

"And what would she be saying to you, troublesome lass that she is?"

In the blackened depths of the shop, a door had opened. Jamie stood there, hands in his pockets.

Fianna went to him. She put her arms around him, and he dropped an arm around her shoulders and drew her into a tiny room in the back of the shop. The cubicle of a room was only slightly less sooty than the shop. After the door closed, the ring of the hammer began once more.

"You can't know what a relief it is to see you, Fianna. It's that glad I am that you made it safe here."

"Jamie, I have something to tell you. It's a horrible thing, and Eamon and you must move quickly. I heard Mr. Whyte talking to someone, secret like. I don't know who the other man was, but, Jamie, I think those two fellows who were sent to Kerry for guns are being held trapped in the cellar of the Whyte house. The man talked of starving them! And torture!"

"Fianna, are you sure? Could you have been mistaken?"

"I don't think so. He was pretty sure of himself. Said he was trying to find out who they met in Kerry about the gunship. But he said—oh, Jamie, he said that he would have to take them to the prison within these two days or they wouldn't be alive!"

"My God, Larkin and O'Dwyer being starved and tortured! You say he may be taking them to Dublin to the prison any time now?"

"He said that."

"Then I have to hurry and get word to the fellows. We have to do something. But, if we do, will they know how we found out about them?" "I don't know. How could he suspect the niece of the grand businessman Marcus Maher and daughter of the wealthy Fitzmichael family? And me a relative of the pompous MP Horace Nugent! One more thing, Jamie. There is a sweet little housemaid there named Annie. Those people are brutal to her. Of course, none of the staff has been allowed off the premises for a week or two, to be sure they couldn't talk to anyone, just in case they heard something from the cellar, but this girl kept that evil old man from molesting me. She did, and now she may be punished. She said she is used to getting slapped, but that he puts his hands on her sometimes. Can you do anything to help her get out of there, Jamie?"

Jamie's face took on a thundercloud of concern. His voice was hard, and there was an angry determination to it. "I promise you I will take care of that. Is there anything else you need to tell me, lass? Are you going to be alright?"

"I'm sure of it. I just wish I didn't have to go to London now that I have found you."

"I can't spend time with you now." He reached into his pocket and pulled out her pepperbox. "I hope you won't be using that pistol on those high-and-mighty Nugents if they insult the Irish. Go along and enjoy your holiday."

She took her precious little pistol and slipped it into the purse. "It's a good thing I didn't have it at the Whytes'. That man would have had five holes in him. Jamie, my love—" Fianna reached up and kissed him. "Promise me you will see me at Leaghanor very soon."

"I can't promise you a time, but I will be there again. Goodbye, Fianna Fitzmichael. Be very careful."

He gave her a swift one-armed hug and opened the door.

"Don't you worry about me, Jamie Rooney. I can take care of myself."

As they stepped outside of the tiny room, Jamie caught sight of the red-haired young man across the street. He was standing at the bottom of the platform steps, casually gazing up the street of the town.

"I wonder who that fellow would be," Jamie murmured.

"His name is Neill McBride. It's a friend of the Whytes he is. Been fishing in the Grand Canal before going back to Trinity College. He's taking the train at the same time that I am."

"Is he now?" Jamie's eyes narrowed. "So it's fishing he's been, wearing that fine suit of clothes. And he'll be riding the train with you, will he?"

The smithy looked up from his hammer and glanced across the road. Then he went back to his work without speaking.

"Jamie Rooney, it's jealous you are!" Fianna was delighted.

"I'd not have to be jealous to wonder at any stranger hanging around you, especially now. I don't know what you may have said at the Big House—maybe something to make them suspicious. Be careful, Fianna."

A shrill whistle called from down the track, and Fianna went out of the dark shop. At the door she turned, and the blacksmith looked up in time to see her mouthing, "I love you, Jamie Rooney," before hurrying across the tracks.

Her boots tapped across the cobbled road. As she neared him, Neill looked her way.

"Well then, did you have a nice visit with your friend the smithy?"

"I did."

He took her elbow as she climbed the steps to the platform. "The wonder is that you could talk to him at all, with all the hammering going on the whole time."

"We talked enough," Fianna responded defiantly. "It's his work I'm admiring. He's an artist with iron, that he is," she said. "And the horseshoe he was beating was ready. He had to strike while the iron was hot."

"So I've heard." That disarming little-boy grin spread across his face.

"Well now, are you suggesting that I'm not telling the truth?" Fianna shot back. "It would be interesting to know how you went fishing in those fine clothes without making a mess of them."

The train had stopped, and he chuckled as he guided her into the car.

"Why, I borrowed some clothes from Robert Whyte and left them at the house when I cleaned up."

Fianna could have sworn she heard him murmur under his breath, "Touché!"

Chapter 8

Neill McBride remained on the train when Fianna got off at Kingsbridge Station. They had talked a bit on the short ride—Neill polite enough but relaxed and quite jovial, Fianna quiet and guarded.

As the train pulled to a stop, Neill stood up to help Fianna from her seat.

"You are certain there will be someone to meet you here?" he asked.

Fianna was not on her feet yet. "Don't you see anyone out there on the platform?"

"I do. A rather slim gentleman all in black and a red-haired lady. Sure now, she's a beauty!"

"I've heard that often enough," Fianna said dryly. "The man would be Marcus."

"So that is Marcus Maher," Neill said with interest. Then he amended, "Mr. Whyte spoke highly of him."

"Mr. Whyte is a pig."

He only grinned and took her arm to assist her to the door of the car, where he left her to step down to Marcus's waiting hands. Neill turned away and went back to his seat.

When Fianna finally crawled into bed in the safety of the Clarence Hotel, she lay there recalling the happenings of the last hours since before dawn that morning. Did she really sneak downstairs and overhear Mr. Whyte talking to a terrible, cruel man? Did she see Jamie, her dear love, in a blacksmith shop and tell him about the dreadful plight of Larkin and O'Dwyer, captive in the cellar of that elaborate mansion? And where did Neill McBride come from, so easygoing and good-natured? He seemed harmless, and she had to like the fellow, but she had to hold her guard too. She was too trusting for this spy business!

Resting in the familiar bedchamber at the Clarence Hotel, it all seemed unreal. But it was very real, and she prayed that Jamie and Eamon and their crew could do something about the captive Fenian men. As the train had pulled out of the station at Ballymoyne, she had caught sight of a horse and rider dashing desperately across the meadow from behind the blacksmith shop. Jamie.

The next morning, Marcus and Brandeen took Fianna to the ferry dock and firmly placed her on the boat to England.

Rodney Nugent met Fianna as she left the boat in Liverpool. Strangely, she recognized him immediately, even though she had only a vague image of him in her memory. Nine years ago, when he had been fatuously wooing her sister, Alice, Fianna had been too occupied with her own distresses to take particular note of him. Her mother had lain ill and demanded constant attention from the little girl.

But there was Rodney on the dock, his rotund little body perhaps just a bit more round after years of happy marriage. Almost no sandy hair was left on top of his head to blow in the wind off the Irish Sea. His smile was lovable, and his mild blue eyes greeted her with delight.

"So happy to have you come to visit!" he said, as he motioned for a baggage carrier to help with the small leather bag Brandeen had supplied.

"Alice is so pleased, and the twins cannot wait to meet their auntie," Rodney continued. "We will board the train right here and be at Saint Pancras Station before you know it. Shall we take a bit of tea on our way, Fiona?" he offered as he settled her into a small, plush chair in the dining car. "I hear they call you Fianna now at Leaghanor. I hope you won't mind that we call you Fiona while you are here. Father would go off on a terrible tirade if he heard that Fenian-sounding name, after all the trouble those rascals gave us on our estate before we left Ireland."

"I expected that. Fiona will be fine." She looked around the beautifully appointed railroad car, amazed at the elaborate brass sconce lamps on the walls, the sparkling white table linen, and the silver service. Were they really going to have tea as they rode through the English countryside? Wouldn't it spill?

As the train pulled forward, she realized that this conveyance was entirely different from the rocking wooden coaches in Ireland. They passed through a tunnel cut into the side of a hill, and over sturdy iron bridges. The train rumbled smoothly along on shining wide-gauge rails. The tea did not spill.

Through lace-curtained windows she saw prosperous villages, red-brick homes, charming meadows carved precisely out of rich green woodlands, country folk dressed comfortably in good woolen sweaters and vests, and gentlemen in tall black hats and frock coats. Everything was clean and neat and abundant.

Inside she burned. So, this was the peasant stock of England. No tattered drugget skirts or shabby, undyed shawls here. The houses were neatly kept and stood on well-tracked roads. The people all seemed well fed and pleasantly occupied with their chores. She saw no families with their earthly possessions wrapped in grimy bundles sitting along the roads—no large, dark-circled, hungry eyes of dispossessed children. And this across the Irish Sea only sixty miles east of Ireland. *Will the people of Ireland ever be able to live like this? No. Not as long as foreigners own the land, as they had for seven centuries.*

Rodney was making cheery conversation on his side of the small table. At last he gained Fianna's complete attention when he asked her about Dublin.

"Dublin is grand," she answered. "I have always loved the city. The bridges over the Liffey and the bookshops and Trinity College and the fine big buildings like the Custom House and Four Courts."

"Then I am sure you will love London!" he exulted happily. "The Parliament and Westminster Abbey and Buckingham Palace! Of course, Dublin is one of the great cities of the British Empire, but we will be sure to give you a grand tour of London while you are in England."

"That's kind of you." Fianna responded to his offer as nicely as she could. He was such a dear little man, purely innocent of the horrors of farm life in Ireland. Well, she had done her little bit toward independence for Ireland. She was a spy for the IRB.

While they sipped their tea, she thought about Dublin. She remembered so clearly Brandeen's angry green eyes as Fianna stepped down from the train, two days late. Just as Brandeen was ready to light into Fianna, demanding to know where she had been and why she had gone off with a pack of tinkers, worrying them to distraction, Marcus broke in. He had an odd smile on his gentle face.

"Well now, Fianna pet," he said gently, placing her hand in the crook of his elbow and leading her to the waiting cab, "I've been receiving all sorts of interesting telegrams. Received one from a certain Mr. Whyte. Said you had come to his home in great distress and he gallantly assisted you."

"He did," Fianna said wryly. "You'll be getting your request for compensation when he gets ready to ship his barley to England."

"I see." Marcus understood. "And this other telegram, signed J.R. Am I to know who this person is?"

"I'm sure you do."

"So that is where he has been keeping himself, is it?"

By that time they were climbing into a hansom cab to take them along the quays of the Liffey to the Clarence. Brandeen had not spoken during the discourse. But her wide green eyes were reading every nuance. Later, as she helped Fianna get out of the fawn-colored suit, she asked questions point-blank.

"You found your Jamie, did you?"

"I did."

"And is he coming home to Leaghanor?"

"Not yet."

"I understand. Marcus had his obligations too. And I know that he still does certain things that I am not privy to. Don't try to talk Jamie out of it, Fianna. The waiting will send you into terrors, and every time you know he is involved in a secret mission, you will be frantic with fear for him. But members of the IRB won't renege on the oath, and the goal is more important than you or me—to him and to Ireland."

Fianna was a bit surprised at her cousin's understanding. But, as she thought of it, she remembered those nights when Marcus had disappeared into the darkness, leaving Brandeen to sit by the fire with her books, no questions allowed.

"I know," Fianna said.

"Of course you do. Now let's be off down Sackville Street to find you a new travel costume for the ferry."

"And a new hat, for goodness' sake! This toque hat is ridiculous!"

So here she was in England. Somehow she would get through these two weeks of aggravation.

Part of the time on the four-hour train ride, things got quiet and Rodney dropped off to sleep. Fianna watched the man a bit. He was not handsome by any means, but his rosy, round face was so kind, so innocent of troubles.

"Just you wait until you see our twins!" Rodney took up the conversation as soon as his eyes opened sometime later, apparently unaware that he had been asleep. "Bobby loves to fly kites, and Betty is marvelous at croquet. Beautiful children!"

When he went on to speak about Alice, it was almost with reverence. Apparently he had never recovered from the adoration he felt for the delicate, fair-haired lass who condescended to marry him.

They lived in the Nugent manse—Member of Parliament Horace Nugent and his wife in the main suite, and Rodney and Alice with their lively, noisy children in a separate wing.

"Do you remember my sister, Amy?" Rodney asked. "She has married well and lives in Scotland. Emily is married too, and has a fine young son. She still lives at the estate, because her husband has a most unusual career. He is an officer of the Royal Irish Constabulary Special Branch now. It would not be comfortable for her to live in Ireland with his involvement in subversive intelligence. Rather dangerous and unnerving for a wife, you see. Perhaps you remember him, Major Spencer George?"

Fianna felt her face go numb. "I remember him only slightly," she said. "I was just a child then." Spencer George, the army officer who had caused so much trouble for the Fitzmichaels, who had put her Uncle Daniel in jail, who had pretended to court Brandeen while he snooped around the Big House of Leaghanor. Now he was a spy with the Special Branch, dead set on rooting out every Fenian in Ireland and standing them before a firing squad or a hangman's noose. *Jamie, be careful!*

At last they were in a carriage entering the Nugent estate. They followed a long, winding drive through thick green trees, a forest such as Fianna had never seen in Ireland, green though her country was. Clusters of forest were virtually nonexistent in Connaught and rather sparse in any other place in her homeland. Elizabeth, the Queen, had stripped the island of its grand oaks to build her fleet of ships and fine houses in England.

Seeing that she seemed impressed, Rodney asked innocently, "It's a beautiful country here, isn't it? Ah, there is the house."

Fianna was awed. They rounded a curve, and it came into sight. Beyond an expanse of rich green lawn stood a magnificent red brick mansion. Dozens of window recesses dotted the facade, and the four-story edifice spread its arms wide across boundless grounds.

The carriage rolled to a stop beneath an ivy-covered portico at one end of the building. Rodney courteously handed Fianna down out of the carriage and led her through high oaken doors into a great hallway. They walked along the mosaic-tiled floor for what seemed like miles. Gold-relief designs covered the ceiling. Gigantic proud portraits hung on the walls. Elaborately carved chairs upholstered in gold brocade were placed at careful intervals along the walls.

"It's like Dublin Castle," she said in amazement.

"Oh, much better than that."

She followed him to a huge room where a grand staircase led to the upper regions of the mansion. The little man was puffing by the time they reached the second level. They turned to the left and climbed a much smaller staircase, and then walked along a somewhat narrower hall to a pair of polished dark wood doors.

"Miss Fitzmichael, I welcome you to *my* home," he said proudly and swung the doors wide.

What a difference! Fianna found herself in a warm, comfortable drawing room with a friendly fireplace and soft chairs. The sound of children's voices rattled from somewhere. A woman came gliding into the room. She had silken blond hair piled into a fashionable coil on the crown of her head. Her gown was soft blue with blue-violet pleats draped on the front of the skirt up to the bustle in back. A froth of pale-blue lace rippled around the rather low-cut V neckline. Her lovely face wore an expression of contentment and happiness. It was Alice.

Moving toward her, Alice gave her sister a gentle hug. "Welcome, dear little Fiona," she said softly.

Fianna laughed and hugged her back. "Alice, I hardly knew you! You look so happy!'

Alice's laugh was kindly. "I am indeed, Fiona. And I would not have known you. You are all grown and become a lovely woman. Come and let me get you settled in your rooms. Sure, you must be tired after the boat and the train and all."

Supper was served in the suite that evening after the lively six-year-old twins had met their aunt and were taken off to bed by their nanny. Fianna found the pair delightful. Both had fair hair like their parents. Little Bobby had his mother's fair complexion and his father's joy for life. However, Betty gazed up at Fianna with large brown eyes very similar to her own. It gave Fianna an odd feeling of kinship that she had not experienced for nine years. She was touched, and felt tears sting her eyes.

Even before her brother, Andy, had died and Alice had left Leaghanor, Fianna had felt alone. Her only friend was Marcus, her schoolmaster, and, when he married the beautiful Brandeen, Fianna had felt betrayed. So she stood alone, daring anyone to challenge her ability to "take care of herself."

The dining room was light, and French doors were opened onto a raised terrace overlooking a small lake. A cool twilight breeze floated in for the comfort of the three seated at a long, glossy mahogany table.

Rodney Nugent had a grand time playing "mine host" for Fianna. Alice did not talk much. Fianna remembered that she never had been very vocal. At Leaghanor, Alice's silence was unhappy acceptance of her situation; it was of no use to fight her mother's domineering ways. This plump, friendly little man, Rodney, changed all that. Gratitude toward him welled up in Fianna. She *liked* her brother-in-law.

"We'll be dining with my parents tomorrow," Rodney said. "They can barely remember you at our wedding, you were so young, and they were in such a hurry to get to England to escape the night raiders. Also, my young guest, there is to be a ball here at the end of next week, just before you are scheduled to go back home. You will have the opportunity to break some hearts."

The next evening Fianna was almost overawed when she was escorted to dine with the majestic MP Horace Nugent and his supercilious wife. The dining room was immense. Sparkling chandeliers and richly carpeted floor tried to intimidate Fianna. Pure white linen (*probably from Donegal*, she thought) covered the long table. Light from tall candles, spaced strategically, flickered on silver and crystal. Certainly, they had white linen and candles and crystal at Leaghanor, but the dining room was perhaps one-fourth the size of this one. It was no wonder that Rodney and Alice generally took their meals in their own cozy apartment.

A person would feel like a bug on a pin trying to enjoy a bit of food in this place.

Emily was there. Her thin hair was tan-colored, parted in the middle, and wrapped on each side of her head in a fashion from ten years past. Her gray gown was expensive but as unimpressive as the pale freckles on her cheeks.

Beside her sat an eight-year-old boy with straight white-blond hair. He was dressed in a diminutive suit, white collar, and ascot—an imitation of the attire of his grandfather. He gave Fianna a look of smug superiority. Fianna remembered that look. He was definitely the son of Spencer George.

Rodney's children were not at the table. They were not yet trained enough, and their exuberant ways would disturb the hushed arrogance in the room. Little Spence was different in that he had been carefully groomed by his grandfather and had received many lectures from his oft-absent father about the importance of his social class.

The one person at the dinner table whom Fianna could not identify was Mr. Hinkley. He was introduced as an Englishman of lordly lineage who had fallen on bad times and so had become overseer of the vast domain of Nugent investments. His narrow face seemed all the more so because of long, thin, graying sideburns. Properly dressed in the dark-gray suit and gray waistcoat of a menial, nonetheless the man's long, slim fingers carefully lifted fork and knife with gracious ease. There was a gentleness in his demeanor that made Fianna like him immediately. What a contrast to Fianna's vague memory of the flashy, arrogant captain of the British army, Emily's husband.

Fianna could not help but notice the looks he cast toward Emily. As Emily served herself from the platters offered by white-gloved butlers, her eyes were demurely downcast, and Mr. Hinkley's eyes saluted the lady over his glass as he sipped his wine. From the manner that Emily kept her eyes, never meeting his glances, Fianna wondered about Emily's feelings. No doubt, Emily as a young girl in the hinterlands of Ireland had accepted Spencer George's flattering advances with delight. But, somehow, the well-bred gentility of Mr. Hinkley might appeal to a maturing lady hungry for true devotion.

The great Horace Nugent made sure that his important presence was felt. He sat at the head of the table, serving himself first from the trays brought by the servants. The grand mane of white hair, his heavy though well-trimmed white beard, and his large hands were a bit awesome. But there was a too-bright glint in those fading blue eyes that made Fianna want to say, *You think you are smarter and bigger than anyone else in the world, but your cheap pride shows through, making you small.*

After dinner the ladies adjourned to a magnificent drawing room, also adorned with imposing portraits of important bygone relatives. The gentlemen remained in the dining room for their coffee and cigars. Spence was sent to bed. In an undisguised effort to ignore the chatter of the younger women, Mrs. Nugent retired behind her embroidery hoop.

"What will you be wearing to the ball?" Alice asked Emily as soon as the drawing room doors closed.

"I don't suppose it matters," Emily responded carelessly. "Spencer won't be here to see me, and no one really cares."

"Not at all!" Alice surprised Fianna with her persistent concern about Emily's mood. "Now, Fiona dear, what color do you think would bring out the gold in Emily's hair?"

"Why then, perhaps lavender. Or rich purple."

"There you are! Emily, you must wear a beautiful new gown in royal purple. Taffeta, I think, so that it will be crisp and rustle when you dance!"

"Do you think so?" Emily began to show interest. A touch of rose appeared on her pale cheeks.

From behind her hoop, Mrs. Nugent interjected, "*Not* purple! Definitely not purple for a matron lady!"

"Well then, lavender." Alice did not back down altogether. Apparently she was accustomed to the objections of her mother-in-law. "Emily, we must dress Fiona handsomely for this ball—her first and only one in England. Who knows if she will meet someone like my wonderful Rodney, who will make her happy all her life!"

Getting into the excitement, Emily stood Fianna up and looked her over deliberately. Finally, she decided.

"Red! Flaming, magnificent red. With those dark eyes and lovely dark hair, she will simply *glow* in red!"

The sound that came from behind the hoop was ignored by the three delighted young women. Alice would have no other color but blue, but it would be a grand, rich blue. "Rodney likes me in blue," she said.

This anticipating was fun and sociable. Perhaps that was what Marcus and Brandeen had hoped for when they sent Fianna to her sister.

The mood changed when the gentlemen entered the drawing room, led by the imperious lord of the manor. Emily became quiet and sat on a chair by a window, careful not to speak or look up. Alice and Rodney were subdued, careful to observe every courtesy in the presence of his father. Mr. Hinkley was, of course, quite attentive to anything Mr. Nugent said, nodding agreement to every word.

The tall member of Parliament stood beside the mantelpiece in his fine frock coat and striped trousers, expounding on the intricacies of the governing body and the British Empire.

"He has given the RIC their head to do whatever is necessary to beat down that Irish rabble," he said, his arrogant, sonorous voice filling the room. "Habeas corpus is too slow. Instant punishment is what it takes. That action at Mitchelstown, that's what is needed. The only thing wrong is that they only killed nine of them! Should have cleaned out the whole mob."

Fianna got a sudden mental picture of Crazy Nan living in a muddy cave alone because her unarmed husband had been killed by police firing from inside a building into the crowd at Mitchelstown. Parnell himself had declared the event a travesty.

"Parnell—" she started to say.

"Parnell is a rabble-rouser!" Nugent spouted loudly, angry that she dared to interrupt him. "The man has outrageous ideas to give Ireland Home Rule. Keeps those ignorant Irish stirred up, raiding and robbing decent landlords! Those people are nothing but animals. Unfit to govern themselves! Parnell was in jail once. The man should be put away for good! He continues to deny that he approves of those Fenian attacks, but I know he does! As long as he is free, there will be no Englishman safe in Ireland."

Warning signals came from Rodney and Alice. Fianna bit her lip and lowered her eyes, forcing herself to keep quiet. Mr. Hinkley cast an apologetic sidelong glance at her.

Nugent continued his tirade for an hour until the family could properly excuse themselves to bed. On the way up the stairs, Rodney tried to console Fianna.

"Please understand, little sister. Father is deep into his parliamentary work. He loves the intrigue and power that the British Empire controls. He gets carried away with it. I'm sure he did not mean to distress you, a guest in the house."

Fianna murmured something to the effect that she understood. Then she said no more and went to her rooms.

She was not distressed. She was furious! All the more angry she was because she dared not come back at him with the kind of blistering words she had on her tongue. She seethed inside like a boiling pot, *glad* that she spied for the Fenians, *glad* that Jamie was fighting these English tyrants, determined that if she ever had the chance, she would do it again!

Chapter 9

True to his word, Rodney gave Fianna the grand tour of London. He chose a fine day when the sun was shining and loaded his ladies into an open barouche. Fianna and Alice rode in the backseat, with parasols open to protect their complexions from the sun, and Rodney rode in the front facing them, wearing his tall, black beaver hat. A picnic basket stuffed with cold meats and cakes and wine sat on the seat beside him. A kitchen maid rode seated on the small platform beside a footman on the back of the carriage.

"The first thing we will do is take the excursion boat along the Thames River, so you will get an excellent view of Westminster and the Houses of Parliament with the three towers rising above. You will see the huge clock they call Big Ben in one of the towers. It is all magnificent!" he exulted.

From the boat, Fianna also saw factories and warehouses and docks along the river. She caught sight of the *Sheeaun*, one of the Fitzmichael Freighting Company ships, loading cargo. Their ships did indeed carry goods to and from England as well as France and America. Rodney's pride couldn't match the swell of pleasure she felt at the sight of her own tall ship in the foreign harbor.

They left the boat and climbed back into the barouche to see more of the city. The boat had let them off near the Tower of London. Fianna could see the tall sides of the White Tower rising from inside the gray stone fortress walls.

Those outer walls made her shudder. They looked formidable, as did the round turrets on certain corners, their narrow windows reminding her of the many persons who had gone behind them, never to come out alive.

Rodney instructed the driver to take them across the Tower Bridge and through the southeastern part of the city.

"This drive will take us to Westminster and Buckingham Palace," he said. "You will see more of the city this way, Fiona, although I must apologize for some districts. I suppose every city has its bad side."

"Couldn't we drive another way, dear?" Alice spoke up. "It breaks my heart to see the way those poor people have to live."

"Just close your pretty blue eyes, my Alice," Rodney said gently. "You have a sweet, tender heart, but there is nothing we can do to change things. Very soon we will stop for lunch on a lovely green with fountains and flowers and shade trees."

"Dublin has the Liberties," Fianna remarked. "Poor people are crowding into those old tenements because they have been chased out of the countryside."

"Just so," Rodney responded, totally missing Fianna's hint that the farmers were driven into the city by evictions.

They went quickly along, past places where the air smelled fetid, and ragged people stood in doorways, watching the fine carriage roll by. Fianna looked past the near buildings and saw dark alleys filled with grimy people dawdling, babies crying, children begging. So, England has its poor and hopeless, but they are confined to a small part of a great city, while Ireland's poor are everywhere, hungry, homeless, and wasting away all over the country.

Westminster Bridge loomed wide and sturdy ahead of them. They crossed it and found themselves passing Westminster Palace, which housed the Parliament. The grand building spread itself far along the side of the river; stately windows and Roman porticos combined with lacy grillwork to make an awesome impression.

As they passed the street side of the building, Fianna caught sight of several young men near the massive entrance doors, grouped around a tall gentleman with a neat black beard. There was something very dignified and remarkable about the man. He stood among them without speaking loud or gesturing, but they listened attentively, almost in awe.

"Who would that man be?" she asked.

"Why, that is Parnell himself! I understood he was still in prison. Here he is at Parliament after all. Father will be very much annoyed!"

"So, that is Charles Stewart Parnell," Fianna said thoughtfully. "I would have thought he wore golden angel wings or fiery red horns, depending on the person describing him."

Rodney laughed. "How clever you are, Fiona! You are right. There are those, like my father, who despise the man. Yet there are many, British as well as Irish, who have great respect for him. He is a most unusual gentleman. Unfortunately for my father and several other members of Parliament, he expounds some radical ideas."

The carriage passed the entrance to the Houses of Parliament, but not before Fianna caught a glimpse of bright-red hair among the cluster of young men. It reminded her of Neill McBride, although, of course, he would not be here in London.

I almost wish he was, Fianna thought. *That good-humored smile would be a welcome sight.*

The driver turned the carriage onto a boulevard that went almost directly westward past an attractive park, and soon Buckingham Palace was before them.

"Now there you are," Rodney said with a certain reverence in his voice. "The palace of our beloved Queen Victoria. She's a grand old girl."

Grand indeed, Fianna observed silently. *It was this "grand old queen" who had knighted Charles Trevelyan for letting nature take its course and starving millions of Irish people to death.*

Rodney was doing his best to entertain his guest, and Fianna tried hard to make the proper comments, expressing awe and appreciation for the grandeur of the city of London. But there was a bitterness in her heart that would not go away.

They enjoyed their picnic lunch sitting on blankets on a green in Saint James Park, the meal spread and served by the kitchen maid. It was a lovely place of shade trees and velvet lawns. Rodney complimented the ladies on their pretty summer frocks with long skirts spread out and ruffled parasols, telling them they were like flowers on the green grass.

"Perhaps we should have brought Bobby and Betty along. Look, there are children playing with a ball over there. They would enjoy playing with other children," Alice commented.

"Perhaps we should." Rodney was agreeable. "We shall do just that the next time we have an outing. This time we are entertaining our sister, Fiona."

"Sure now, I wouldn't mind having the little ones with us," Fianna protested. "I have never been around little children, except for little Kells. I find your young ones delightful."

"Of course you do." Rodney glowed. "They are the most beautiful and wonderful of all children!"

Alice and Fianna laughed at Rodney's deliberately outlandish praise of his offspring.

After a while of lounging on the well-groomed green, they climbed into the carriage again and Rodney ordered the driver to turn toward home.

The night of the ball, Rodney escorted two beautiful ladies down the grand staircase, one on each arm. His round face was rosy with pleasure and pride. The entrance was made at just the right moment, when a crowd of gloriously gowned ladies and elegant gentlemen were already milling about in the glowing entry hall. The chandeliers were lighted with hundreds of burning candles. At the foot of the staircase, a number of young men already stood watching them descend, waiting anxiously to meet the "stunning" young lady in the flame-colored satin gown.

On the third floor, two small persons in white nightgowns peered through the banisters, watching their father and mother and Auntie Fiona until they disappeared into the colorful throng. Then their nanny pulled them back inside the apartment, where milk and biscuits waited for them before bed.

Mr. Hinkley, resplendent in new black, escorted Emily down the steps, hovering carefully so that she would not make a misstep. Her pale cheeks were colored prettily with the excitement. The lavender taffeta gown fit her nice figure and "rustled" as Alice said it would. She glanced shyly up at her escort as he led her into the lavish and brilliantly lighted ballroom.

Fianna couldn't help the thrill of excitement that she felt as the orchestra sent infectious music throughout the halls of the huge house. Dancing couples swirled to the waltz and polka, the ladies in radiant colored gowns. Wealthy people chattered and sipped fine wines. She was caught up in the dazzling, overwhelming ambiance as in a glorious dream!

In the scarlet satin gown, superbly draped on the front of the skirt and caught up in a saucy bustle-type bow in the back, she did indeed seem to be a heartbreaker. The low neckline revealed the smooth, clear skin of her throat and shoulders. Her rich auburn hair gleamed in copper highlights and was piled high, with a tiara of Alice's glittering in the curls. A narrow bracelet of diamonds, also borrowed from Alice, was clasped around the left wrist of her long white gloves.

Young Englishmen in splendid, slim black suits and white gloves brought her glasses of punch and plates of delicious tidbits and begged for dances. She laughed at them arguing over which one would be favored with the next dance. It was wonderful to be plied with flattery. Fanning herself from exertion, she could feel her cheeks flush rosy, and her brown eyes sparkled with glints of gold.

"I say now," a tall blond boy argued, "I have had only one chance at the lady. I'm sure it is my turn around the floor with her!"

Coming through the crowd was a fellow balancing a tiny plate of cake and ice cream on a napkin.

"You will have to be waiting a bit for a dance, lads. It's fair exhausted I am, and I did promise that boy there to sit and eat with him," Fianna teased.

It was shameful, the wicked pleasure she took in the glares that came from matrons clustered here and there on the sidelines, heads together, gossiping about that scandalous girl flirting the eligible fellows away from their unmarried daughters. And an *Irish girl*, at that!

Sitting in an alcove with the accommodating young man who had brought her desserts, she took time to realize that her family would surely be delighted if they could see her on this wonderful, relaxed, carefree evening. She was fawned over and spoiled by young fellows who were sought after by many other pretty girls. How grand!

As the evening went along, she moved in a trance, glorying in the popularity and gaiety. The music and conversation flowed around her. The fiery red gown swished delightfully through spinning dance steps. Forgotten were Ireland's miseries for the time. She set aside her craving for Jamie. It was a merry time, such as she had never known.

Then something brought her down from the rainbow clouds of delight. She caught sight of a familiar face far across the ballroom. A tall man had just entered the room. He wore a neatly trimmed Prince Albert beard, and his dark-blond hair was perfectly parted in the middle. He was dressed smartly in the black uniform and gleaming brass buttons of an officer in the Royal Irish Constabulary, clearly intending that his impressive attire would make a grand entrance at the party. *It was the man from the train!*

"Who is that?" she asked a young man who was pressing a glass of wine toward her.

"That man? Why, don't you know? He's a bit of a relative of yours. That is Emily Nugent's husband, Major Spencer George.

Chapter 10

Spencer George! He was on the train with her from Ballyhaunis to the bogging down in the riverbed not far from Ballymoyne. And she didn't know him! Now she recognized him. He had changed somewhat in nine years. That neat blond hair was darker. The prim mustache had become a full beard, albeit perfectly groomed. In that rather shabby brown suit he had worn on the train, he was unrecognizable.

That arrogant look was the same, on the train as well as here. Clearly he had not recognized her either. The way he had tried to become familiar with Fianna was far from the way a proper married man should behave. Emily's husband. Gentle, self-effacing Emily. *How dared he?*

And his high-handed attitude, shouting orders at Fianna. She might not have gone with the Gypsies if he had left her alone. But she was glad she did. She would not have found Jamie if she had stayed with the train.

What had he been doing in County Mayo? He was a major in the Special Branch of the RIC. His entire mission was to search out members of the Irish Republican Brotherhood and destroy their plans. Nine years ago he thought he had done just that in

Cullymor. A wry smile tugged at her lips when she remembered how he had been fooled.

But what was he doing dressed in that old brown suit and hat, traveling on the train eastward? The only answer could be that he was traveling in disguise, possibly trying to gain information from the country people by appearing to be one of them! She would tell Jamie, warn him of this evil reptile. It seemed that he was home at the Nugents for a visit. Knowing what she did about Jamie and Eamon and Crazy Nan, Fianna would have to be very careful if he was around her.

Dutifully, with his proud father-in-law beaming over his wine glass, Spencer danced his first dance with his wife. His eyes roamed the room, ignoring Emily's smile and attempts at conversation. Fianna felt it immediately when his ice-blue eyes caught sight of her. Smoothly, he steered Emily in Fianna's direction so that, when the music stopped, they were right in front of her.

"Well now, aren't you the foolish young woman from the train?" he asked. His voice was loud and strident, and a contemptuous smile was on his smug face. "Emily, you must introduce us properly."

"Of course." Emily obviously wished he was not suddenly so taken with Fianna's striking appearance, since this was her first sight of her husband in months. "Fiona Fitzmichael, this is my husband, Major Spencer George."

"Fiona! Of course! I thought you looked familiar on the train. If I had known you were a relative, I would have kept you from going off with those tinkers if I had to tie you down! Quite a beauty you've turned out to be, compared to the washed-out urchin you were."

Emily looked puzzled. "You saw her on the train?"

"I did. When that rattletrap train got bogged down in a swamp, this young lady took herself off with a pack of Gypsies. It's a wonder she was not abused and found dead on the road. Do I understand you found a plantation house where you could get help?"

"I took care of myself. How did you find out that I went to a house?"

"Word gets around," Spencer answered jovially. "Not much the RIC doesn't know. How is Brandeen these days, and that mousy schoolteacher husband of hers?" The look on his face told Fianna that Spencer was certain Brandeen was sorry she had lost him for a husband.

"She is happily married and a mother."

Emily stood quietly listening to the exchange. She accepted Spencer's habit of ignoring her when others were around, especially attractive ladies. Hurt and insult showed on her face, but it was clear from Fianna's crisp answers that he was not going to be encouraged.

"You must dance with me, Fiona!" he announced. Before she knew it, the man had his arm around her and swept her into the throng of dancing couples.

Fianna was angry. They had left gentle Emily standing alone at the side of the dance floor. In spite of the whirling steps, Fianna caught sight of Mr. Hinkley moving quickly along the wall toward Emily. *God bless the man!*

"You look lovely in that gown," Spencer said, flashing his toothy shark's smile. "We will be seeing a lot of each other. I have come to arrange some matters with my father-in-law. He is a member of Parliament, you know."

"Of course, I know. He seldom lets anyone forget it."

Spencer laughed. "Do I detect a bit of aggravation in your charming brogue, Fiona? Remember, we are relatives now. You and I must get to know each other better."

That I will not! Fianna instinctively recoiled from his touch and turned her head as if watching the other dancers, but caution spoke to her. If she rebuffed him too strongly, he could become an enemy. With his training in the RIC, he might find out some things about her actions that had to be concealed—for her sake and the sake of others.

"We won't have much time to get better acquainted," she said, looking up at him with a tentative smile. "I am leaving for Dublin on the day after tomorrow."

"Indeed? That will not be a problem. I cannot leave my position in Ireland too long. I will escort you back on the ferry myself."

"I wouldn't want to interfere with your visit with your family, and your wife and son."

"Don't worry about that." The lecherous gleam in his eyes made it clear that he intended to make it worth his while.

At last the dance was over. Fianna fluttered her fan.

"Here now, my lovely Fiona, you're too warm from all this exercise. Let us go out onto the terrace where it is cooler."

"I think I must go freshen up in the powder room. Thank you, Spencer, for the nice dance. I'll only be a minute."

"I'll be waiting." There was that gleaming smile again. Fianna darted for the curtained alcove that led to the ladies' powder room. Inside the elaborately appointed anteroom, Fianna dropped onto the plush seat of a gilded chair. She looked at herself in the gold-framed oval mirror.

It was herself she saw, but then not quite. The rich auburn hair piled high, the gleaming tiara, the smooth white skin of her shoulders and above the low-cut bodice of the brilliant red gown—it all looked foreign to her. Her cheeks were soft and brightly tinged with rose, and her eyes shone from the exertion of the dance.

"Is that me?" she asked the mirror. The startling beauty, the fine costume—was that the girl from the stony west of Ireland who rode astraddle her horse and went fishing with the stable master's son? The same girl who carried a pistol in her purse and would actually have shot the Gypsy if she had feared physical harm?

It was. But that girl in the mirror was going to have to be polite to Spencer George and Horace Nugent and Mrs. Nugent and to any other pompous, arrogant English persons who came her way for at least one more day. The eternity of two weeks was just about past, and she would go back to Ireland where she could be herself again.

I've got to go home! I'm sick to death of putting on a show of capitulating to their remarks about the Irish. And now Spencer George! I can't take much more of this bowing and scraping to British society. If she had not had almost daily good times in the upstairs apartment with Alice and Rodney and their wonderful children, she could not have borne it this long.

When she emerged from the room, she hung back to keep out of sight of the ballroom. The curtains of the alcove shadowed the area, and Fianna became aware of a dark hallway leading off the space. It had to be a servants' hall, enabling them to bring more food and drink to the buffet tables. If it led to the kitchen quarters, she might be able to run up the back stairs to the apartment and calm down. As long as she was dressed for it, she would try to avoid Major George and enjoy the ball once more.

Silently, she slipped into the hall and followed it for several feet until she found a door. It was slightly ajar, as if left that way for the waiter to nudge it open while carrying a tray. Her hand was on the knob when a voice on the other side stopped her. It was the detestable Horace Nugent.

"So, gentlemen. The plan will be put into motion now that Major George has come. He will take our mission back to Ireland without any other go-between, which will insure secrecy. I trust my son-in-law. I'm sure he can find the right man to do the job, and the man will know of no one in on the affair but George. Once it is over, Spencer can dispose of the actual assassin as he pleases, and the whole thing will be completely covered."

Another male voice spoke, rather thin and whining. "Here now, Nugent, are you sure this will work? I want Parnell out of the way as much as either of you, but it begins to seem rather extreme."

"What now, Forster?" Nugent became angry. "What is one more Irishman put under the ground? You will not back out now. I have your signed letter of intent, along with the others, safely locked in my desk at Parliament. You have guaranteed your contribution to pay the assassin. Have you forgotten how he walked out of prison and into the halls of Parliament just as you were dressing him down? He made a fool of you! If he continues to stir up the rabble, we may be in for an actual war. We would conquer them, of course, but why have to deal with it? Something has to be done to stop him and, by God, we will do it!"

Fianna stood in the dark hallway listening to the most outrageous, appalling scheme that could ever be imagined. Murder!

The outright murder of Charles Stewart Parnell! She was stunned. Did she misunderstand?

"We will indeed!"

That voice came from the left side of the room, which appeared to be the library of the mansion. Fianna could see the corner of a large fireplace. From that side of the room, another man sauntered into view. He was slim, very foppish, with curled blond hair and a carefully trimmed blond mustache. His clothing had a stylish military look, with double-breasted coat and narrow trousers.

Rolling a cigar daintily between his fingers, he continued, "I'll have him dead if I have to do it myself, by heaven! Carrying on with my wife as bold as brass, and the whole of Parliament knowing it!"

"Yes, and the whole House of Commons knows that you have taken advantage of it, Willie O'Shea." Nugent's voice was snide. The tall, haughty man moved into Fianna's sight, white-bearded chin high and eyes glaring, challenging. "Got yourself a nice position as an MP from Connaught by playing games with Parnell and turning your head from his affair with your wife. You know that the only way you can gain respect and keep your position is the elimination of your wife's lover without any connection to you!" The dandy lit his cigar in silence, apparently unable to disagree with Nugent's facts. The other man spoke up again, nervous.

"Are you sure no one will be able to trace the assassination to any of us? What of the money?"

"See here, man." Nugent was getting more impatient. "We are sharing the cost so that no one would find an unusual amount withdrawn in our accounts, if they dared to investigate. Together the three of us have guaranteed enough to get the job done by a professional and assure his silence. You have pledged your share in your letter of intent, and I will hold that letter so you cannot renege. This needs to be done; Parnell needs to be put away, and we will see to it."

The man mumbled something, and the dandy nodded his affirmation. Then Nugent burst out, "Ah, here he is, coming through the door! The final factor in this plan. In a few days, it will be over and done with. Come in and close the doors tight, Spencer, my man!"

Fianna saw Spencer George come through the double doors on the side of the room opposite to the service door where she hid. She felt a tremor course through her body. The conversation she was hearing was worth her life!

Chapter 11

Slowly she drew back into the dark hall. She could hear Spencer George casually greeting his fellow conspirators, pleasantly assuring them that they need have no fears, that the mission would be completed within days and all would be better for them and for England, of course.

Carefully, she eased her way along the hallway, grateful that the red satin gown did not rustle like taffeta. As soon as she dared, she fled out of the alcove. The festivities were still in high form—music, laughter, eating and drinking, dancing. Before her eyes, it all seemed like a churning whirlpool of colors and gibberish—a nightmare!

It was madness! Four prominent, respected men were plotting like a den of filthy thieves to assassinate the finest man in Parliament—the strongest, the most popular, the hope of Ireland for freedom! She had to get away from the noise, the confusion of partying. She had to think!

Stumbling, pushing through the crowd along the wall, Fianna made her way through the wide French doors and out onto the terrace. Couples were there, talking, sitting, standing, leaning on the low balustrade around the flagstone floor. She put her hand on the solid brick wall of the house and followed it to a corner where a stone bench was partly hidden by potted foliage. Sitting down, she laid her head back against the rough wall and closed her eyes to shut out the activity around her.

What could she do? No one, not even Parnell himself, would believe her if she tried to tell what she knew. How could she, a lass from the west of Ireland, convince anyone that three honorable elected government representatives would even consider such a monstrous idea. She rehearsed it in her mind over and over. Was it real? Had she truly heard this outrageous plot to kill Parnell?

It was madness! Handsome, dashing, sure of his invincibility—the man stood before crowds of people, openly injecting pride and unyielding passion against tyranny into the people of his homeland. His position in Parliament was indeed an irritation to the British MPs, because he never failed to stand tall and lead the other ninety-nine Irish delegates toward self-government for Ireland. Parnell's presence alone was enough. When he was released from Kilmainham Gaol and walked into the meeting hall of the House of Commons just as Forster was blasting his name, Parnell said not a word, but the speaker was so embarrassed that he stumbled over his speech.

Aside from the horror of murdering such a good man, the assassination would surely beget a full-fledged revolt. It would be a bloodbath—Irish blood because, as so many times before, the people's pikes and pitchforks would never stand against the English soldiers' rifles and bayonets.

The horrendous vision overwhelmed Fianna. She sat there trembling. The knowledge put her life in danger. Never, never must she let on to anyone in this household that she knew about the plot! She would have to sit at the dining table tomorrow with those *killers* and act normal until she could get away. Somehow she must get home to Ireland and give the information to Marcus! But time was short. Major Spencer George was assigned to hire an assassin, and he would surely act swiftly.

Gradually her terror began to be replaced by fury. The monsters! Well then, they must never know she had heard it, but if she had the chance, she would stop it from happening, somehow!

At the sound of a soft, dignified voice close to her, her eyes opened, startled.

"Forgive me, Miss Fitzmichael," Mr. Hinkley said quietly. "I hope I did not frighten you. I'm sure you are resting from all of this unusual activity. I had trouble finding you, but you see, there is a nice young chap asking to dance with you. He is the son of one of the Irish MPs, and I have a feeling he is longing to hear the sound of gentle Irish brogue. Do you feel up to the exertion, or shall I excuse you to him?"

Fianna thought a second before she responded, "Sure, I'm a bit lonely for my countryfolk too. I believe I might enjoy his company."

"Fine, fine." The gentleman smiled. "Miss Emily was sure you would. She is so thoughtful, you know. Here, let me help you rise, and I will escort you to the young man."

Mr. Hinkley bowed just a bit to keep Fianna's hand comfortably on his arm while he led her through the crowd. She was still shaken and trying to accept the reality of what had happened. Indeed she would be glad just to talk to a good Irishman for a bit. Of course, she would not tell him anything.

A young fellow waited in anticipation near the buffet table. He was neatly dressed for the occasion in black dinner coat and starched white cravat. His dark hair was combed close to his head, and his blue eyes lighted when he saw Fianna. Hinkley made the proper introduction the best he could without knowing the boy's name.

"Just call me Colin," he said to Fianna. "It's grateful I am to you, sir, for fetching her for me. Kind of you to honor my whim."

"Certainly." Hinkley's long face crinkled into a smile. "Do have a good time, children."

He disappeared into the crowd, on his way to find Emily George, Fianna was sure.

"Will you dance?" Colin asked. "Or are you weary? I will be glad of your company in any way. I had no idea you would be so beautiful."

"Thank you," Fianna said sincerely. "I believe I will dance." It would be better to be moving than sitting still, all jittery. "And isn't this a grand *cèilidh*?"

"Careful, lass," he teased as he took her hand for the dance. "Don't be using the Gaelic in this house. You could be hanged."

"You are all too truthful." Fianna sobered. "I hate it here!"

"Do you now? And your own sister married to one of them."

"Rodney Nugent is a grand little man, not at all like his pompous father."

"Indeed, indeed. I've had occasion to meet the man. Now then, Fianna Fitzmichael, I had a purpose to seek you out. A message, and here it is. 'Jamie sent me.'"

Jamie? Fianna would have stopped still in the middle of the dance floor, but Colin kept her whirling to the music without missing a step.

"Listen to me, Fianna," he said close to her ear. "I know you have had connections with the IRB. I don't know this man Jamie, but I was told to use his name. There are some very important letters that must get to Dublin. As soon as it gets around that they are missing, there will be a grand move on to find them before they get into the hands of rebels at home. Certain MPs will be frantic to get them back. Guards will be everywhere, searching everyone who has passage from England to Ireland, men and women, including the ferryboats. Will you take them?"

More than ever, the room spun around Fianna. Smuggling! How could she do it? No one would be exempt from the search, especially any Irish person, male or female. A cold chill traveled swiftly over her body.

"Letters, did you say? What kind of letters?"

"Suffice it to say, they are letters of intent. You need not know any more than that. It would be knowledge too dangerous for you to carry."

Fianna bit her tongue. Could it be that these were the same letters she heard Horace Nugent exulting over? Should she tell this young man, this apparently patriotic IRB agent, what she already knew? No. After all, she really did not know if he told the truth or if Nugent somehow found out about her eavesdropping and sent him to trap her. And the information she held made it immensely more dangerous for her to be involved with smuggling those infamous letters into Ireland if he was really working with the IRB.

"Who told you about Jamie?" she asked cautiously, moving mechanically to the music.

"I can't tell you that," he said firmly. "Just be sure that you are the only one we know who can do this. We don't want to do this to you, but if those letters are not made public, there could be terrible trouble. I'm not sure how you'll be doing it either. But your family connections make it more possible than anyone else we know. My orders came from one who is sure of your loyalty to Ireland. It must be done swiftly. There is no time to waste."

"I see." If they were the assassination letters, he was telling it true. They must get to Ireland before Spencer George.

He had called her Fianna. He knew someone who knew about her spying and her family. Could it be Marcus? Perhaps one of Eamon's group? Suddenly she realized that too many people knew it all.

If indeed the letters were the proof of the plot to assassinate Parnell, then sure, time was important. But Nugent stated positively just a few minutes ago that they were locked up in his desk at the House of Parliament.

"How did you get these letters?"

Colin smiled. "Access to Parliament. Never mind the rest."

"And how will you be getting the letters to me?"

"When do you leave for Ireland?"

"Day after tomorrow. I'll be taking the ferry from Liverpool."

"They will be in your hands in time."

"And who will I be giving them to if I can get them there?"

"When you're needing to know, it will be told to you."

A thrill of fear sent a chill over Fianna. So much jeopardy. So little knowledge to work with. *What am I doing?*

Then she remembered Nugent's words overheard in the hallway—his confident desire to have Parnell murdered, casual, determined, not the least compunctious. After all, "What's one more Irishman put under the ground?"

Fire flashed in her eyes. She looked up at Colin. "I'll do it!"

"God bless you, lass!" he whispered and whirled her once more before the music stopped. Escorting her to a seat by the wall, he bowed over her hand and disappeared into the throng.

Fianna rested there for a few minutes before some of her young admirers clustered around her again. Strangely, now that she had committed herself to performing an unspeakably perilous task for the Brotherhood, she felt exhilarated! She danced and flirted and immensely enjoyed being the belle of the ball, keeping an eye out for Major George. He did not appear again on the dance floor, no doubt still closeted with his cohorts.

Everyone in the house slept late the next morning. Everyone except MP Horace Nugent. He was out early and off to his seat at the House of Commons. By noon the family was up and having brunch when he arrived back at the mansion, his face purpling with fury!

"Thievery!" he shouted. "Nothing sacred! Treason! Someone will be hanged for this!"

Frantically, his wife tried to find out what was wrong. Rodney went scurrying down the grand staircase, warned by the servants that his father was home and in a rage. He had no better success trying to calm the man than his mother had. Nugent marched through the house raving.

"It was that man! That weakling! I should have known he was too big a coward to allow him to take part in this! It had to be him!"

"To take part in what, Father?" Rodney asked, following the tall man through the halls. "Are you sure you know who did some terrible thing!"

"Had to be! But it could have been the other one. Whimpering turncoats!"

Spencer George came out of his apartment, dressed in a dark-red brocade robe. As soon as Nugent spied him, he ordered him to come to the library with him.

"It's over! We are undone!" Nugent shouted. "We must get those letters back!"

"Of course," Spencer spoke in a strong, firm voice, smoothing oil on the troubled waters in that unctuous way of his. "We will get them back, certainly. Calm yourself, sir. I will take personal charge of the matter."

They went into the library and closed the door.

From the second-floor balcony, Fianna stood with Alice and the children, watching the uproar. When the library door closed, Alice herded her little ones into their own quarters. Fianna followed.

"Does he often get like that?"

"Often he goes into tantrums," Alice answered, a frown puckering her lovely white brow. "But I have never seen anything like this. I fear he will go into apoplexy."

Well you might fear for him, Fianna thought. *If my thinking is right, he is in for grand embarrassment and will possibly lose his seat in Parliament for conspiring to commit murder, if indeed the English think that hiring an assassin to kill an Irishman constitutes murder.*

For the rest of the day, the family was careful how they walked. Nugent remained in the library. Major George paraded around the house in grand authority. He called for the London Police from Scotland Yard. They could hear him loudly berating the officers for lack of security in government offices. Fianna had an odd feeling that she had heard his voice behind walls at some other time, but she couldn't remember where. Possibly it had happened when she was a child at Leaghanor.

He spouted orders at them as to procedures they did not follow and what was to be done to repair the damage of lost valuable papers. Guards, searches, punishments, investigations. He was in his finest element.

Fianna wondered just how he would explain the letters if they were found by the authorities and they had *read them*.

That evening the entire family, except the twins, gathered for dinner. Horace Nugent was almost silent, eating little, drinking a lot. Spencer enjoyed taking charge of the table. He paid little attention to his wife, but frequently he barked orders to young Spence, such as "keep your back straight" and "remember, manners reveal the measure of the man."

Emily sat with her eyes downcast, attending to the scant portions of food she accepted on her plate. Mr. Hinkley gave furtive glances her way, sympathy written in his kind blue eyes.

Finally, Spencer announced, "I'll be leaving for Dublin tomorrow. The place to find those missing papers will be in Ireland, I swear. Also, I will be able to escort our Miss Fitzmichael safely back to her relatives. She can't be trusted, you know."

Fianna felt her face go red. *What does he mean? Does he know something about my mission?*

The man took a drink of his wine and added, "She might run off with a pack of tinkers again!"

Obliging little smiles went around the table. Only young Spence gave an audible hoot. His father nodded to him, approving.

The thought of traveling with Spencer George all the way to Dublin sent a ripple of ice through Fianna's nerves. If those papers really did come to her, she would have to carry them right under his nose!

"I can take care of myself," she said, and her thoughts went to the heavy little pepperbox in her purse. *How would he feel if he knew about that? I must be sure he doesn't know.*

"Ho, you've proven that, haven't you?" Spencer mocked her. "And why should Rodney have to go all the way to Liverpool again?"

"I don't mind…" Rodney protested.

"Don't you think you should spend more time with your wife and son?" Fianna asked sharply.

"Duty calls," Spencer responded pleasantly. "And my son has a fine example to emulate—his grandfather. I could not ask for a finer model of a man to entrust with my boy's upbringing."

Mr. Nugent only slightly looked up to acknowledge the compliment. His face was dark with uneasiness.

After dinner Fianna went to her bedroom. "Must get some rest for the trip," was her excuse. She flung her clothes into the open chest that sat on her bedroom floor ready to be packed and shipped when she left. It was certain to be rifled through by Peelers on its way to Dublin. Sitting in her loose nightgown, she brushed her full, dark hair and studied the mirror. Surely she did not look like a secret messenger.

Everything was becoming more and more complicated. The papers had not arrived. Perhaps they would not come; perhaps the IRB had decided to find another way to get them into Ireland, where the information could be exposed. And, if they came, how would she smuggle them across the Irish Sea, especially with Spencer George sniffing around her all the way?

Finally, she fell into the bed, ready to lie awake, waiting to be contacted, wondering what the major had in mind with those salacious looks he gave her. If she did get the papers, how could she hide them where they could not be detected by sight, feel, or sound?

As her head hit the pillow, she felt something touch her shoulder. Quickly she sat straight up. A dark edge showed beneath the pillow. She reached under and pulled out an oilskin packet, tightly sealed, about six inches square.

The letters had come.

Chapter 12

The next morning she was ready for the Great Adventure. Alice was surprised when Fianna appeared, not in her simple travel suit, but in a sprightly Scotch plaid taffeta ensemble. A snug black velvet jacket outlined her figure above a long skirt with crisp layers of bows at the waist in back. The neckline was a *V*, edged with ruffles of the same taffeta, as was the pretty parasol she carried. A colorful little toque atop a cascade of rich auburn waves in back completed the picture.

"I want to look my best," Fianna said casually. "If I look nice, I will feel more confident on this journey."

"I see," Alice said, with a tiny frown between her eyebrows that told she surely did *not* see.

Emily was also surprised at Fianna's costume; however, that lady was busy trying to remember the many last-minute instructions for their son being rattled off by her husband. She desperately wanted to please him, but it was more than obvious that would never happen.

The two couples and Fianna stood in the early morning in the immense and crowded Saint Pancras Station in London, taking leave. The roof of the structure was high and arched to accommodate smoke belching from the locomotives. Fianna kissed Alice good-bye, quite reluctant to be apart from her after the happy reunion of these past days. They had become truly acquainted for the first time ever. Rodney turned red and smiled when she gave him a hug in gratitude for his loving care of her sister.

The big, shining black locomotive already standing in the station began to rumble and wheeze. Spencer George led Fianna to the long coach cars and helped her up the steps.

The grand major was also surprised but very pleased to see Fianna dressed so gaily for the trip.

"I hope you chose that delightful costume for my sake," he beamed.

"As a matter of fact, I did," she answered briskly. *Begin the tease. It is the truth after all, but not for the reasons he wants to believe.*

Spencer settled back in his seat beside Fianna, that sharklike smile spread across his face. It was clear that he believed that his attentions toward Fianna had paid off. She seemed to be finding him as attractive as he thought he was.

The major was out of uniform again, clad in a fine black suit and tall hat and immaculate black dress boots. He carried a shining walnut cane topped with brass—the picture of the affluent British gentleman. No one would guess that he was a tenacious, ambitious policeman under that garb. *He was on his way back to Ireland*, Fianna thought, *back to his incognito role.* The shabby brown suit and cheap pampootie boots he wore on the train in Ireland were obviously just another sheep's clothing for this avaricious wolf.

She felt uncomfortable, sitting so close to him. She could almost feel his lascivious imaginings in the touch of his arm against hers. Fianna sat up straight on the expensive plush seat and tried to lean toward the window.

"Relax, dear Fiona," Spencer said. "No need to sit up so stiff in these comfortable seats. It isn't anything like those cracker-box coach cars in Ireland. Remember them? You are expected to rest back in repose and enjoy this trip. After all, it will take nearly four hours to get to Liverpool, and after that the crossing of the Irish Sea on the ferry. We must learn to enjoy the company of one another."

"I know." She smiled what she hoped was only a shy smile at him.

The crossing, she thought. Spencer George hovering over her all the while, she tried to keep him off guard and at bay at the same time. He was sure to eventually make definite advances to her. How was she going to handle that? His licentious intentions were like an aura on him, a virtual scent of disgusting lechery! She dared not rebuff him literally. He would get angry. He could cause a great deal of trouble.

If ever he became suspicious that she was working with the IRB, it could mean her arrest and trial and surely the death sentence. The accusations of what the English called "treason" would surely affect the family. The slightest bruise of his conceit would be disastrous. And yet, she was *never* going to let him take advantage of her! Nausea swept over her at the thought. She touched the place where her sturdy leather purse hung rather heavy. *I will kill him if I must!*

How she despised him! His treatment of Emily was cruel. Gentle Emily was caught between a neglectful, disrespecting husband and an overbearing father who not only admired Spencer George but was his partner in a murderous scheme. It was plain that Mr. Hinkley adored Emily, but he would never speak about such a thing to a proper married lady.

Major George could also destroy Fitzmichael Freighting Company. Up to now, the family had quietly gone about building a prosperous shipping company, even though they were Irish. Fianna's grandfather Old John Fitzmichael had taught them to play down the ethnic facts and deal with the British customers carefully.

When she boarded the ferryboat at Liverpool, Spencer attended to their small luggage and then escorted Fianna on a stroll along the deck. They watched the cliffs and green banks of England dwindle behind the silver ripples of the steamboat's wake.

She felt just a bit sad to be leaving Alice after having at last learned to love her and the children. And, sure, Rodney was a dear. Beyond that, she couldn't get away from England soon enough. The tension of having to constantly be on guard, not to offend the delicate senses of the aristocracy, was multiplied a hundred times by the task she was involved in.

"The wind is chill out here," Spencer commented cheerfully. "Perhaps we should take a cabin for the length of the trip."

"No need to go to that expense," Fianna said. "Sure, I'd be happy to have a bit of tea. The breakfast we had at the lovely Midland Hotel by the railway station has long since lost its good."

Spencer did not seem particularly pleased with her request, but he politely guided her to the tearoom. After all, there was plenty of time before they docked at Dublin.

Through the wide windows of the agreeable restaurant, they could watch the green water frothing in the northern gale. Fianna relaxed just a little, glad to use up some of the passage time surrounded by waiters and people at other tables. Nevertheless, she sat stiffly in the white wrought-iron chair, nervously playing with her sandwiches.

"Come now, dear, don't be dawdling. We must not waste the whole trip in this stifling room."

"I'm sorry. I cannot eat too quickly," she offered as an excuse. "It's the water, you know. It makes me ill if I gobble my food. I'm sure you understand." She gave him a coy smile.

"Perhaps we should not have come inside here then, where you can see the waves through the windows. A cabin would let you rest from the sight." He called the waiter for the check.

Fianna could see that she couldn't keep him at the table much longer. She put away a little more of the fancy breads before she remarked, "Look there now, isn't that the red-haired boy we saw on the train when we got bogged down?"

"I believe it is," Spencer said, frowning at the young fellow who leaned against the ship's railing outside the window, watching the water. "We must take pains to keep from drawing his attention, or we will have him bothering us all the way across."

What a wonderful idea! Fianna discarded the thought as soon as she had it. To deliberately attract Neill McBride to them would certainly make Spencer furious. It wouldn't do the young man any good either, to irritate a man with Spencer's power.

Out on the deck again, Spencer led her to a pair of chaises in an alcove between the cabins and the service areas. "Here is a spot where we can enjoy the view and be out of the wind. If you become too cold we can retire soon to a nice, cozy cabin."

Cabin again. He was so blatantly trying to get her alone inside one of the sitting rooms on the boat. She wouldn't do it! But how to stall him until they finally docked?

For a while other passengers walked back and forth in sight of them, settling themselves for the rest of the trip to Dublin. Finally, there was no one around. Spencer leaned over and casually laid his arm across the back of Fianna's chair, his fingers touching her shoulder. His face and that white smile were close to her.

"There now, isn't this nice? We're finally alone here without interruptions. Very soon I think I will persuade you to go to the comfort of a cabin with me where we can truly become very well acquainted." He winked.

Here it comes. Fianna forced a sweet smile and looked up at him, hoping that her dark eyes did not speak the revulsion she felt. She was so tense that she trembled.

"Yes, it is nice out here." It was impossible to keep her voice from shaking.

"Why, Fiona dear, I believe you are cold out here already! I will call the steward to take us to a cabin where you will be warm."

"I'm not thinking we need that," she murmured, desperate. "The fresh air will keep me from being seasick."

"Seasick? Nonsense. The Fitzmichaels love the sea. What other reason for operating a shipping company? I will call the steward immediately."

"I'm different, major. Brandeen and Marcus wanted me to take ship on the route around the southern coast of Ireland with them to get to Dublin, and I refused. I couldn't bear the sailing ship rocking along all that way. That is the reason I was alone on the train. Please understand," she pleaded frantically.

"I'm sure that I understand, dear Fiona, but you must trust me. I know what is best for you." His voice was not quite cajoling.

Just as Spencer started to rise up, another passenger strolled into view. The man stopped and leaned an elbow on the rail, looking across the waves foaming in the wake of the prow. Spencer glared. It was Neill McBride.

Suddenly the wind caught the young man's wide-brimmed hat and tossed it back into the alcove. He turned and came chasing it into a corner.

"Pardon, sir," he said, as he picked up the hat off the floor. "I apologize for intruding."

"Why, it *is* the young fellow from the train," Fianna said, utterly grateful. "What are you doing on this boat?"

He grinned. "Gathering information for my thesis on the Roman occupation of England in 67 BC."

"Happen you to remember Major Spencer George here?" Fianna chatted. "He was on the train with us when it bogged down."

Neill looked puzzled for a moment as he studied the man's face before he said, "Why, it is indeed. How do you do, sir?"

Fianna glanced at Spencer as if she was sure he would agree, and she said, "Won't you come and sit with us?"

One look at the thunder on Spencer's face and Neill said, "I believe I won't right now. I enjoy watching the waves."

"Don't let us keep you from your pleasure." Spencer's voice was acid.

The young man nodded politely in Fianna's direction and left, disappearing around the corner of the cabin wall.

Just as Spencer was leaning over Fianna again, his eyes searching her face for signs that she was captivated by his proposal to spend time together in the privacy of a ferryboat cabin, a uniformed steward appeared. He walked to Spencer and asked abruptly, "We are more than half across the passage, sir. Will you be needing your cabin now? I have others waiting if you will not."

"Ah, yes. The cabin I ordered. Surely you want to go inside out of the cold now?" Spencer winked at Fianna.

What to do? She placed her hand over her mouth and looked, she hoped, nauseous. "I think I had better not."

Frowning, frustrated and perturbed, Spencer waved the steward away. "Apparently we will not take a cabin today."

"I must go to the rail." Fianna rose quickly and headed for the open area of the deck. Spencer sat in his place, irritation building in his sharp blue eyes.

As she passed the corner of the cabin wall, she caught a glimpse of the red-haired boy talking to the steward, that disarming grin spread across his lightly freckled face.

Fianna stood leaning over the rail for a while, in plain sight of Spencer George. Several times she fell forward, clutching desperately on the railing, as if losing her lunch. When she turned back, she tried to be sure that Spencer had decided not to insist on the cabin anymore. He looked angry.

So be it. Let his arrogant conceit be frustrated. He thinks women should fall over each other to let him paw on them. He is just a paunchy middle-aged man trying to be the lothario he thought he was in his youth.

Careful! Fianna scolded herself. I have hours yet with this vermin, and I have to keep his vanity pampered. I don't dare reveal how much I despise him or he will make me sorry. And he has the power to do it!

Sitting gingerly down in the chaise, she dabbed her face with her kerchief and sighed, "I'm feeling a bit better now."

The man sat with his arms crossed, eyeing her skeptically.

She placed her hand on his arm and gave a wan little smile up into those ice-blue eyes. "It's so kind of you to worry about my well-being, Major George."

He looked at her for a moment and then asked, "Who will meet you at the dock in Dublin?"

"I'm not sure. Marcus and Brandeen are out of the country again. But the suite at the Clarence is always available to me."

"Indeed? A private hotel suite? How convenient." He let go that blazing, carnivorous smile again. Spencer sat back on the chaise and relaxed, an odd little smirk of anticipation settling on his face.

A battery of grim-faced police along with soldiers lined the Dublin piers when the steamer pulled alongside. Fianna stood on the deck with the rest of the crowd of passengers, watching the inquisition. Each passenger was halted as he or she came down the gangway. Everyone else was obliged to wait on board. Men were told to remove their coats and hats to be searched—pockets, jacket linings, even the insides of sleeves. Ladies were enraged as the guards rummaged through their small bags and looked over their persons, front and back. If there was the least seemingly unnatural bulge or depression on their skirts or bodices they were hustled to a small building on the dock where a large, uniformed matron waited. Soon after, they could be seen stumbling out of the place, red-faced and furious, some in tears. English or Irish, it mattered not.

For some time, Spencer George stood close behind Fianna in the crowd—a bit too close to suit her, for more than one reason. He was admiring the work of his officers, commenting loudly on their professional skills and absolute impartiality.

"The only way to do it," he bragged in a low voice, so that only Fianna could hear. "Nugent need not fear. His property will turn up soon enough."

"So, that is what they are looking for?" Fianna asked. "The things that were stolen from Mr. Nugent?"

"That they are! Mark my words, my dear, the RIC will not let them fall into the wrong hands. *I* have seen to that!"

Such an admiring look she tried to cast in his direction before turning to watch the shameful harassment on the dock.

Dear Saint Brigid, don't let me get caught! That big woman with the police will find them sure if I am searched!

Real terror shot through her while she was forced to stand with the most arrogant and ambitious Peeler of them all, pressing himself against her back and bragging about his authority.

The major of the RIC began to fidget. He drummed his fingers on the railing. He changed his position the best he could in the pressing mob of anxious people.

"If those officers only knew who you are…" Fianna murmured.

There were still many waiting before he and Fianna would reach the gangway. Spencer let out an expletive and pushed his way through the crowd.

Forcing people against the ropes, he made his rude way down the incline and onto the dock. The guards were there instantly, bayonets ready for the insolent man advancing on them.

"Put those away," he ordered and produced papers from inside his coat. As soon as they looked over the papers, they saluted him, muttering apologies.

"Of course, of course. Don't you think I understand what you are doing? It was on *my* orders that you are on this duty!" He looked up and called to Fianna, still standing by the ship's railing, "Come down, Miss Fitzmichael! We must be on our way!"

Grudgingly the crowd parted enough to let her squeeze through. Emotions tumbled over themselves in her breast. Her heart was pounding so hard she was sure he could see it.

The people who let her by obviously had their own idea of the reason the pompous gentleman allowed his young companion to leave while they stood waiting, tired and impatient. It was clear that he was of some high rank, and this young girl was not his daughter, sure! Fianna's cheeks went red, and she kept her eyes lowered at their despising stares.

When she reached the floor of the dock, one of the policemen hesitated and then told Major George, "Sir, orders are that everyone must be searched. They said the smuggler could be a woman or child or anyone."

"Do you know who this young lady is?" Spencer asked archly. "She is a relative of MP Horace Nugent, just coming from visiting his home! He is my father-in-law. Now, we will have no more detainment! You may search her bag, as my orders directed, but be quick about it. Come, my dear. It's been a long journey, but it will be over soon. Our carriage is waiting."

Just before taking Fianna's elbow, he stepped close to the guard and whispered something, motioning toward the crowd on the gangway.

Then Spencer led her to the waiting hansom cab. As she moved away, she saw the guards force their way through the waiting people and take hold of Neill McBride, yanking him down to the dock.

Fianna looked at Spencer George, ready to ask him to intervene for the boy. Then she saw the look on his face and closed her lips tight. There was a gleam of smug revenge in his eyes that set her cold. So, it was this evil man himself who turned the guards onto Neill!

She knew the reason. He was angry with the boy for his accidental hindrance of Spencer's obscene plans for Fianna. What would the guards do to him, an Irish boy whose innocent friendliness got in the way of Spencer's lechery?

Dear Saint Brigid, forgive me for hating this man so! Just a bit longer and she would be rid of him! Once those letters were safely out of her possession, she would turn on him like a viper! She would become herself again and tell him just how much she despised him! *Oh, hurry and tell me what to do with the letters!*

It had worked though. The fancy costume, the coy looks—everything had come about just as she hoped it would. Better, because without Spencer, her person would surely have been searched at the docks. But she felt a sickness in the pit of her stomach at the thought of the brutal British police and soldiers turned loose on Neill. If Marcus happened to be at the hotel, perhaps he could find a way to help Neill.

Spencer was very solicitous, helping her into the cab with grand courtesy. He sat beside her, bragging of his power with the guards, while they traveled toward the hotel. Lantern lights on the corners reflected on wet streets as they rode beside the River Liffey. A pleasant glow and muffled voices, sometimes joined with music, came from the pubs along the way.

In the darkening light, Fianna began to be alarmed. Suppose Marcus and Brandeen really were gone on one of their business jaunts? She never knew. How could she get rid of Spencer George? The night gave her an eerie feeling of threat, and her own real vulnerability swept over her.

The carriage rolled along Sackville Street and crossed the Liffey on King's Bridge. Then they were in front of the charming brick-and-white hotel facing Wellington Quay.

"Here we are, Fiona dear." Spencer took her key and opened the door to the Maher suite at the Clarence. He stepped aside, directed the porter to place her small bag on the floor, dismissed him, and closed the door.

Fianna began to remove her gloves. "Thank you so much, major, for being so kind and helpful. After your day of being so thoughtful, I'm sure you're wanting to go along and get some rest."

"Rest I will get." He leered as he stepped close and touched her shoulder. "My dear, don't I deserve a reward for bringing you back to Ireland safe and sound? I believe I should have at least a kiss and maybe something more for my chivalry."

He leaned toward her, and she backed away, turning to place her gloves on the small entry table.

"Come now, Fiona. I know what you want. The air has been electric between us all the way from London. It's time for us to stop playing coy and come together, lovely Fiona."

He was right behind her. Both his hands were on her shoulders. She could feel his breath against her throat. His hands were tight and unyielding as he moved them down her arms and around her bodice, drawing her back against his body.

Dear God, he's going to try to force me!

She reached for her purse and the gun inside. *I'll kill him first!*

Chapter 13

"ello, Spencer."

The pair turned quickly at the voice coming from an opened door to a bedroom.

"I see you haven't changed in nine years." Brandeen stood there in a green satin brocade dressing gown, hairbrush in hand and her magnificent mane of red-gold hair cascading over her shoulders.

"Why, Brandeen, you look lovely! Certainly not the picture of a matronly married woman. I wanted to be sure our little Fiona was recovered from an embarrassing experience at the dock. She narrowly missed having her person searched by the guards. If I hadn't been there, it could have been dreadful for the poor child." Spencer George stepped quickly away from Fianna, adroitly assuming the attitude of the gracious protector.

"Is that true, Fiona?"

"It is."

"Then I must thank you, Spencer. As always, the grand RIC to the rescue. Now, Fiona, you must hurry and refresh yourself from your journey. We have a dinner engagement."

Fianna gladly moved away from the man and started for her bedroom.

"I see that she will be fine now, so I will take my leave. Good-bye, lovely Brandeen." That salacious smile again.

He bowed elegantly toward Fianna. "I will see you again, Fiona. Soon, I hope. We have unfinished affairs."

"Sure then." Fianna smiled at him, relieved, glad to see him get out of her life, but keeping up the pretense to the last. She still had those letters.

"Good day to you," from Brandeen, a final dismissal.

He left. As soon as the door closed behind him, Brandeen asked, "Did he harm you?"

"Not at all, unless you take into account that he is a persistent lecher and a colossal, conceited bore."

"And what is this about guards threatening to search you at the docks?"

"Some important papers turned up missing from the Parliament. It seems that they could do MP Nugent a lot of harm if they come into Ireland. The old man was in an awful stew when I left London. Major George there promised to get them back for him before they got into the hands of the Brotherhood. Every passenger off the boat, except for his Royal Irish Constabulary personage there, had to have his or her luggage searched and sometimes their clothing. They searched my bag. Sure, he did make them let me be, he was in such a hurry to get me alone here!"

Brandeen gave a short laugh. "For that I am grateful. Marcus is coming back from Brest tomorrow. I don't think he is involved with any of that."

Fianna shook her head as she started toward her bedroom. "How can you ever be sure?"

"Jamie?"

"Indeed." Jamie had to be part of it somehow. They had used his name.

Now that the terrible stress of manipulating Spencer George was finally over, Fianna returned to thinking about the purpose of this whole charade. The life of Charles Stewart Parnell was in danger! If she could get the letters into the hands of the Irish Republican Brotherhood, there was hope that the entire plot would be called off. Surely it was postponed for now, because any attempts to murder him could be swiftly traced to those three back-stabbing aristocrats in the British Parliament and their sly perpetrator, Major Spencer George.

At the "dinner engagement," Brandeen herself was the only other guest. They had a good dinner in the beautifully designed hotel dining room. The crystal chandeliers reflected softly on the creamy embossed plasterwork of the ceiling.

Brandeen needed to hear all about Alice and her children and the ball and the rest of it. Fianna gladly rehashed everything, careful to leave out the conversation she overheard from the dark hallway and the dance with a young man named Colin.

The lady's brow drew together when she heard about Emily's distress. "The man is a pig! I remember Emily and her sister, Amy, when they came to dinner at Leaghanor. Flighty, harmless little things. She did not deserve to have a man like that deceive her just to raise himself up in society and rank. How Horace Nugent managed to raise children like Rodney and Emily, I cannot imagine."

"Spencer brags about being a member of the RIC Special Branch. He got on the train at Ballyhaunis—the train that got bogged down. I didn't recognize him until I saw him at the ball all decked out in his RIC uniform. On the train he was dressed in an old brown suit and hat. It's sure that he's infiltrating the Fenians, possibly up in Mayo. That seems to be where he was coming from."

"That isn't good." Brandeen frowned.

"That's true. I will have to be sure that Marcus hears about it."

There was silence at the table while the ladies finished their ices and thought about the danger to the rebels.

Suddenly Fianna spoke up. "Look there! That red-haired fellow just going into the pub door off the lobby. I saw him on the train and again at the Whytes' house. He was on the boat coming across."

"That's odd."

"Odd, perhaps, but certainly fortunate! He happened to meet us on the deck of the ferry when Spencer was trying to seduce me. And then that old lecher had him arrested at the dock, out of spite, I'm sure."

"Then we must thank him." Brandeen called a waiter and sent a message to the young man, asking him to come and join them.

He came, smiling but looking a bit puzzled.

"I understand I have you to thank for being gallant to my cousin on the ferryboat," Brandeen said.

"I only made a nuisance of myself when I saw the gentleman making unwelcome advances to the young lady."

Brandeen nodded. "Come and join us for tea. What is your name?"

"Neill McBride. Thank you, madam, I would be honored."

"I've been so worried about you," Fianna rushed to say. "I saw the guards go after you. Were you hurt? What did they do to you? How did you get away?"

"Just dumb Irish luck. Someone shot several rounds from a pistol down at the far end of the pier. The people on the boat started screaming, and the guards ran off to see what was going on. Left me standing there with my coat all ripped apart. So, I walked away, that's all."

"Thank the saints!" Fianna was relieved. "Sure, I was that worried about you."

"Were you now?" That engaging grin appeared.

"I was."

The talk went on for a while until Brandeen rose from her chair. "Don't bother, Neill," she said, as the boy started to rise. "Fianna, I only got off the ship from Brest this afternoon myself. Marcus and I have had a rigorous trip, although very worthwhile. But I'm very tired. Mr. McBride will escort you to your door when you are ready to come up then?"

Neill nodded.

She gathered her purse and gloves and left the dining room; her expensive white shawl hung like a stole around her arms.

"A lovely lady," Neill remarked.

"We get along."

Neill stirred his tea for a couple of minutes. Then he spoke quietly.

"Jamie sent me."

Fianna's mouth dropped open. *Fenians everywhere!* Finally, she asked, "So then, it was no coincidence that you were on the ferryboat?"

"You had to be escorted...from afar...from London to Dublin. No one dared take the chance to smuggle those papers across the Irish Sea. Only you. You are a brave girl."

Neill kept his voice low, careful of the attendants and other guests in the dining room. Fianna was reeling. How many of the IRB were there? They turned up at the most astonishing places!

"You were at Robert Whyte's house."

"I was. Robert happens to be a mate of mine at Trinity College. Of course, he has no idea that I might be an Irish patriot."

"Did you know what I was doing at the blacksmith shop?"

"I did."

"Did you see what happened at the dock today?"

"That I did. Someday we may have the delightful task of thanking the major."

"And wouldn't that be a pleasure now?"

The young man sobered then. "You have an important item in your possession?"

"I have, and I'll be thankful to be rid of it!"

"Not yet. It's grand that you brought it from London, but I'm afraid it must go with you a bit farther. After the incident on the dock this afternoon, I could be suspect. I dare not take the papers to their final destination."

He pulled a small tablet from his pocket, and a pencil, and made a note. "Here is the address. Please take it there quickly."

"Tonight?"

"Definitely not tonight! But as soon tomorrow as you can."

"Strange that you were at the Whytes. Or was it planned?"

"A bit of both. I drop by there often, but it would have been difficult for me to learn anything with Robert beside me every minute. The informer we have in the house was forbidden to leave the premises. Thanks to you, we now know why."

"It was terrible. Have Larkin and O'Dwyer been rescued?"

"Barely in time. They were caught on the road being transported by the police to Richmond Gaol. A Quaker family in Queen's County took them in and brought them back from the dead. It's glad I was to get you out of there."

"Were you now?"

He gazed at her a long minute, her luminous brown eyes, her auburn hair glowing copper highlights under the chandeliers. Then he said, "That Jamie must be one lucky fellow for his name to be magic to you."

"Will you be seeing him?"

"Wouldn't know him if I did."

Fianna studied the darkness outside the draped windows of the dining room, thinking about the young man across from her. His appearance was so easygoing, so boyishly good-humored. Yet there was a secret side of him, a side of intense dedication that made him risk his life to carry out an important mission for the Brotherhood and win freedom for Ireland.

Fianna said, "You were indeed lucky that someone made a noise that took the guards away from you today. I wouldn't be wanting anything to happen to you."

"That was not luck."

"Indeed?"

"What is Jamie to you?"

"We grew up together at Leaghanor, my family's home in Connaught. His father is our stable master."

"Ah, he's like a brother to you then?"

It took only a second for her to decide to nod and leave it at that. "So he says."

"Kind of you to worry about me."

She only nodded. Something was stirring inside her, something different than she felt for Jamie. "I'm thinking it's time to get some rest. The feelings I've dealt with today are all mixed up and distressful, and I'm that weary."

"Of course." Neill stood up and helped her with her chair. He placed her hand on his arm and started to hand her purse to her. "Lass, what in the world makes your purse so heavy? By the saints, you've got a gun in there!" he whispered.

"Only my little pepperbox. The fine Major George doesn't know how close he came to feeling its fire."

A hearty laugh burst from the boy. "I'm thinking you don't need much looking after!"

"It's sure I did today. If I had killed him, it would have spoiled the mission, wouldn't it now?"

"It would." He was still chuckling when they reached the door to the Maher suite.

Fianna looked up at Neill McBride. He was taller than he seemed. His red hair lay in curly waves with just that little golden cowlick curled up in front. Those dark-hazel eyes betrayed the serious, intense truth of the man.

"Are you really a student at Trinity?"

"Sort of. I am supposed to be working on a graduate paper, but I don't have to be there all the time. Why?"

"In case I want to see you again, in case I need you. Will I be seeing you?"

"Never know. It's best that way."

She dawdled, standing there near him. She didn't like to hear that she might never see him again. She wanted to reach out and touch him, to keep part of him with her.

Neill's grin was gone. He stood there almost as if he had the same troubled feelings about their leave-taking.

Then he said, "Forgive me, Jamie."

Gently he took her in his arms and pressed a kiss on her soft lips.

He turned and left her, hurrying off into the dimness of the luxurious hotel hallway.

Chapter 14

The next morning as Fianna sat at breakfast in the suite, she told Brandeen, "I'll be taking a carriage ride this morning."

"Will you now?" Brandeen buttered a scone, pretending not to be surprised. "And where will you be going? Perhaps with that nice-looking red-haired boy?"

"With no one. And where I go is of no importance to you."

Brandeen looked up. How familiar those wide, stubborn brown eyes. How many times as a child "Fiona" had set her chin and made it clear that Brandeen had no authority over her. They were, after all, really only cousins a few years apart in age. Marcus could demand answers and information. But Fianna was not required to answer Brandeen's questions, and she would not, especially when the answers were so desperately confidential.

Going back to her scone, Brandeen said calmly, "I hope you will be back by midmorning. Marcus will be coming soon, and I want to get some shopping done before we start back to Leaghanor. Some things for little Kells."

When Fianna came from her bedchamber dressed to leave on her carriage ride, Brandeen remarked in surprise, "You're wearing the same ensemble today. Aren't you tired of wearing that velvet jacket and plaid taffeta after you wore it all day yesterday?"

"It is the same and, indeed, I am tired of wearing it." Fianna pulled on her gloves and picked up the heavy leather purse. Instead of the frilly little toque, she nested her straw boater over her dark auburn hair and opened the door and left.

The driver of the hansom cab frowned when Fianna told him her destination.

"Not a good part of town, the Liberties," he said. "Beggars and thieves, rebels and homeless there. Are you sure that's the right address?"

"It is," Fianna answered. "And if you'll not be taking me there, I will hire another."

"I will, lass, if you are determined to go. But only to see you safely there, if I don't get meself hung up on a lamppost and me throat cut while we're about it."

She settled back in the carriage and watched the buildings go by. They turned off Wellington Quay and crossed the Liffey on a different bridge. Fine shops and pubs lined Sackville Street. Well-dressed gentlemen stood on street corners in clusters, discussing the market. Ladies in lovely gowns smartly caught up in bustles strolled together in and out of stores.

As she rode along, tucked into the back of the carriage, Fianna let her thoughts roam to the hall in the hotel the night before. Neill McBride kissed her. Not a brotherly kiss. It was a tender gesture, holding her so close, so protecting in his arms. It left her with a feeling that he was drawn to her thoughtfully, definitely and surely yielding to a growing ardor for the young woman who was Fianna Fitzmichael. She felt treasured, exalted.

What about Jamie? Suddenly she realized that her need for Jamie Rooney was not so desperate. *Be careful now. Jamie is my own true love. Isn't he? Don't be letting a single kiss from a virtual stranger spoil all my hopes and dreams. Everything will be the same when next I see my Jamie. Surely it will.*

Before long, the cab passed the grand pillars of the General Post Office. As they turned a corner, Fianna found herself in the midst of an open market. Shabby-looking old women spread out their goods on tables over every inch of Moore Street, barely leaving room for their customers.

Then the atmosphere changed. Ahead, the domed roof of the Rotunda rose amid the roofs of tall tenement buildings. The ugly bricks of tall apartment dwellings were dark and soiled. A pungent odor surrounded her—human waste and rotted food.

On a filthy, narrow side street, the cabbie pulled to a stop. Around them the tenements stood so close and so tall that the street was in a constant grimy gray shadow. Furtive figures could be seen, disappearing into doorways and behind corners, no doubt watching the young lady alight from the carriage.

The cabbie looked around nervously. "You won't be long now, will you, lass?"

"I will not." She looked at the dank, grubby wall before her and compared the number to the writing on the scrap of tablet paper.

"I'll be waiting for you," he muttered. "But, by all the saints, hurry!"

Fianna entered the building. Thankfully, the number she wanted was on the ground floor. She tapped on the door nearest her.

Scurrying sounds came from inside, the rustle of paper, the slamming of drawers. At last the splintery old door opened a crack and a face appeared.

"I have something to be delivered here," she said.

A voice from within said, "Ask who sent her."

Fianna was a bit taken aback. She was sure that Neill would not want his name revealed to anyone. After a few seconds hesitation, she decided.

"Jamie sent me."

"Let her in."

Jamie's name was like a password!

The door was opened by a young man in shirtsleeves with a black apron over his front. As soon as she stepped inside, he glanced around the hallway and shut the door.

She found herself in a fairly large room with high ceilings. The walls were filthy with soot and cobwebs. There was a heavy desk and a long table spread with a few papers. The windows were so filthy that no one could possibly see out or in.

At the desk sat a small older man with slightly thinning hair on top and a neatly trimmed dark beard. His face, under smears of black ink, was very pale. One arm of his white shirt hung limp. Fianna realized who he was. His arm had been torn off when he was a child working in a cotton mill in Lancashire, England. The whiteness of his face was prison pallor after years in Mountjoy Prison.

"Michael Davitt!"

"I am." A kindly smile broke across his thin face at her awe. "It's time you were coming, lass. It seems that you have something of great importance for me."

"So I have. There were guards waiting at the dock when we got back to Ireland, looking for it."

He frowned. "How did you get past them, child?"

When Fianna told him, he chuckled. "What delightful irony! Sure, it's too bad that I cannot print that in the newspaper."

The newspaper! Fianna looked around. "Then this is the place where you prepare and publish *United Ireland*."

"It is for now. Now hurry, lass, and give me your message. This is not a good neighborhood for you to be found in. And, should that cabbie I heard out there get suspicious, I could be back in an English prison for another seven years."

"I'll need some privacy."

"Privacy, is it?" He smiled, and the apprentice in the black apron grinned. "I can't imagine where you have tucked away my gift. Tommy, you'll be letting the lady into the privy. But hurry yourself!"

The young man opened another old door, revealing a tiny washroom. As soon as Fianna slipped into the tiny room and the door was closed, she took off the black velvet jacket. Sliding out of her plaid taffeta gown, she stood there in her white petticoats, turning the dress upside down and inside out. Carefully she ripped loose hand-sewn threads attached to the inside of the waist and pulled out the oilskin packet. Dear saints, what a tizzy Spencer George would be in if he knew that the object of his desperate quest was concealed inside her crisp, fussy gown. He nearly touched it.

Well then, she would be rid of the fearsome responsibility in seconds now, and glad of it.

Quickly, she redressed herself, buttoning her jacket. Straightening her skirt, she pulled on her gloves and took up her heavy purse. Then Fianna Fitzmichael emerged into the big, dirty room once more, the perfect picture of a demure, innocent young lady.

Michael Davitt made a bit of a laugh. "You are indeed amazing." He slipped the letters out of the oilskin and glanced at them. Then he looked closer, and shock and alarm filled his eyes. "Do you know what is in this packet?"

"I do. No one told me. It happened that I was in the house when Horace Nugent found they were gone."

"No matter. All of Dublin will know it by tomorrow, and the rest of Ireland soon after. Go now, child. You have done your people an unbelievable service and put yourself in terrible danger. I wish I could tell the whole country what you have done."

"I wonder if the cabbie will know what is going on in here."

"By the time this paper is on the streets, this office will be gone. Go, go!"

"I'm glad it is over. It is an honor to meet you, sir. Good-bye, Tommy. Good-bye, Michael Davitt."

She found the cabbie still sitting nervously on top of the hansom cab, looking continually around in all directions for the hoodlums who were sure to burst out of the shadows and cut his throat. As soon as Fianna stepped into the cab, he slapped the horse into motion and they went clopping swiftly through the threatening streets of the Liberties.

When they pulled to a stop in front of the Clarence, hands reached up to assist her out of the carriage. "Well, little lady, aren't you the early bird? Where have you been this lovely soft morning?"

It was Spencer George.

"She's been where she ought not to be," the cabbie scolded as Spencer handed him his fare.

"And where would that be?"

"Had me take her to the Liberties, that's what she did. Could have been hung up on a meat hook!"

"Fiona!" Spencer chided. "Whatever took you into that part of Dublin? The place is crawling with criminals of every kind and nests of rebels."

"I went to see a friend." She was thinking fast. "A student I met at Trinity Library. Got herself in trouble and was disowned and thrown out by her family, poor thing."

"Any friend you have living in the Liberties is making her own luck, likely in the employ of Piano Mary. You will never go there again."

"I'm sure you are right. It was awful. Such ugly poverty and smells." Fianna was all properly chastised and embarrassed, to the surprise of the cabbie. *Oh well, it was probably love. Love changes people*, he thought. He slapped the reins and moved off to find another fare.

"I came to take you to breakfast this morning, you wayward girl. Now it will have to be early tea. You're wearing the same charming ensemble as yesterday. Can I hope it is for sentimental reasons?"

"You can." *Hope all you want.*

He found a dim corner in the hotel dining room and ordered for them—fruit and cheese and tea. Then he sat across from Fianna, smiling.

"Major, you are wearing that brown suit you wore on the train. You hardly look like yourself without your fine uniform. Why do you wear that sad-looking costume?"

"I have my reasons," he said with a smile. "Just call them my 'work clothes.'"

"Too bad." Fianna lifted her teacup. "You looked so grand in your uniform, and you were so fine looking with me on the ferry. Are you ashamed of that old suit?"

"That might be one of my reasons." He winked at her and took hold of her hand. "You intrigue me, Fiona. I believe I'm going head over heels for you."

"What of Emily?" she asked wide-eyed.

How much longer am I going to have to play this charade? I suppose I should keep him deceived until the United Ireland *exposes the letters. Brandeen called him a pig. Sure, that is an insult to a fine, useful beast.*

At her question about Emily, he sat back, frowning a bit. "Well, what of her? She has a happy little life, while I must go out into the field and lay down my life for my career. Now, will you go to the races with me in Phoenix Park this afternoon, my dear?"

"Oh, I would love to be doing that. I love the races. Sometime while we are in Dublin, I'm sure I will go. We always do. But, you see, Marcus is coming back from Brest today and, sure, he will expect me to spend the day with himself and Brandeen, catching up on news of the Nugents and all."

Spencer's frown became darker with frustration and anger. It was clear that he had stayed in Dublin another day fully expecting to get Fianna alone and satisfy his baser urges.

"Well then, I suppose I will be getting on with my assignment. It does seem that you could make just a little time to spend with me."

"Where will you be going, major?"

"Just out into Westmeath a little way. Would you like me to come back soon?"

"Of course, I would," she lied cheerfully.

Brandeen found them in the back corner of the hotel dining room, sipping tea and nibbling tiny slices of cheese. She was dressed in suit and hat, apparently planning to go out. She glared at Spencer George.

Fianna spoke before her cousin could begin scolding. "You're here then, Brandeen. The major was just asking me to go to the races in Phoenix Park. I told him that I was sure we'd be going sometime while we are here in Dublintown."

"Of course. We never miss horse races." Brandeen's voice was crisp and impatient. "Are you finished with your refreshments, Fianna? We must be getting along to the docks to meet Marcus. I hope he won't have to be subjected to the same harassment that you had yesterday."

"Ah, but he will!" Spencer assured her. His face took on that smug, egotistical smile as he bragged. "I have given orders that people coming from the Continent must be searched also. Ah, yes. The search will continue until I have those papers securely in hand."

"I can't be thinking what kind of papers would be worth the trouble to bother hundreds of people. Don't your soldiers have something better to do, such as bayoneting Irish babies?"

"Brandeen, your sharp little tongue still amuses me." Spencer's eyes belied his remark. "Fiona, my dear, perhaps we can have a small rendezvous when I return."

"Indeed." Fianna appeared to be reluctant as she took her leave of the man. As she walked beside Brandeen through the doors and out onto the steps in front of the hotel, she hissed, "Thank the saints you came! I thought I was never going to be rid of him."

Brandeen's green eyes flashed suspicion. "Strange it is that you can't bear the man, and yet I am continually finding you in compromising situations with him."

Fianna froze in quick anger. "Think what you will then."

Chapter 15

Their trip to the docks in the cab was made with even less conviviality than usual between the cousins. But Fianna relaxed as soon as she saw her favorite relative disembark.

His slim form was searched by the policemen. He had to remove his black suit coat, and one of them proceeded to rip open the lining. Another Peeler opened his bag and yanked things out, stuffing them back in halfway before dropping the bag to the floor and going on to the next victim. Finally, thoroughly inspected, Marcus was allowed to move on down the dock to meet his womenfolk.

"It's infuriating," Fianna whispered as she hugged him. "The liberties they take with passengers, and it's all done on Spencer George's orders. He bragged about it."

Marcus gave her a wry smile, his gentle schoolteacher face wry with sardonic amusement. "I'm used to it, lass. We are Irish, you know."

"I know. And haven't I just come back from London and that pompous orator Horace Nugent?"

Marcus took his ladies back to the Clarence. All three of them were rather weary from their travels. Fianna finally got out of the tired taffeta ensemble and changed into a crisp, flowered-print chintz day dress. Marcus relieved himself of the torn suit coat and rested in comfort in a large, soft chair, perusing the legal contracts that Brandeen had brought back from France in her luggage.

"It certainly is good fortune that you brought these papers with you," he commented. "Those soldiers might have thought they were subversive. I wonder what they are looking for."

"Something stolen from Horace Nugent, according to Fianna." Brandeen tied the sash of her green brocade dressing gown and dropped onto a settee by the fireplace. "She was escorted on her journey from England by Major Spencer George, and he is crowing about having control of the search."

"Indeed?" Marcus looked up from his papers at Fianna, who was settling her full, glossy skirts into an armchair. "So, the grand army major brought you safely home to Ireland, did he?"

"He is no longer in the army, if you remember. He transferred to the Royal Irish Constabulary, and he is serving in the Special Branch, proudly certain that he is going to round up all the Fenians in Ireland."

Marcus frowned. "I am not happy to hear that. Can you tell if he has made any progress in his mission?"

Fianna glanced at Brandeen and then back to Marcus. "I only know that he wears a tacky old farmer's suit when he travels on the train. Otherwise, he shows up dressed in top hat and cane or his RIC uniform."

"He does that? I see." Marcus's frown was thoughtful. "It would be helpful if that information was circulated."

He went back to his papers. Brandeen studied a brochure on packet boats. Fianna curled up for a nap.

That evening, they went to bed early, with a promise from Marcus that they would go to watch the races in Phoenix

Park the next day. Both of the ladies were delighted. Marcus's women, raised in the wild, stony country of Connaught, rode their own wonderful horses over the hills with the wind blowing their hair. They wore riding clothes designed by themselves that allowed them the freedom of sitting astraddle with a sure grip on the saddle.

The next morning, they prepared to leave for the park early. Just as they came out onto the steps of the hotel, they heard an uproar moving along the street. Looking around they saw everyone down the street to their left—gentlemen, cabbies, fish- and flower-mongers—holding newspapers in their hands and exclaiming loudly. An urchin in ragged pants and a grubby tweed hat was running along the quay, his arms full of tabloids. As he reached Marcus's group, he ran quickly up the steps and thrust one of the papers into his hands and then kept on going down the cobbled street.

A cluster of soldiers came out of a pub. The boy ducked down a side street and was gone before the officers realized what he was spreading.

"Will you be looking at this?" Marcus exclaimed, holding the paper out to Fianna and Brandeen. It was the *United Ireland*. "No wonder it is that Spencer George and the whole RIC were desperate to find those papers! This tells it all!"

Fianna read the headline:

"MPs in despicable assassination plot. C. S. Parnell in danger!"

Huddling closer together, they read the subheading:

"*Three British devils lay plans to murder the grand Irishman, Charles Stewart Parnell*"

Marcus quickly hurried his ladies back inside the hotel entrance, keeping firm hold on the newspaper. He took them immediately back to their suite and closed the door.

"Well now, what do you think of that?"

Brandeen was wide-eyed and outraged. "They can't conquer him by legal means. He makes fools of them every time, so they resort to murder! And look here, one of them is Horace Nugent. Fianna just left his house. What an evil man!"

Marcus looked at Fianna. A strange, private little smile tugged at her lips as she endeavored to read more of the newspaper story. She seemed not at all surprised.

"I think we had better stay here for a while," he said, "whilst we try to digest this news."

Later he cornered Fianna in the hall of the apartment.

"What do you know about this scandal?"

"I know enough not to talk about it."

"Fianna." He stepped close to her. "Child, be careful. You know I love Ireland, but I don't want my beloved pet to be hurt. Or worse."

Fianna gave a little laugh and hugged her mentor as she assured him, "It's alright, Marcus. I was in and now I'm out. But I'm glad I was. It's grand! And no one suspects me, not at all."

Marcus shook his head. "Fianna, once you are in, you cannot ever get out. Somewhere, someone knows. I want you with me or Brandeen every minute from now on, at least until we can get out of Dublin. I'll be telling Brandeen as much as she needs to know. I have very important business meetings this week, and then we will go to Cullymor, where we know everyone."

"Don't you be worrying about me, Marcus Maher. I have my little pepperbox and I can take care of myself."

Marcus's blue eyes grew stern. "Do as I say!"

For the rest of the day, they remained in the rooms of the suite. Each of them, in their turn, studied the newspaper story. The editor, with a name obscured in anonymity, claimed to have in his possession certain "letters of intent" in the handwriting of the perpetrators of the horrendous crime. Undisputable proof.

Fianna rejoiced! No one knew her part in it except that young man at the ball and Neill McBride. And, of course, the unknown person who left the letters under her pillow at the Nugents. Marcus was right. *Someone knew.* But those who knew could not tell their own part in it. It was over, she was safe, and she had succeeded in performing a major act in stopping an English brutality.

That night she couldn't sleep. Her mind was in turmoil. First there was pride. She had helped the IRB pull off a magnificent coup!

Parnell was safe, at least from Horace Nugent and his two high-standing cohorts. They were held in disgrace. They would be screaming about lies and libel, not knowing where those infamous letters were that proved their evil intrigue. And Spencer George could not put together an assassination with all of the world knowing that he was Nugent's son-in-law.

The English Parliament would be shaken by the revelation that three of their own were aspiring assassins. Many of them would likely be pleased to see "another Irishman put underground." Surely, all of the persons named would cry innocence! They would claim forgeries and lies and swear that the whole thing was an Irish plot to discredit their reputations. The "grand old queen" would refuse to believe the conspiracy, of course.

As the night hours wore on, as she turned from side to side on the luxurious hotel bed, Fianna's thoughts moved on to the memory of Neill McBride's kiss. It was soft and sweet, not requiring any obligation. Did it mean anything to him? Did it mean anything to *her*?

It must not. Jamie was her love. She had plans for them together. She would make him come back to Leaghanor with her, where he could settle down and raise horses. He must take himself out of danger in the rebellion. Jamie had been part of her life since she was a child. He must never be hurt.

Neill was different. He was himself alone. She was sure that his underground work with the Brotherhood would not allow him to become attached to anyone, least of all a girl he had only met for brief moments.

So, why did he embrace her? Such a gentle, deliberate kiss, as if he was telling her that she was a valuable creature in her own right. She liked that. He was not friend or family, but he wanted to be close to her, even if only for the moment. A small thrill began to grow inside her heart.

She wished she could see Neill now. And wait until she told Jamie. She could tell Jamie!

Fianna had to get up. She paced to the window. Only the faintest hint of morning light grayed the thick fog outside the hotel. She could not even see the low wall that divided the cobbled street from the dark water of the Liffey only thirty feet away.

She loved the fog. At Leaghanor she would go out into it, surrounded by silence and mystery, wrapped in the whiteness as if she was the only person in the world.

For two days she had been cooped up inside. She had to get out, breathe the fresh, cold air. The fog would surround her, conceal her from everything that was fearsome, protect her from trouble. Excitement and exhilaration filled her. She had to *move*!

She dressed herself in the crisp, polished chintz gown with only one simple straight shift beneath it. There would be no one out in the early morning to notice that there were no layers of petticoats under the loose skirt. Then she slipped quietly out her bedroom door. Crossing the sitting room, she spied Brandeen's beautiful white lace shawl laid over the arm of a chair. It would be cold outside. Fianna wrapped her arms in the rich, fluffy folds and silently let herself out the door.

No one was at the front desk of the hotel, so no explanations were necessary for her venturing out in the cold fog all by herself in the wee hours. It was so early that no doorman or porter was standing outside the doors. No one to disturb her thrilling mood.

Stepping out under the hotel marquee in the silent whiteness, she paused, once more relishing her delight when she had stood there first seeing the headlines of magnificent Michael Davitt's *United Ireland* newspaper.

As Fianna moved away from the door, the cloud swallowed her. She was invisible. She stretched her arms, breathing deeply of the chill air scented with fish in the river and the country smell of horse dumplings on the roadway. The world hung close, unmoving around her. As she stepped forward, her feet almost pranced.

What was that? Out of the corner of her eye, she thought she saw movement below, to the side of the hotel steps. When she turned her head, all was blank nothingness. Listening, all she heard was the burbling flow of the Liffey rushing toward the sea.

Carefully, Fianna let herself down the steps until she felt the rounded cobbles of the street under her slippers. Which way? Perhaps just a little stroll to the right toward Ha'penny Bridge. It wasn't far, and she would be back in the rooms before Marcus and Brandeen woke up.

Her soft footfalls patted hollowly in the street. Far away she heard the echo of horses' hooves plodding steadily along, probably mongers bringing food and fresh fish into the city.

Fianna crossed on the cobblestone-paved street until she reached the very low barrier that bordered the running water. She wanted to be near it, to listen to the water lapping against the stones of the embankment below. The only sound in the wispy whiteness was water and her footsteps.

Or was it?

Was there another sound? A rustling, perhaps, of coarse cloth. Or a soft footfall that was not hers? An ominous chill went through her. Standing absolutely still, she waited. Nothing.

Stop it. My imagination is spoiling the beauty and comfort of the lovely white fog. Relish it. Love it.

She walked slowly on. Again, footsteps. Then Fianna laughed to herself. Of course, it was the echo of her own steps coming from the stone and brick buildings over on the other side of the river. She tried to relax and stroll on.

But something would not let go of her. It was a feeling of something menacing nearby. Her arms prickled with cold that did not come from the fog around her. Her back felt vulnerable, chilled.

She should go back. Why hadn't she brought her pepperbox out here?

The soft, yellow glow from the lamplight on Ha'penny Bridge was beginning to appear in the mist ahead of her. The bridge railing arched up over the river. Fianna hurried her steps just a little, suddenly anxious to reach the light and the iron bridge.

She found herself almost there. An iron railing led to the base of the bridge. She reached out and laid her hand onto the cold metal bar. The fog was still so thick that she couldn't see more than the nearest spikes.

Suddenly, unmistakably, soft footsteps were behind her! Her hand closed quickly over the bar. She turned. A figure loomed up before her, face hidden inside a deep hood, body encased in a loose, dark robe. Hands reached out and grabbed her shoulders and pushed *hard*! Her feet tripped backward, scraping up and over the low river wall. She felt her feet slip off the stones into midair!

Fianna screamed! The sound echoed in the silent whiteness. Ice-cold water swallowed her feet, her legs, her waist, and then her thrashing arms. It filled her mouth; it washed into her eyes. It covered her head.

Chapter 16

The grip she had on the iron railing halted her fall just enough to send her feetfirst as she plummeted down into the black water. The polished cotton chintz skirt billowed out over the water. Air caught underneath the almost-waterproof cloth. For scant seconds the ballooned skirt held her there with her head and shoulders above the freezing water. She screamed again! Then she sank.

Fianna, choking under the water, felt something fall into the river not far away.

Hands groped to find her and clasp hold anyplace they could, pulling at her hair, her sleeves, finally getting a firm hold on her arm and lifting her. She burst up above the water, strangling and gasping for breath. Blinded by wetness in her eyes, she reached around, trying desperately to take hold of something solid.

"Easy, girl!" a water-choked voice shouted. "Don't be fighting me now! We'll get out of here if you don't fight me!"

She was frantic, terrified of the depths of nothingness under her, but she tried to get control, her hand clinging to the sleeve of the person who clutched her arm. Voices of people invisible in the white mist gathered above. Shouts of alarm brought more people. Someone called down, "Call out so we can find you! Hold on to the wall if you can."

Her rescuer swam and pulled her close to the floodwall that bordered the black water of the Liffey through Dublin. Fianna was against a pillar of stones under the end of the bridge.

"Hold on here now, the best you can, until they can help you," the voice beside her panted hoarsely.

She clung tightly to the person swimming there and let her other hand wrap over a jutting brick. It was wet and slimy, but desperation made her grip so hard it hurt.

Blinking water out of her eyes, Fianna tried to see who it was. In the dim light and fog, she could barely see the shape of a man's head and shoulders. His hair was plastered to his head, darkened by the black water. His face was turned away, trying to make out forms to go with the voices of the men above them.

"Here now!" a man shouted down to them. "I'm hanging down a rag of a blanket. Get a hold on it, girl, and we'll try to pull you up."

Voices of many men shouted encouragement up there on the street. "Grab it, lassie!"

"Reach up, up! That's it!"

"Lost it! Try again!"

Fianna's rescuer had her by the waist, pushing with one hand while he clung to the wet stone bricks with the other, making a great effort to help her reach the dangling cloth.

Finally, she clutched it, and the fellows above pulled until a large, rough hand got a firm hold on her.

"Got her now! Give me a hand here, boyo, and we'll have her out!"

"There she be!"

Up on the solid stone street, Fianna was freezing. Her skirts clung to her body, sopping wet. She was grateful that she had only dressed in a single petticoat instead of the customary three, which would surely have drowned her with the weight. Someone wrapped a smelly but dry horse blanket around her, which thankfully covered the embarrassing outline of her legs under the wet skirt. Brandeen's white shawl was lost. Somewhere on the Liffey, it floated toward the sea.

Immediately, men clustered around Fianna, mostly tough old fellows in rough clothing, probably hawkers who were up early delivering fish or milk to the fancy houses and hotels in that part of the city. They had heard the scream through the white fog. They began comforting, scolding, questioning.

Into the crowd came Marcus, tucking his nightshirt into his breeches, alarm and anger in his eyes.

"What is this, Fianna Fitzmichael? How did it happen? What were you doing out before dawn in the fog? Answer me, girl!"

Fianna, lips trembling and purple from the cold, long, wet hair clinging to her neck, flared back, "Don't you be railing at me, Marcus Maher! I'll go where I please!" Then, to her own surprise, she said, "Someone pushed me into the river."

Truly, with all the terror of nearly drowning, with the frantic efforts to stay afloat, with the cold and shaking and trying to move, she had forgotten about it. Someone deliberately shoved her into the river!

Shocked, the men standing about began to pound her with questions.

"Someone pushed you in, did they, lass? And who was it?"

Fianna didn't know. She shook her head. Could it have been a trick to play on a foolish girl out alone? No. The vision of that figure looming over her told her that it was an act of deliberate, deadly malice.

She did not know why; she only knew it was true. Exhaustion suddenly took over, and she felt her knees buckle. "I'm freezing." Her lips trembled so hard she could barely speak.

"Sure and you must be. Will you let one of us carry you, child?"

"I can take her." Marcus scooped her up, coarse blanket and all.

"Well now, there's more to that skinny fellow than it looks!" the group agreed heartily as Marcus turned toward the hotel.

Her voice shaking, Fianna thanked the fellows and asked, "The man who rescued me, where is he? Was it one of you?"

"Not us, lass," the first fellow answered. "Never saw him before, I'm thinking. Anyone see this child's hero, men?"

"I believe I did. Saw him turn and swim for the other side of the river as soon as we got the lass up onto dry ground, he did. Don't know him. Disappeared in the fog."

"Strange," they all agreed.

Over Marcus's shoulder, Fianna watched the men gradually dispersing into the slowly evaporating fog, still discussing the event, likely heading for the nearest open-early pub where they would ruminate over a pint of stout about the morning's adventure.

"Good men," she murmured through stiff cold lips.

"The best," Marcus agreed. "Ireland makes the best."

Brandeen met them on the hotel steps under the marquee, boldly wearing her dressing gown in public because of her concern over Fianna's disappearance out of her bed. Her green eyes were wide with alarm. Immediately she began to question Fianna and berate her for wandering around all alone in the early morning fog.

"Not now, my love," Marcus said, as he slipped Fianna out of his arms and set her feet on the marble floor of the hotel entryway. "First we must get her inside and dried off. Then I have a great deal to ask her. Especially about the statement that someone *pushed* her into the Liffey!"

"Pushed?"

Upstairs in the suite, it took Fianna some time to cease the racking shivers. Brandeen toweled her down and rubbed her hair dry. She produced a soft flannel nightgown and packed the girl into thick comforters warmed by the peat burning in the fireplace.

Then she called out, "Marcus, have they sent up that hot tea? Come in with it then. She's all dried and tucked in and shaking like an ash leaf."

Marcus came in carrying a tray. While Brandeen poured a steaming cup of tea and steadied Fianna's hands to drink it, Marcus pulled a chair near to the bed and the questions began.

"What in the name of all the saints were you doing out in the street so early, and in a blinding fog at that? After that newspaper story, anything could happen to you, and it appears that someone wants to be sure it does. You're saying that someone *pushed* you into the river?"

Fianna sipped the tea gratefully, finally beginning to stop shaking so she could speak. "I couldn't sleep. I thought I would take a little walk outside where I could think things over. Forgot to take my pepperbox with me. Then it happened. But first, I want to know who rescued me."

"I didn't see anyone who looked like he had been in the water when I got there. You didn't see him clearly?"

"I couldn't. Water was in my eyes."

"Could it have been an accident? Perhaps the same person saved you."

"No, I'm sure of that. I heard footsteps behind me just as I got to the bridge railing. Not heavy footsteps like brogues. I turned and there he was…"

Fianna held her head in her hands, trying to see in her mind the figure that burst out of the white mist.

"Describe him, lass," Marcus urged her.

"It's tall, he was. Wearing some kind of a hood. It was a monk's robe, I think that's what it was. He grabbed my shoulders and pushed me backward. I had hold of the railing, but I fell."

Remembering, Fianna shuddered as she once more felt the sudden icy chill of water, the helpless floundering.

"Settle yourself down now, pet," Marcus soothed. "He deliberately took your shoulders and threw you backward?"

"He did! Marcus, he tried to murder me!" The realization finally struck her with full force. *Fear* coursed through her. Someone was dead set to kill her! "Marcus, he must have hated me!"

"Not necessarily, lass. It sounds as if he had planned it carefully, at least if you were to be his victim. But if you were the one, he could easily have been ordered or paid to do away with you. Remember, I told you—"

"I know, I know. Marcus, I'm *afraid*!" Fianna's chin came up. "I will be more careful," she stated. "But that doesn't mean you can tell me what to do, either of you!"

Marcus studied the girl's face for a few seconds. Then he said, "Leave us, Brandeen. I need to know some things. It will not be safe for you to hear them."

For a second, Brandeen looked at Fianna, her stubborn, willful cousin piled up with warm covers to recover from an attempt to murder her, but still rebellious. Then she nodded and left the room, closing the door behind her.

Immediately, Marcus got up and sat on the side of the bed, taking Fianna's cold hands in his to warm them. He told his pet in no uncertain terms, "Now then, you will tell me what has been going on with you. *All of it!*"

"I can't do that, Marcus. You know I can't."

"Fianna, you know that I have operated in the Centre of the Irish Republican Brotherhood for many years. Of late, I have stepped aside, deducing that I could be more useful to the Brotherhood if I can present myself merely as a prosperous tradesman. But I must know what you have been doing."

After a moment of thought, Fianna began to talk about her odd experiences. She told him about Eileen McCrory on the train, and the arrogant way of Spencer George, out of uniform.

"I likely wouldn't have gone with the tinkers if he had not tried to give me orders, but my pepperbox took care of me then."

She explained about Crazy Nan and the little band of Fenians huddled around the old woman's table in the mud hut. "The surprise was that *Jamie* was there. My Jamie, one of the IRB!"

"Thanks be to all the saints that he was. We may never have seen you again if he had not vouched for you."

"Och, surely not, Marcus. They're grand fellows—all but that suspicious John Conor."

"Grand fellows or not, Conor was doing right not to trust you. Now, go along and tell me more."

Fianna's lips pressed together in aggravation at his appraisal of the story. Then she continued. When she mentioned the developments at the Whyte house, Marcus got up and paced the floor.

"Dear God, Fianna! If that man Whyte hadn't believed your pitiful fabrication, I can't imagine what they would have done to you, himself and that monster partner of his that you overheard! Starvation, torture! You could have been raped and murdered!"

"Well then I wasn't, was I? And I have been told that the two Fenians who were being held there have been rescued and nursed back to health. Truthfully, the Whytes' sweet little housemaid got me out of the spot, God bless her!"

"Bless her, indeed! Go on with it then."

Proudly then, Fianna told about meeting Jamie at the blacksmith shop in Ballymoyne, about Neill McBride chancing to be at the Whytes in time to escort her to Dublin.

"It turns out that he wasn't there by accident, after all. I didn't know he was a Fenian then. I only knew he had been on the train and was kind to an old woman."

On she went, about London and having overheard the plot of MP Horace Nugent to have Parnell murdered. Fianna told him about Nugent's two cohorts and Spencer George's role in the plan. And the young Irishman, Colin, asking her to smuggle letters on the ferry to Ireland.

"I didn't even tell him that I already overheard their scheme and knew what the letters were about. I didn't tell Neill either. You know quite well that I can keep secrets."

"You always could, and to my benefit, pet." Marcus stopped pacing and stood gazing at his young protégé. A certain respect was growing in his blue eyes as he listened to the uncanny story.

He smiled a bit when she related how she toyed with Spencer George on the way to Dublin and the delightful way he made sure she wasn't searched at the dock. "And there was Neill again, dallying about the deck of the ferry, almost always in sight."

"I praise the saints that he did. That Major Spencer George is a dangerous one, Fianna. Stay away from him from now on. He served his purpose, but to continue the game now would be putting your life in worse jeopardy, if it hasn't already."

"Neill 'dropped in' to the hotel that same evening and, after Brandeen left the table, he told me what he was and gave me instructions. Marcus, I went to see Michael Davitt, the editor of the *United Ireland* newspaper!"

"Did you, now? Lord bless the dear little fellow. How is he doing since his sojourn in an English prison?"

"He is very pale and thin, but so bright and clever. That is the reason I was so pleased to see the story of the assassination plot in the *United Ireland*. Now then, Marcus, that's the whole of it."

Marcus seated himself on the side of the bed again and took her hands in his.

"Fianna Fitzmichael, my little pet. I have to be saying I am that proud of you. But my heart is lurching all over in fear for you. You have left a trail of vengeful enemies behind you. Tinkers hold grudges. And old Whyte. Don't you think he's going to wonder how the Fenians found out about him hosting a torture chamber in his cellar? Spencer George. Do you know what would happen to his high position if anyone learned that his lechery made a fool of him, especially since he was so deeply involved with the assassination scheme and was responsible for recovering those letters? Then there are the Fenians themselves. You were never obliged to take the oath. Some frantic zealot may have decided to eliminate that one weak link in their chain of secrecy—you, Fianna."

"Sure, I very much doubt that it is Spencer George. He's off up in Mayo, occupied with his sneaky business. I doubt if he has even heard that he has failed and the word is out on their evil plot. He is so sure of his power and station and grand attraction for women that he can't see beyond his beard. And that nice young Irishman at the ball in London would never do such a thing. I just wish I could see Neill McBride again. I like him. And I miss Jamie."

"Don't trust *anyone*! Are you hearing me, Fianna? You must get clear away from all of those people you have been associating with these past three weeks."

She looked down at his long fingers wrapped around her hands and responded, "I hear you and I understand you. But, Marcus, I have done many things on my own now. Now that I see what could be, I will be careful, sure. The memory of that hooded figure in the fog and how I couldn't breathe under the water will make me alert to the slightest danger. Please don't be distressed about me, my dear, wonderful Marcus. I can take care of myself."

Marcus threw up his hands. "How many times have I heard those words from you? *No!* Fianna, my pet, *I will take care of you!* Right now business matters will keep us in Dublin for three more days. One of our own ships will then take us around the coast and back home to Leaghanor, where you will be reasonably safe. Until we take ship, you will stay in these rooms."

"I'll go mad!"

"Then go mad it will have to be. Most of the time, one of us will be here with you. However, there will be times when Brandeen must go with me, because both partners in the company must sign certain papers before a notary. You'll be staying here with the doors securely locked. *This is the way it will be!*"

Two days. Only two days did Fianna stay in the rooms. She paced. She tried to read. She watched for the meals to come up to break the terrible boredom. In the hours that she was there, Brandeen tried to talk to Fianna about going home, riding her chestnut mare over the mountains, seeing little Kells. Fianna couldn't think about such simple pleasantries, not after the tension of the past few days. She went into her bedchamber and shut the door.

Finally, on the third day, she gave Marcus an ultimatum.

"I have to get out of here! Staying in these rooms thinking about all of the dangers you told me makes my nerves even worse! I must go to the races, at least. We never come to Dublin without seeing the races in Phoenix Park."

"That I will not! Fianna Fitzmichael, will you get it into your pretty head that you are in mortal danger."

"In broad daylight, Marcus, no one could do anything. I promise not to go out alone again and, sure, not in the dark. But you will be with me, and there will be people all around. And I've got my pepperbox! I will go mad locked up inside here for another day!"

Marcus looked at her sympathetically. She was bold and ready to dare the world instead of waiting for an assailant to come to her. It would be several hours before dark. Perhaps an hour at the park would help to release some of that tension. Certainly it would be easier for him and Brandeen to deal with her.

"Very well. Brandeen, my love, let us take this nervous kitten out for a stroll."

"You're sure?"

"I hope so."

Within minutes Fianna was dressed in a loose white blouse, suede jacket, and split riding skirt. She wore riding boots. Marcus laughed.

"You're not thinking they will let you get astride one of those high-strung racehorses, now do you, lass? You must be daft!"

"We'll see," Fianna said with a laugh.

They rode a hansom cab along beside the quays, past the place where Fianna was pushed into the cold, black river. With a shudder, she turned her head, determined to shut out the memory and concentrate on the bright day.

At Phoenix Park it was a grand day. The green was glorious in the sunlight and deeply shadowed trees. It was crowded with spectators, mostly Anglos with Irish grooms and toadies. A few decently attired Irish mingled with them. Once or twice Fianna's group spotted grubby Gypsies selling trinkets. The trio strolled across the open space toward the racecourse, happy to be out in the air.

At the rail, they watched several races, delighting in the fine animals, the proud jockeys, the shout of the crowd as the ponies sped by. Even Marcus, as composed and controlled as he kept himself, could not help shouting for whatever horse he favored, and Brandeen laughed aloud at him. After a while they left the track to find a cool drink.

Sitting under a tree enjoying the normalcy of the surroundings, Marcus was glad he had let Fianna coax him into bringing them. Tension and worry had begun to bother all of them.

"I'm going back to the races," Fianna announced. "There is a beautiful roan filly running in the next one. I may talk you into buying her for me."

Marcus and Brandeen laughed.

After some hesitation, Marcus said, "Go along then. Do you have your pistol in your pocket? Just stay out in the open and hurry back soon!"

"I will that!" She patted the place where the loose, full skirt hung over a pocket and took off across the green toward the flying flags and the grandstand, her relatives watching her carefully. She was not out of sight until she disappeared into the crowd of revelers.

Marcus leaned back against a tree, sipping refreshing sarsaparilla, his eyes fixed on the cluster of people at trackside, watching for Fianna to emerge out of the crowd. Brandeen settled her skirts on the grassy shade and shared her husband's relief in the open air.

After a bit the sun began to get close to the treetops on the other side of the park. The crowd had erupted in cheers at two more races. Marcus became alarmed. Hurrying to the mass of people, he called on a pair of acquaintances to help him search. They elbowed through the crowd, calling Fianna's name. They checked inside the stalls and asked the jockeys and grooms.

Finally, they made their way past the starting line to the far side of the track. Behind a stand of young ash trees they found the tinker encampment. None of the Gypsies would admit to having seen the girl. But there was a place where one of the gaudy wagons had recently stood. It was gone.

Chapter 17

The crowd was jocular and good-natured, everyone squeezing around in an effort to get next to the white fence rail and see the ponies burst from the starting line. Fianna strained to see over heads, watching for that pretty roan filly. The gun went off, sending the horses dashing away.

She couldn't see! Too many people between her and the rail. With difficulty she edged her way through until she was on the outskirts of the mob almost behind the starting line. At least she would see them coming back around the track.

No one else was behind her, only a cluster of trees. Everyone was leaning hard over the fence, trying to watch the horses as they turned the far curve. She leaned forward, concentrating on the pack far down the track.

Suddenly a pair of sturdy arms swung around her upper body, a coarse hand covered her mouth, and she felt herself being dragged into the woods!

She found herself in a clearing where several tinker vardos stood, their singletrees dropped to the ground while the hobbled horses grazed nearby. Fianna forced her head to turn in the tight grip to see her captor. She saw a pair of bright, dark eyes.

"Rony! Let me go!" were the first words out of her mouth when he removed his hand. She struggled against his hard, tanned arms and reached for the pepperbox in her skirt pocket. The tinkers again!

"No, lassie." He laughed and jerked the pistol out of her hand. "No more pistol threats. We've got you this time."

Fianna screamed. Rony laughed, that sharp white grin, holding her tight against his soiled blue shirt. The crowd was roaring so loud no one could possibly hear her. Fianna thought she saw heads duck back inside the doors to the other Gypsy wagons. Before the noise died down, Rony crushed her mouth again with his rough hand.

The Gypsy father stepped close and took charge of the gun, dropping it into a pocket of his worn, oversize breeches, while his son fought for control of Fianna's writhing body. He finally got her arms pinned to her sides.

"Let go of me!" Fianna shouted, kicking at his legs with her boots and trying to reach Rony's leering face with her fingernails. Her dark-red hair fell out of its bow and whipped around her face in loose strands.

"We've been waiting for you! He said you'd be coming to the races, sure. We will earn that reward money and put an end to your troublemaking ways. But first, you and I are going to get better acquainted!"

He half carried, half dragged Fianna to where the brightly painted wagon stood. She struggled with all her might, but he held her arms tight with one heavily muscled arm and smothered her face under his other hand. The tinker woman was sitting in the wagon watching the scene with satisfaction glittering in her sharp eyes.

"Remember her, Mam?" Rony asked. "Remember this fine lady and how we gave her a nice ride from the bogged-down train and she threatened the Da with her gun? The man said she'd be coming to the races, and she did."

"How will you be doing it?"

"Och, I'll get to it. I want to enjoy making her pay for her smart ways."

With his mother's help, Rony managed to get a scrap of rope around Fianna's wrists and bind them together in front of her.

"Best get her out of sight."

Rony scooped Fianna off her feet and rolled her through the open back end of the vardo, where she fell into the bottom. She landed half onto the hard wood and half on a bag of grain, still squirming against the rope. On one side her arm was pressed against an old trunk. Looking around for something to use to get free, all she saw was a jumbled mass of goods hanging against the wagon walls—pots, rags, cups.

The woman crawled into the front of the wagon. Fianna kicked and flung her feet apart, but the woman grabbed one booted foot and wrapped a rag around it and then quickly wrapped the other ankle, pulling them both tightly together.

This can't be happening! It's not possible! There were hundreds of people only a few yards away, shouting and laughing, and she was being brutally kidnapped. Marcus warned her, but it just couldn't happen! *It's not real!*

"Let me go!" she screamed, bouncing against the boards.

"Rony, what are you going to do about her loud mouth?"

The men were hitching up the old horse to the front of the wagon. As he boosted himself up to sit beside his father on the driver's seat, Rony looked back and grinned.

"Here it is." He untied a red kerchief from around his neck. "Tie her mouth with this."

In spite of Fianna shaking her head and pulling away, screaming curses on them, the woman stretched the damp, smelly cloth through the girl's teeth and tied it behind her head, catching a good deal of auburn hair in the knot.

It was no use. No one who would care had heard her screams. If anyone in the other Gypsy wagons heard her, they chose to ignore it and go silently out of sight.

Only minutes before, she was walking deep into the excited crowd watching the races. Marcus and Brandeen were casually resting under a tree on the wide green lawn of the park, teasing her about the pretty filly she wanted to buy.

Now she lay tied up and helpless, bruised and crooked, on the jouncing wooden floor of a tinker's wagon, going only the saints knew where!

As Marcus had warned her, it was obvious that the tinker family was angry about Fianna getting the upper hand in their last encounter and planned to repay her for their frustration. Rony himself was furious that she had scorned his manly intentions, handsome as he was sure he was.

She was tensed almost to the breaking point, her joints begging for release from the awkward, miserable position and the squeezing bands around her wrists and ankles and face. But something else was pecking at her mind. The *man* said she would be coming to the races. *He* was willing to pay for her brutal treatment, even her death!

Who was *he*? Her mind ran over the names that Marcus had pointed out to her, names of people she had tricked or embarrassed or simply those who knew she was a smuggler for the IRB. Old Whyte. Spencer. Even John Conor, the Fenian who didn't trust her. Michael Davitt. There was a man who had suffered so much in the hands of the British that he might be almost madly zealous to be sure there were no leaks in the Brotherhood. What about the young man in England who had enlisted her help? Or anyone in his unit of the IRB in Britain. Neill?

Impossible! Neill was fine. How she wished Neill knew what was happening to her right now. But he went quietly on his way, performing his work, even after caressing her. The thought sent thrills of fear through her mind. *Could anyone be so coldly dedicated to the revolution as that?*

Fianna squirmed around, trying to get more comfortable on the boards of the wagon floor. The woman watched her, not smiling, with malicious amusement in her eyes. The wagon trundled along through the trees. She heard the noise of the crowd at the racetrack gradually diminish until she could tell they were out on the cobbled road away from the park. Soon it became the wobbling but muted sound of wheels rolling over earthen tracks.

For a long time, the wagon rolled along, Fianna feeling every bump when they rolled over a stone or turned the horse aside on the path.

Where are they taking me? They must be traveling miles. Why? We are getting so far from Dublin, far from Marcus, from anyone who might help me! Where is Jamie? Where are my family at Leaghanor? There is no one to help me!

Then her words came back to her. *I can take care of myself!*

Was I a fool to say that? I thought I could handle anything. But now I don't have my pistol. I was caught off guard and here I lie, bound and watched and threatened with murder. What can I do for myself?

Suddenly she heard someone passing them on horses. Fianna bounced in the wagon, banging her heels against the floor. If she could just get the attention of the people on horses outside.

The Gypsy woman leaned forward and slapped her so hard it made her ears ring!

Fianna had never been slapped before in her life! At first it stunned her with shock and fear. Then anger flooded into her. Her eyes stared at the woman with fury. That earned her another brutal slap!

Rony looked back and laughed. "You'd best be behaving yourself, royal lady. Your head won't be on your shoulders by the time we get there if you don't!"

Get where? Fianna dropped her eyes so the woman could not read the hot anger flaming out of them. She must take herself in hand and try to get some kind of control of the situation. At least keep herself from being hurt. If she could do that, perhaps she would find a way out of this trap.

Twilight and then black night came on. Fianna was in agony. Her hands were numb from the tight cords. Her back ached from the awkward position, and she couldn't move into a better one. And the evil-smelling kerchief was stretched so tight across her mouth that it cut into her cheeks. Every muscle in her body agonized with pain.

She moaned, whimpering for some relief. The Gypsy woman glared at her.

"Cry if you will, rich girl. It won't be long until you won't be in pain. In fact, you'll not be feeling anything at all, never again."

Fianna didn't need more explanation. The meaning of that statement was quite clear. The cold wash of fear came back, but she fought it this time. *I will do something as soon as I have the opportunity,* she demanded of herself.

The tinker woman seemed to doze off in the front of the wagon. Fianna could hear the men talking—the father very serious and Rony merrily responding with delight over his coup.

Did she sleep or go unconscious? Fianna wasn't sure, but at one point she felt the wagon moving up a hill, making her head lower than her feet. Dizzy nausea filled her. She forced sounds from her throat behind the kerchief—sounds of distress and alarm, fear that she would vomit and strangle.

Rony's voice came from the wagon seat. "You can take the gag off her now, Mam. She can scream all she wants. No one can hear her from out here."

In the dark, the woman crawled over Fianna to untie the knotted rag. It felt as if she pulled half of Fianna's hair out with the cloth.

"Where are we?" Her numb lips shaped the words with effort.

Slap! "Never mind where we are. It won't matter to you."

Before long then, they trundled to a stop. Rony jumped down off the wagon seat and came around to the back. Dropping the gate, he dragged Fianna out of the floor and stood her on her wobbling, squeezed feet.

The faintest light was turning the short summer night into early day. Fianna could see that they stood on a weedy, rocky path in front of an ancient pile of stones that once had been a castle. It sat high on a hillside, and she had the impression of open fields and meadows far below.

Rony pulled from his belt a razor-sharp knife. He held it in front of Fianna's alarmed, wide eyes and twisted it back and forth, catching the light so that it gleamed menacingly. Instinctively, she drew back, and he laughed again. Then he swung it downward and slashed the rags that bound her ankles.

"I'll not be carrying you, lassie," he teased. "There is no one around for you to run to and no one to hear if you want to scream."

Fianna made no effort to speak. It would do no good and, sure, she was tired of being slapped. Fury warred with terror inside her. But good sense kept her from fueling Rony's threats.

"Good girl. Keep quiet and be an obedient lass, and we will have a grand time together, you and I—at least for a while."

He shoved her forward up broken stone steps. She stumbled through a huge doorway bordered by splintery wood that had once been doors. Inside, the huge, empty room was dank and shadowy. Far above on one side, she could barely see where stones had fallen, allowing white, misty light to leak through.

Still gripping her upper arm to lift her feet, Rony pushed Fianna on into the wide room. Spiderwebs drifted from the walls and caught in her hair. He shoved her down onto the bottom step of a high, cracked, and crumbled staircase.

"See how fine our hotel is?" he said. "All those folk who look on us and sneer as we travel on the roads—they don't live in a castle, do they now? And no one comes to bother us or chase us away, because it is haunted, don't y'see? They see lights and strange sounds in the night." He laughed and Fianna knew who the haunts were. "Now tell me your name. He didn't bother to tell it—only to describe you, and, sure, it was easy enough to remember you and your huffy ways."

"I am Fianna Fitzmichael, and you'll be answering to my family, that you will! And who is this madman who wants to do away with me?"

"Fianna, is it? Finn MacCool's whole army rolled up into one little girl. We'll see how much of a warrior you are. As for his name, I don't know it. No matter. I know where to find him when the job is done, that I do."

"And where would that be?"

Rony's eyes narrowed. "You'd want to know it, wouldn't you? Well, it wouldn't do you any good anyway. Sit there and keep still, or you'll be feeling the back of me hand."

The tinker family went about bringing in provisions from the wagon. A small fire was built in the monstrous, big fireplace in the great hall of the castle, and a spit rigged up to ride a chunk of pork over the coals. The family watched Fianna as they moved about, coming and going. There was always someone in the room with her.

She sat still, hands tied in front of her, moving her toes and sore ankles slightly inside her boots. *I've got to do something! I've got to try!*

By the firelight, Fianna could see how the steps behind her rose far up into the dark shadows of the decaying structure. The steps were broken and cracked, but not totally crumbled away. What was up there? Were the ancient castle floors completely rotted, or was anything left of them? A dark, recessed area suggested a hallway.

Could anything up there be worse than what she faced down here? She could only imagine the brutality of Rony's coming attack on her. His pride was dangerously pricked, and he wanted revenge—and the pleasure of being paid to do it made it even more enticing. It was plain that the Gypsy woman wanted to hurt her for bruising her son's conceit. Fianna had to take the chance.

In an instant, when Rony was outside and his father went out the door as the mother was coming in, Fianna jumped to her feet and ran up the staircase into the darkness of the upper floors. Her short riding skirt made her dash for freedom possible. It was only the sturdiness of her boots that kept her ankles from giving way as she leaped from step to step, watching for the most level, undamaged parts.

There was a shout from the mother, and Rony came running into the great room.

"Up the stairs!"

Fianna found herself on the second floor of the cold, bare, broken building. Flagstones had once been laid over the beams of the upper floor. She felt them give as her boots pelted them through a dim, narrow opening. Rony, by that time, was hard behind her, reaching for her.

A room! Darting into the open space, she saw a window to the outside. It was only a slim slot set deep into the castle wall, but it was wide enough. Fianna ran to it and jumped backward into the window opening.

"Stop!"

Startled, Rony stopped just inside the door.

"Come a step nearer and you won't have to worry about keeping me anymore! All I have to do is throw myself backward and I'll fall out the window. I would rather die down there on the rocks and be done with it than let you touch me one more time, you filthy pig!"

He made a forward motion and she leaned farther back, her whole upper body hanging precariously out into the air. "I go—!"

"No!" He stood still, thinking, and an amused glint came in his eyes. "I should let you do it, you know. You would be dead and I will get my money. You'd be killing yourself, would you then? I don't think so. No, I believe I want you to have time to think about what I am going to do with you." He pulled out that sharp blade from his belt and twirled it in the light. "Stay where you are and think about it, Fianna MacCool. We'll be down there in the great hall drinking and feasting, and you will be here, cold and hungry and thirsting. A bit of spiders and rats, and you may be more agreeable. Sure, I'm thinking you'd be more trouble running loose down there than locked in this room."

Fianna looked around. Locked in?

"Ah, you didn't see it, did you, lassie? This room has a door. Not a grand one, sure, but not so rotten that it can't keep you safely tucked away up here as long as I please. By the time I come, you may find Rony handsome and very welcome."

Fianna's eyes followed his as he examined the room. It was bare except for undistinguishable heaps of rotted things here and there. Filth and webs and grime in the large stone room with high ceilings and one bleak window. There was a large fireplace in one wall, full of grit and dust. That was all.

"Indeed, this will do fine, and I can get a bit of rest down below," he said and pulled the slab of thick, old wood that hung in the doorway to the dark hall. "The bar is rusty but it will do. That's good. Good-bye for now, rich and proud wench."

He managed to push the door closed on its corroded hinges, and Fianna heard the iron bar fall into the groove. She was alone. *Alright now, get your mind to work on this situation and "take care of" yourself.*

Her body ached from bouncing on the hard wooden floor of the wagon. With her hands still tied, her fingers tingled, almost bloodless. For a few minutes, she tried to pull at the knots with her teeth, but her efforts were fruitless.

Sliding down from the window aperture, she walked slowly around her prison, to the deep window ledge and the grit-covered floor. She saw some dust-filled cracks, but nothing movable. At the fireplace she leaned over and walked in, looking up. Not a glimmer of light came from up in the chimney. The space was large—big enough to walk into—but the floor was covered with ancient ashes and cinders, rat tracks, and the remains of a few dead birds.

She examined the door, trying to break away the rotted wood with her fingers. She found the wood to be nearly petrified, impossible to crack off. A couple of kicks with her boots were useless. If she got out of the room, where could she go? The only path away seemed to be downstairs into the hands of the tinkers.

With her hands hanging tied together helplessly, she left the door and went to the window. Through the opening Fianna could see far away. The blue-gray outlines of the Wicklow Mountains undulated across the horizon. A patchwork of greens spread out below, traced by streams and rows of hedge. Sparsely dotting the countryside were a few tiny gray cottages, but more frequent were dark spots where evictions had left heaps of rubble.

There were no people for a mile or more, if any at all. It seemed they had traveled all night from Dublin, leaving the city and coming into the open country in the midlands. Marcus could be terribly distressed and alarmed, if not furious with her for being so careless. But how would he know that she was kidnapped? With Fianna's record of willful impulsiveness, Marcus and Brandeen might even be thinking she was off on one of her forbidden adventures.

Directly below the window, she could see only scrub and weeds, vines and thorns among the rocks. This must be Kilalea Castle, long ago cursed by Cromwell with the blood of innocent people, said to be inhabited by banshees and the hooded ghosts of Druids performing sinister rites to Bel. If she could possibly find a way to signal from the castle window, and if someone could see it from so far away, they would only cross themselves and breathe a prayer to ward off evil. Despair poured over her body, leaving her sick, exhausted, hopeless.

The thought of hooded figures sent a chill over her, remembering the one in a monk's robe who had tried to drown her! *He didn't get it done, so he sent the Gypsies!* He, the man, wanted her dead and silent, and would get it done one way or another.

Sounds echoed from below. Fianna smelled smoke from the fireplace downstairs. She heard laughter—Rony exulting over his successful abduction.

Fianna's lips were dry and her tongue too parched to wet them. Her stomach ached. She had never experienced real hunger before. She felt caved in, weak, hurting, and desperately terrified. She could not get away, ever! When Rony was through with her, she would be disposed of. No one would ever think to look for her in the haunted castle.

Her own words tormented her. *"I can take care of myself." Admit it. I cannot!*

Hands tied, locked up, hungry, and thirsty, no way out of this cold gray room, Fianna knew that only a miracle could save her life.

Letting her exhausted legs give way, Fianna slid down to the floor under the window and curled up, raising her suffering hands to her face, listening, dreading.

His knife is so sharp! Dear Saint Brigid, help me!

Something made her take her hands down from her face. Her heart nearly stopped! In the dim light, she could see that someone was in the room with her. Rony?

No. It was smaller. It stood silently in a shadowed corner of the fireplace. She opened her mouth to try to scream, but it moved forward. Fianna blinked in disbelief.

It was a leprechaun!

Chapter 18

The little figure moved forward, out of the darkest corner of the fireplace, and placed his finger on his lips.

It was a man. Perhaps. He was a small, wizened creature with wispy, long gray hair and a neatly cropped beard. The clothing he wore was fashioned from years past—the waistcoat, a cutaway coat with tails, and funny little buckled boots below his breeches. The white cravat wrapped around his short neck was almost in shreds with wear, and it was faded, as was all his costume. Fianna could just make out his figure in the dim light—head too big for his body, tiny hands and feet.

As soon as he could be sure she was not going to scream, the undersized creature moved closer to her.

"Quiet yourself now, lass." His voice was hoarse and rather stiff, as if he wasn't accustomed to speaking much. "Don't move now, and I'll be getting those ropes off ye."

His stubby fingers worked at the cords as quickly as he could, and soon they fell away. Fianna rubbed her numb wrists and stared at him. He gave a sort of muted chuckle.

"Don't make any noise," he whispered. "I'm not sure if sound will echo downstairs. Think the faeries have got you, don't ye now? Or a leprechaun? That's it, child. I'm a leprechaun. Keep silent now and follow me." The best he could, he helped her to her feet.

"Come along then." The little person went to the fireplace, entered its dark depths, and disappeared. Then he stepped back into the dim light. "Come, I say! They are getting fair drunk down there and they'll be coming soon. Come!"

Fianna moved. She was so stiff that she could hardly take steps, and her body hurt all over. At the fireplace where the elf had once more disappeared in the dark, a tiny hand grasped hers and tugged her into the blackness at one side. She leaned over in order to fit into the space and stepped along gingerly, unable to see a thing. Then he left her for a second, and she heard shuffling and then the scrape of stone on stone. If there had been the least reflected light in the place, it was gone. He took her hand again.

"Had to brush away our footprints in the dust or they might be able to tell where we went. With that slab of stone in place, it should be totally impossible to find this ancient passage. Step down, now," he whispered. "Down and down. It's stairs, d'ye see?"

Fianna felt like she must be in a dream. Had she fallen asleep on the cold floor? Was this a hallucination, a frantic imagining? She seemed to be floating in the pitch-dark, each footstep reaching into thin air to find the next level below.

With her free hand, Fianna felt a hard, scratchy wall beside her. Using it to steady herself, she continued to descend the steps, responding to the firm grip of the dreamlike person who led her. Down. Down. There seemed to be no end.

Finally, he stopped. "Hold still now, child. Do not move!"

He let loose her hand. She heard his feet pattering short steps across the floor. Then there was a spark of flint and steel, and a tiny light began to glimmer.

"Careful, now. Look below you."

Fianna looked down. In the candlelight she saw a chasm two feet wide directly in front of her feet. The bottom was lost in inky blackness.

"Step careful, lass. There now, right over the trap. Centuries ago, many a hapless prisoner fell into that hole to God only knows where, but they never came back out. And here we are in my charming quarters."

Standing safely on the other side of the gap, Fianna looked around. It was a large room. As far as the light reached from the stub of candle, she saw chains attached to the walls and lying in rusty heaps on the floor.

"It was the castle keep, down here," he said. "The entrance is just about completely closed up with fallen stones and rubble. I feel secure here away from people.

"Sit ye down here." He laid what had once been a fancy, embroidered pillow on the floor beside her. "There you are. I'll make you some tea. Ye're needing it."

As soon as Fianna released her knees to sit, they began to tremble. She trembled all over. *What's wrong with me?*

"Och, lass, you've had a bad time of it," the little man said soothingly, as he brought a kettle from over an iron pot full of hot coals in the corner. He poured steaming water into a pottery teapot on the table next to Fianna. The table was no more than a board laid across two stones, but it suited the size of the resident there. On the table was a stack of books and a clay pipe. Old cushions and pillows were piled in a corner, obviously for sleeping.

Her host offered her hot tea in a stained beaker; her hand shook as she accepted it. "No wonder it is that you shiver. I heard them talking and laughing about the rough ride they gave you in their wagon. It's an evil family, they are. Not all tinkers are such. And your poor hands—the ropes have left deep welts. I'll do something about that. Take your tea, now. Don't spill it on you. It's thundering hot. It will be good for you."

He steadied the cup with his small fingers as she sipped the bracing tea. It felt so good on her dry lips and mouth, and the hot liquid warmed her inside, making her feel less like she was walking in a fantasy.

"There now, that is real, isn't it? And I'm real too. There are folk such as me in the human race, you see. But sometimes we get tired of being stared at and tormented by mean boys. And there you have it—the reason I live here and have for many years. Those tinkers, they started coming three years ago. Found out that the village people won't come near. The shee live here, don't y'see? That's me," he said with a chuckle. "The tinkers don't know about me a'tall. And I don't let them. I know this castle inside out—every passage and room and cranny. They just come to use it to rest and drink their poteen."

Slowly Fianna's head began to clear. It was real. The stunted little man, dressed like a leprechaun, for sure, in his very old clothes. This was his home, this battered old building. He remained here because he was different, and the outside world was cruel to anyone who was different. They didn't see beyond his size to know the gentle heart of the man who walked bow-legged across the room on his tiny feet to put the kettle back.

Fianna coughed, the warm tea soothing her throat so she could speak. "It's thankful I am that you found me. I had no hope of getting free. That Rony is vicious with his knife."

"I know, I know. Terrible way to treat a lass. I was glad when I saw that he left you in that room where the secret passage is, used by the castle lords to cause unwanted guests to disappear for good."

"Living here alone, how do you provide for yourself? Tea? Food? Everything?"

A hoarse laugh broke from his wide mouth. Fianna looked around quickly, fear in her distressed, brown eyes.

"Don't you fear, child." The man plumped himself down on one of the pillows. "We are in a closed room in the lowest cellar of the building. I can slip out and watch them and listen to them, but they cannot hear us as long as we are here. As to provisions, well now, you know the Little People have to be pandered to. I have a route in the countryside hereabout. Ah, the loaves and bits of meat and barmbrack left on the doorstep of many a farmhouse to keep the faerie curses from making the cattle sick or spoiling the milk. Sometimes the door is left open when the cows are brought in from the meadow. I slip out from behind a rosebush and into the house. They never miss a spoon of tea leaves or a cup of stirabout meal or even an old clay pipe. To tell the truth, there's many a torn-down cottage where once was not exactly prosperity but at least sufficiency. My borrowing takes longer now between occupied dwellings. I say a prayer for every house I visit."

"I see." Fianna laid her head against the stone wall behind her and closed her eyes. Gradually the trembling lessened. This whole experience—the kidnapping, the threats and mistreatment of the Gypsies, the appearance of a real live leprechaun—was beginning to take on reality. "God bless you, sir, for saving my life."

"Indeed, indeed." He smiled and settled himself on the cushion, tiny knees up under his chin. "Now then, what must we do with you? The tinkers will soon be looking for you. Or, maybe they will look for your dead body on the ground under the window. With a bit of Irish luck, they will be afeard and clear out, believing that the banshee carried you away. If they think you have freed yourself somehow, perhaps they will think you'll be sending the RIC to arrest them. I feel you should be prudent and stay here awhile, at least a day and a night. I can take you out in the dark tomorrow morning."

"I can't stay! My family is frantically looking for me, sure! I've been such a careless fool, so sure that I could control any problem that came my way. I have helped the Fenians, and now someone is after me. The tinkers said they would be *paid* for murdering me!"

The dwarf frowned thoughtfully. "Much goes on these days that I don't understand, but if it means helping the Irish Republican Brotherhood, then I would be glad to do what I can. Years ago, before I gave up the struggle of living in the outside world, I saw the hanging of the croppy boys and the starving of women and children. Let us wait through the day and see what the tinkers will do. If they go away, I can spirit you out across the meadows and get you on your way. If they don't leave today, we will have to wait and try to slip out in the dark tonight. You must rest while you can. Lay your head down and sleep, so your strength will build up again. I will go now to see what is happening."

The kind gentleman raised himself up off the cushion and started toward the dark opening of the stairs. Turning, he said, "By the by, could I be knowing just who I have rescued this day?"

"Fianna Fitzmichael is my name, coming from Cullymor in County Mayo. And you, sir, what is your name?"

"Fitzmichael, is it? I know of your family. It would be your grandfather perhaps who took his whole company west of the Shannon in order to smuggle Indian maize from America to feed the people? He was a good man. My name is Jonathon Brehon."

He was gone. Fianna leaned back once more, praying that somehow she would get out of here and away from the tinkers. Somehow she must find out who was behind this vendetta against her!

But she was so tired. She took one of Jonathon Brehon's pillows and laid her head down on it on the table. She couldn't sleep. How could she sleep when her life was being threatened? But she had to rest herself just a bit.

She opened her eyes. Suddenly she realized that she had been asleep. The miserable position she took to lay her head on the pillow on the low table had cramped her body and woken her.

Jonathon wasn't there! How long had he been gone? She paced the floor by the pitiful candlelight. It was sad that he lived here in this dark dungeon, pinching bits of food and provisions in order to survive without being tormented.

He seemed so kind. But was he? Of a truth, she was at his mercy now, trapped in this horrible, dark place. *What if he made a deal with the Gypsies? What if they caught him? What if he never came back?*

Panic was setting in. All of her confidence and common sense was getting her nowhere. She continued to pace, moving about the bare, dusty cavern. Looking at the hanging wall chains made her feel eerie, wondering about the men, and possibly women, who were manacled and tortured there.

What time of day was it? Or was it day? Perhaps it was night. It was impossible to tell while she was buried down in the depths of the building. She kept her eyes fixed on the dark staircase across the bottomless chasm.

When finally she heard steps coming, her nerves were so tight that she nearly jumped. With a hearty chuckle, Jonathon appeared out of the opening and hopped over the crack in the floor.

"Sure, it's as I thought. They are frightened. Looking everywhere they are, even for tracks under the window, as if you could jump down all that way and run off. I will go and check on them again to be sure they are packing up to leave."

"No!" Fianna burst out. "Don't you leave me here alone again! I can't bear it."

The little man studied the girl's face. "Of course, I will not. It did not come to my mind that you would feel trapped down here. I apologize, lass. Let me give you a bit of soda bread and honey. You must be starving. And here now, let me be looking after those hands of yours. Cruel those ropes were. Poor child."

Fianna dropped to sit on the pillow again. She felt foolish, allowing her fears to mount until she exposed her vulnerability so shamefully. Silently, she gladly ate the food he offered.

He went to a small chest in the corner and came back with a very small pot of ointment. "It is only dog fern and shamrock and butter—but see now, I'll just touch a bit of it on your poor bruised and scratched wrists. There now, you'll be feeling better."

"Jonathon Brehon, are you a healer?"

"My father was a physician," he admitted. "I learned much from watching him. No one would ever let me treat them, of course. They thought I had been cursed because of my size. After my Da died, I escaped from the life they call civilized society."

She sat at the low table, munching on the hard soda bread. They talked, Jonathon and Fianna, for a long while. Slowly she felt better, but still constrained and without control.

At last he said, "It must be dusk by now. I will slip out and see what goes on."

"Please..." Fianna began.

He patted her hand with his stubby fingers, gentle and reassuring, "I won't be long this time, child. I promise. But I cannot take you with me to spy. It is not safe. I will be back quickly. Just rest and wait."

In minutes he was back, pleased. "It appears they are gone, lass. Their stuff is cleared out. You are wearing boots. That is good. We have some walking to do. Now follow me very slowly and carefully."

He led Fianna through a pitch-black maze of staircases and deep, narrow halls. Finally, they came to a heavy wooden door. When he pushed it open, fresh cool air caressed her face, and she breathed deeply with a sigh.

"Hist!" Jonathon whispered and she held her breath. "They could still be about, you know."

Jonathon went first, stepping gingerly out of the doorway. Fianna did not move out of the shadow of the doorway for several seconds. Things outside seemed almost bright after the inky blackness inside. Clouds overhead reflected a soft, very pale glow on the weeds and thicket. She and Jonathon seemed to be coming out of the side wall of the castle, not far from the main gateway.

Suddenly a dark figure leaped out of the brush and yanked Jonathon into the air!

"I knew it! I knew someone used this path! What have I here? By all the saints, it's a *púca*!"

Chapter 19

Rony had the small man by one arm, holding him high while he crowed over his captive. In his other hand, he was holding a pistol. Fianna's pepperbox!

She burst out of the doorway and leaped on Rony's back, scratching his flesh, tearing his hair! He dropped Jonathon and tried to fend off the harpy that clung to his back, reaching for his eyes with her fingernails. The pepperbox went flying to the ground. Instantly Jonathon caught the situation and retrieved the pistol.

"There now!" he shouted. "You can let him go, lass!"

Fianna jumped away and scurried around behind Jonathon. He held the pistol firmly in both hands, pointed toward the strong young man.

Rony laughed. "What a fool! A pint of a man with a pint of a gun! Da," he called out. "Come and see what we have here!"

From the front corner of the massive stone building they heard the sound of running feet. Quickly, Fianna took the gun out of Jonathon's hands.

"Do you think it is funny, you filthy thug? I have it now and I will use it!"

Suddenly Rony lunged forward. Instantly the pepperbox shot fire into the dark, and he fell.

"My leg! You shot my leg!" Dark blood covered the upper leg of his trousers.

"It will be your head next," she declared. "I doubt you have a heart to strike." Then to Jonathon, "Let's go!"

"Fianna Fitzmichael, you witch! I'll get you for this night, I will!" Rony screamed after them as Fianna and Jonathon disappeared into the bushes.

They could hear the Gypsy father shouting with alarm for his son. Fianna grabbed Jonathon's hand and ran through the brush toward the front of the castle, causing his feet to barely touch the ground. She stumbled in the dark tangle of woody stems and vines but kept going, determined to circumvent the Gypsy man. She could hear him crashing down weeds along the wall on his way to help his screaming son.

As they broke out of the underbrush near the front wall, Fianna saw the woman standing there with a lantern, peering into the darkness, shouting to her husband, to find out what had happened. In the faint light, Fianna saw that the old horse was bridled, ready to be hitched to the wagon.

Without stopping to think, Fianna let go of Jonathon and ran to the woman. She turned the woman's shoulder around to face her and slapped the Mam as hard as she could, knocking her to the ground, speechless. Then she ran toward the horse.

Jonathon's legs were short but quick as he followed the girl. Fianna jumped astraddle and hoisted Jonathon onto the horse's back behind her. Pulling up the long buggy reins, she kicked its flanks, and the startled animal charged off down the hill into the night.

When he caught his breath, Jonathon shouted, "Where are we going?"

Sure that they were far from catching distance of the tinkers, Fianna slowed the horse to a walk. "I'm not sure. I don't know where we are."

"If you follow this bohreen we're on, you'll come across the railway after a bit. The road there leads to Ballymoyne."

"Ballymoyne." Fianna was relieved. "The tinkers have brought us right into the territory where I first met them. I know the blacksmith at Ballymoyne. He is a friend of Jamie's. I think I can trust him, but of late I'm not sure who I can trust."

"I understand."

They trailed along the bohreen and then the road, able to see in the pale moonlight filtering through thin clouds overhead. It was still dark when they reached the smithy. Fianna and Jonathon slipped down off the horse, and Fianna led it inside. She found a bucket of water next to the anvil, used to cool hot metals, she surmised. Many folks, she knew, believed that the blacksmith's water would heal ailments. It shouldn't hurt a horse. Tethering the animal in the back of the shop, she set the bucket down so he could drink. Then she led Jonathon into the tiny room where she had met with Jamie. Lighting a half-burned candle that sat on the rough old table, she dropped onto one of the crude chairs and rested her elbow on the table, chin on her hand. The teapot sat there, partly filled with cold tea. She and Jonathon shared the strong tea gratefully.

Sitting still, Fianna's eyes began to blur. She shook her head to try to clear her thoughts.

"Now then, lass, if you'd be adding it up, you haven't had any real sleep for nearly forty-eight hours," Jonathon figured. "Lay down your head on your arms on the table. It will be somewhat comfortable, although far from a perfect resting place. Close your eyes and I will keep watch. Sleep now."

Before the gentleman finished speaking, Fianna had done just that.

It was some time later when she heard Jonathon's voice from the outer room. "Stop right there, young man. I can see you are not the smithy, so what are you wanting here?"

Startled words came from the visitor. "I beg your pardon. Who are you? And what are *you* doing here? To tell you the truth I am searching for a young lady, a friend of mine. She came up missing in Dublin two days ago. I was going to ask the smith if he has seen her."

"Jonathon?" Fianna stood in the doorway, holding onto the frame for support. She began to slide down, eyes closing against her will.

Neill caught her up in his arms and stepped into the room. Still holding her, he sat down on a chair and drew her onto his lap, arms around her, smoothing her tangled hair away from her face.

"What do you want, Neill? I don't trust you or anyone anymore. Only Jonathon. He saved my life. Someone wants to murder me…"

Her head fell against the collar of his tweed jacket, and her eyes closed. Neill looked at Jonathon. "Are you Jonathon? Is that true?"

"Jonathon Brehon is my name. I am grateful to say that I happened to be in the right place when help was needed. A family of tinkers held her captive—"

"Wait now! A family of tinkers, did you say? *Again?*"

The kindly gentleman hopped up on the chair opposite him and told Neill what had happened to Fianna as she had told it to him. He explained his presence in the crumbling old castle. "I suppose I will not be able to return to my small hovel in the dungeon there and will be obliged to find a corner somewhere else in the world. Ah well, so does life go on."

"My name is Neill McBride, Mr. Brehon. Don't you worry yourself about a place to live. It will be arranged, I promise you. You have my greatest thanks for what you have done to protect this impulsive lass. It's not an easy task."

Jonathon's wide mouth smiled. "It has been my pleasure, sir."

"I have another promise to make." Neill frowned thoughtfully. "I will promise you and Fianna and everyone else that that particular family of tinkers will never bother anyone again, especially that bloodthirsty lecher called Rony."

Fianna was starting to come awake. "Neill, what brought you here? How did you know I was gone?"

"I just got off the train here in Ballymoyne. I went to the hotel to see how you survived the cold water of the Liffey, and I met with your uncle, Marcus Maher."

"The river! Neill, it was you who kept me from drowning! It *was* you, wasn't it?"

"Just another case of being in the right place." He verified her idea without taking a bow. "What were you doing out there in the fog? How did you happen to fall in?"

"I didn't fall in. I was pushed!"

Alarm filled Neill's hazel eyes. He held her more closely. "And now you have been abducted by the same tinkers, and they said they were paid to do it?"

"They did."

"When your uncle told me you were missing, I remembered that the smithy was a friend of yours, so I came to see if he knew where you were. I thought perhaps you had left Dublin on your own to find your Jamie boy."

Annoyed, Fianna tried to sit up, but she found Neill's arms around her, holding her snug to him. "There you are now, thinking I did this for a lark! I suppose Marcus thinks so too."

"It seems not so. He is quietly sending out word to all of his connections to look for you."

Jonathon spoke up, "If you will excuse me, I believe I will step out and light up my dudeen."

"Jonathon, don't leave! Please stay with me."

The little gentleman looked at her sharply. "I will stay nearby if you really want me."

"I do."

He nodded and left the room.

Neill still held Fianna gently, but securely, on his lap. She was wide-awake now, her dark-brown eyes gazing up into his. He studied her face, her eyes, the smooth curve of her chin, her soft, full pink lips.

"You are very right—you should never trust anyone, not even me." Then he bent slightly and covered those lips with his own.

It was so gentle, so tender. Fianna relaxed against his chest and gave herself fully over to the delight of it. Neill held her there, his lips roaming over her face and her hair, and she loved it. No one had ever given her such adoring touch. She wanted it to go on forever, and with Neill McBride!

His dear, boyish face. His pixilated grin. Those hazel eyes that could crinkle with fun or be so seriously intense, his kindness—all those things had become precious to her. *He cares for me!* Out of all the pretty girls he must know, girls like those on the train with their giggles and flirting, it was Fianna that he wanted to hold in his arms like this, Fianna in her grubby, creased, and soiled clothes, her skin dusted with grit and spiderwebs.

They were not brotherly kisses. She could feel vibrant desire as he held her close, her body against his. Touching her cheek and her eyes, before once again claiming her lips, his kiss was ardent and hungry. Yes, she could spend her life in his arms with purest joy. She raised one hand and let it wander up to caress his cheek and move softly around to the back of the crisp red-gold waves of his hair, resting there and urging his tender embrace.

Finally, as he pressed another kiss on her willing lips, he said, "What about Jamie?"

"Jamie?" She couldn't say more. She didn't know what to say. *Jamie.* The love of her life. She had pledged herself to marry him. *What of Jamie?* She drew back from Neill, confusion in her eyes.

"I see." Neill carefully set Fianna on her feet and rose from the chair. "Daylight has come now. Now that I know you are alright, I will be going along. Get in touch with your uncle right away and, by all that is holy, let him keep you safe!"

He left the room. Fianna heard him bidding a polite goodbye to Jonathon out in the barn. That was it.

Shaken, she dropped onto the chair. When Jonathon entered the room again, he found her sitting there, her eyes staring at the old teapot but not seeing it, confused, troubled. Jonathon settled into the other chair and toyed with his dudeen, certain that he should not intrude into her pondering.

Fianna's mind was churning. It was true—she always thought she loved Jamie. Well then, she *did* love Jamie. He was her dearest companion, her mainstay throughout her growing-up years in the lonely country in the west of Ireland. She wanted nothing but the best for him. His dreams, his plans, must come true.

But Neill! To him she was a new person, not an old friend with long-promised obligations. Neill took her as she was, and he seemed to adore her. The love he expressed for her came from some kind of sudden, magical magnetism that simply happened. She couldn't deny that the same wonderful attraction had seized her also. Now that she understood about her darlin' Jamie, she must see Neill again, soon! She had to explain. And she would have to tell Jamie too—shamefully after all of her declarations of desperate love. Would he understand?

She became aware then of the little gray-haired man sitting across from her, patiently pulling on his pipe. How sad that such a wise, kindhearted, and generous person should have to live like a thief, and in a cold stone castle keep at that. She decided that she would take him to Leaghanor, if she ever got there herself. He would be treated like the hero he was, God bless him! His very old clothing was torn, from Rony's mistreatment and snagging bushes. She would do something about that too.

It was a while later that another voice broke in. "By the saints, what have we here?"

The smithy stood in the doorway, staring at Fianna in the dim early morning light. "Why, it's our spy lass! And tired out by the look of her. Cold too, I swear. I'll make you hot tea."

As he started to move around the table to get to the tiny stove and the kettle, he saw Jonathon. The burly man's eyes went wide.

"What is it?"

Instantly, the little man stood up to his full height. "I'm not an 'it,' I'll have you know!"

Fianna smiled. "Sure and he is not. He is a fine gentleman, and he saved my life. Smithy, will you be greeting Jonathon Brehon, my hero."

"Hero, is it? I'll have to be hearing about this. Jonathon Brehon, I'm thinking you'd like a hot cup too, wouldn't you now?"

Carefully, to be sure he left room for the small person, the huge blacksmith edged around the table to the stove. Dumping several chunks of peat into the belly of it, he stirred them up to a nice little blaze.

"I'll go to the stream down back and get water. Make yourselves comfortable."

By the time he came back, Fianna and Jonathon had stretched themselves and moved out of the small room into the back of the shop. They stood, concealed from view of the street by remaining deep in the shadows of the sooty barn, as they watched the night begin to fade into morning. Fianna's fine white silk blouse was soiled, and her heavy riding skirt was wrinkled unspeakably. She wanted to take off her boots, but the floor of the shop was covered with tools and bits of iron and soot.

"A message was coming to me yesterday," the smithy said. "Told me that Marcus Maher is worried to distraction about his favorite niece, he is. And I'm hearing things, Fianna Fitzmichael." He put the kettle full of fresh water on the stove and came back into the open barn. "I'm hearing there is a grand uproar about the Parliament trying to do away with our Parnell. Saying it may have something to do with you."

"Did you hear such foolishness, now?" Fianna stood still, staring out of the barn.

"Also told me that your life may be in danger, missy. Where have you been these past two nights?"

"No matter. I'm here now."

"So then—Marcus wants to find you right away. I thought me that Jamie might know, so I sent for him. He's sure to be coming along soon."

"Will he then? I will be glad to see him. We're needing to talk."

The smithy looked at her with curiosity. "I wonder that you are not more happy to be able to see him."

She didn't respond to his wondering. "I'll go make the tea," she said.

Fianna could hear Jonathon making polite conversation with the blacksmith while she spooned tea into the pot. Then she heard the big man say, "Ah, here comes our Jamie boy now!"

Stepping out of the tiny room, she moved quietly toward the opening, careful to stay in the shadows so that no one outside could notice her.

Jamie came walking along the street on the other side of the railroad tracks, nearing the shop. Then, out of the morning mist, a figure appeared from around the corner. A girl.

Fianna saw Jamie's ruddy face break into a smile. His steps quickened. His sturdy arms encircled the lass. He pressed her into the recess of a doorway. Fianna saw his head bend down to kiss her. As Jamie drew back, she could see the girl more clearly. It was the housemaid of the Whytes. It was Annie.

Chapter 20

Annie. The country girl—the one who shyly told Fianna that her sweetheart wanted a horse farm, a place to breed fine horses. Of course. They were going to gather together enough money to buy horses. Annie was working at the Big House, suffering abuse and insults, to add her pitiful stipend to Jamie's earnings.

Memories came flooding into Fianna's mind. Jamie's statement that he had a contact person at the Whytes' house. Apparently Annie was not employed there only for the bits of money. His frantic protestations when Fianna suggested that his "contact" might not be there anymore. Pieces started falling into place like a puzzle coming together.

Indeed, Jamie had stood up for Fianna with the Fenian men. He had virtually put his life in danger to protect her. He had said he loved her and he surely did—"like a sister," he always said. And so it was. Jamie was her dearest friend. But not her lover.

She watched the pair, so clearly in love, standing close together in the growing morning light, and Fianna felt a certain sadness. She wanted to do so much for Jamie. But it was plain that Annie would be the one to help him realize his dream.

And there was something else flowing into Fianna's heart. Was it...release?

The smithy had stopped gathering his tools and materials for his day's work. He stared at Fianna intently, studying her dark eyes, her mouth not compressed in anger as he had expected. He remembered her full-blown affection for Jamie when last she was at his shop.

Watching the couple across the street sharing their love so sweetly, he murmured to Fianna, "I'm sorry, lass."

"It's alright," she answered. It was indeed *alright*.

Jamie crossed over the railroad tracks alone, Annie having disappeared around the corner again. As soon as he entered the blacksmith shop, he stopped and stared. The emotions that played on his face were almost amusing. There was embarrassment that Fianna had surely seen him kiss Annie. Surprise to find Fianna there. And relief, unbelievable relief, that Fianna *was* there!

"Fianna! Praise the saints, you are alive! I heard you disappeared right out of Phoenix Park in Dublin. I thought you might be off on one of your escapades, but then they told me someone had tried to drown you! What is going on?"

"Don't you know?" Fianna had a sudden flash of temper. "Time and again I was given messages from you. 'Jamie sent me,' they said. I have smuggled and lied and found myself in grand trouble because of you. Now I see that you are in love with Annie. *You used me!*"

"Fianna, I never did that! I don't know what you are talking about. Dear God, has someone been putting you in danger by telling you that I wanted you to do things? Tell me!"

He held her, his hands tight on her arms so she couldn't move, his round, ruddy face close. His alarm, his anger at her jeopardy, was very real, like a brother berating a beloved sister. She saw it now.

She stopped fighting. She laid her head against his thick chest.

"They must have been using us both, Jamie. To tell the truth, I didn't mind it all. It was an adventure and, if I could trouble those pompous Anglos, I was glad to do it. I think I only got angry because I thought you were using my love for you to serve the Brotherhood."

Jamie grinned, that wide, endearing grin. "So it's alright, my loving little Annie, just as long as I didn't make a fool of you? That's my girl, my Fianna!"

"Someone is trying to silence me, Jamie." She pulled away from him and addressed both him and the smithy. "Someone deliberately pushed me into the Liffey to drown. And the tinkers who kidnapped me said that someone, a man, was going to pay them to kill me. If it were not for Jonathon, I would be tortured and killed by now. Jonathon? Where is he?"

"He just slipped out the door," the blacksmith said.

"Jonathon!" Fianna ran to the door. Jamie followed.

She caught sight of the little man sliding into nearby gorse at the side of the meadow. Catching up with him, she grasped his coattails.

"What have you got there, a leprechaun?" Jamie came up behind her.

"Indeed," she said with a smile. "A magical gift from the saints. Jonathon Brehon, my dear friend, why are you going away?"

"You're not needing me now," the small man replied with dignity. "You have many friends, I see. I must be going about my own ways."

"Jamie, this gentleman saved my life. He rescued me from the Gypsies. In so doing, he no longer has a home. Please tell him he will be welcomed as a hero at Leaghanor. He can live there in comfort."

Jamie assessed the situation quickly and, with typical Irish hospitality, he said, "Indeed you will, sir. Come along with us now."

"I think not," Jonathon insisted. "Big people can't help but laugh at me, and I won't have it. I'm an Irishman. I have my pride."

"Mr. Brehon," Jamie reached down and took Jonathon's right hand. "If you have saved our own Fianna, you will be greatly respected at Leaghanor. If they laugh at you, they will have to deal with me. Please come inside now. People will be about the town soon, and I want Fianna out of sight. And you too."

They hurried back inside the shop and the back room where the kettle bubbled merrily.

Over cups of bracing tea, Jamie studied the situation.

"I think you would be more safe at Nan's until Marcus can come for you," he said thoughtfully. "But getting you there is a problem. In the daylight you would be easily noticed. If those Gypsies or that one, the man who hired them, learn where you are, they might be bold and attack you without warning."

Nothing was said for a while. The only sound was the ring of the blacksmith's hammer out in the shop while they thought over the problem, Jamie and Fianna sipping their tea at the table and Jonathon perched on a stool near the stove.

Then Jonathon mused, "I have never seen a lady ride so disgracefully and so skillfully astride a horse as this one. No one might take note of a young man riding with you, Jamie."

An hour later, two young men left the smithy's on horseback, one with a bag of flour over the saddle in front of him. The other wore an old American Civil War wide-brimmed campaign hat pulled down low to shade the eyes. There were many of those old hats around, brought by American soldiers who had come to Ireland after the war.

Fianna had discarded her petticoats and tucked her riding skirt into an old pair of brawn trousers that the smithy kept at the shop. They were so large that she had to tie them with a scrap of rope to keep them up. The jacket made of drugget cloth that she donned over her white silk blouse was ancient and filthy from hanging in a corner of the sooty shed.

The riders, Jamie on a horse borrowed from the smith and Fianna on the tinker's cob, cut across the meadows instead of following the bohreen to Crazy Nan's. After reaching the far side of the first hillock, Jamie shook loose the bag on his lap and Jonathon sat up, sputtering.

"The flour dust in that bag is choking," he said, coughing. "I'm not sure I want to be carted about like a rabbit!"

Jamie laughed and helped the little man adjust his seat so that he faced forward on the pommel, a more dignified position.

"We won't be too long riding," he said. "We'll be at Crazy Nan's in a bit."

"This Crazy Nan," Jonathon said. "Who is she? Has she a story?"

"She has." Jamie told the gentleman Nan's tragic tale while they rode. "Lost her husband in the Mitchelstown Massacre, she did. And then she was tossed out into the road without kith or kin to help her. The other evicted farmers took pity on her and made her a house of sorts under a mound. It's a damp cave, but there's no other place for the old woman. She's got the countryside thinking she's gone mad over her troubles and that she's consorting with faeries and demons."

"So she behaves like a witch to deter people from coming around. I understand." Jonathon's pale-blue eyes grew soft with empathy. He, too, used the superstition of the country folk to gain protection and privacy.

They arrived in front of the pitiful wattled cave and dismounted quickly. Nan met them at the door with broomstick at the ready. She looked at the strange rider with suspicion until Fianna tossed off the broad-brimmed hat, shook out her auburn hair, and smiled. Then Nan saw Jonathon, and her yellow-green eyes stared. He took note of the woman's straggly white-and-red-streaked hair, wrinkled face, and odd-spaced teeth as he politely said, "God bless this house and all here."

"Nan, old girl, let me introduce this gentleman who only yesterday saved Fianna's life." Jamie spoke quickly before Nan could embarrass the small man. "This is Mr. Jonathon Brehon."

Jonathon stepped forward and extended his stubby hand. Nan took it, hesitantly at first, but then with an awkward curtsy. She seemed to recognize a worthy human being in the diminutive person with his courteous manners. Nan set the kettle on the hearth while they told her the story of Jonathon's heroics.

"So it's a castle you've been living in. Like a king you'd be then."

"Not at all, kind madam," he denied gently. "It was in the dungeon I had to live because of the tinkers. I got along well enough. Like you, madam, it was necessary to become a *púca*."

"A *púca* indeed." Nan nodded her head and went about her chores. Her manner seemed different from the feisty hag she usually portrayed. Fianna watched in wonder. Then she realized that Nan understood Jonathon's feelings of being different. The old woman was making an effort to let him know that he was respected in her home.

When invited, Jonathon hefted himself onto a chair at the table. With careful good manners, he gratefully partook of tea and stirabout, taking care to thank the provider of the feast. Nan only nodded and went back to her hearth.

"I heard about the plot to murder Parnell," Nan said. "*Himself* told me this morning when he came to see was tonight's plan still ready. The whole country is in an uproar about it all."

"Have any of the fellows been about, Nan?" Jamie asked as he took a cup of tea from her hand.

"None but that fool Conor. Talks too much. Telling everyone about the girl's spying at the Whytes. Oh, and the Cobbler was here about four days ago. Conor reminded him about tonight, you know." She gave Jamie a knowing look.

"The Cobbler?" Fianna asked Jamie.

"We call him that because he makes pampooties, those all-of-a-piece boots with no heels, to sell to support his family up in Mayo. Evicted from his farm last year. He's fair outraged about it all. Hates the British. He isn't around all the time because he goes to take care of his family."

"Conor told him about the Whytes, he did. The Cobbler thought it was grand."

Fianna felt her face go numb. "Conor is telling *everyone* about me?"

Jamie read Fianna's thoughts. "So everyone is knowing that Fianna spied for the Brotherhood? And someone is trying to get the girl killed. Not only was she kidnapped at the asking of a stranger, she was pushed into the Liffey to drown!"

Nan's yellow-green eyes grew wide in her weathered face. "Conor has told no one but the Fenians. They are all under the oath of secrecy. It should go no farther."

"What about *himself*? You are the only one who ever saw him, Nan. What do you think?"

Himself, the one who was the link between the superiors in the Brotherhood and outlying Fenian crews, came occasionally to bring news or leave instructions with Nan for the unit who met there. "I don't believe that. He moves about alone, walking. And he never heard Conor's tales. No, I will not believe he is an informer."

"Fianna, the man who tried to drown you. Did you see him? Would you know him if you saw him?" Jamie was trying to put together some kind of pattern.

"I'm not sure. All I remember is a tall figure in a monk's hood. I heard his steps behind me, soft shuffling sounds they were, and I turned..." She shivered with fear at the memory.

Jonathon scraped the last spoonful of stirabout from his bowl and devoured it avidly. "Has any information ever leaked before about your Fenian activities?"

"Has it?" Jamie frowned in thought.

Nan's eyes widened. "What about Larkin and O'Dwyer getting caught? We never figured out how someone knew they were going to meet the gunship in Kerry. They suffered dreadful in the Whytes' cellar before this girl found out where they were and the fellows rescued them from the RIC guards on the road."

"True," Jamie murmured. "We planned their trip right here at this table, and they went from here. No one had time to tell it around."

There was silence for a few minutes while they thought about the collection of facts.

Finally, Jamie put into words what they were all thinking. "We could have an informer in *our crew*." He paused in thought. "Whoever is behind all this knows who Fianna is and that the tinkers gave her a ride. That could be anyone who was here the night she came to us."

"Or anyone John Conor told," Nan said.

"Has the lass met all of your Fenian men?" Jonathon asked. "No? Then perhaps she should remain in hiding where she can see them all tonight. She is a bright one. Perhaps she will recognize something that you do not."

"Will you do that, Fianna?" Jamie asked.

"To do something that will explain all of this, I will be delighted! I will hide outside, myself and Jonathon, in case the Gypsies told that evil murderer about him. If I see anything that will help, I will tell Jamie."

"Will you be wearing those clothes?" Nan asked, eyeing the coarse, baggy trousers and the bulky drugget jacket.

"I will. Right now I must stretch out and rest." Fianna dropped the jacket onto a chair and lay down in the cupboard bed. "Don't be closing the doors on me this time."

In the late afternoon, the light steps of small feet wakened her. She opened her eyes, not sure where she was. Fianna had caught sleep in so many different places in the past weeks that she had to get her bearings again. Turning over on the rough hay-filled mattress, she caught sight of Jonathon coming in the door with an armful of small branches. She didn't dream it. She really had been kidnapped by tinkers and saved by a leprechaun!

The little man smiled at her. "Just gathering a few kippeens for the fire for our hostess. I apologize if I woke you."

"Time you woke up anyway, lass." Jamie sat at the table. "You'll have to be leaving the house soon because the men will be coming when dark is setting in. I'll want you to go around to the stone wall behind this mound. They won't see you down by it in the dark. I'll be making some excuse to go out after they've all come and bring you back. You can peek through that window hole and tell me what you see."

Fianna crawled into the bulky jacket again, checking to be sure her pepperbox still hung heavy in the pocket. Jonathon sat on the stool beside the hearth smoking his dudeen. He looked so comfortable there, as if such a place was suited for him.

He got up as soon as Jamie started for the door. Quickly, Jamie took them outside the thin wattle walls and around the drumlin to a place where a drystone wall bordered a bog. He left them there, curled down behind the stones, out of sight.

Darkness fell over the meadows, and the pair was able to stretch a little from their cramped position. Several times they heard horses' hooves walking stealthily past them toward Nan's hovel. No voices.

It was an hour after pitch-dark when they heard Jamie softly call, "Fianna!"

She left Jonathon in hiding and met Jamie in the dark. Silently he led her to the wall of the cave. The wattle was so thin that she could hear muffled voices inside.

Fianna stood still, listening carefully. She could hear Eamon and John Conor clearly, and other voices discussing a raid they were going to make in the night.

Suddenly cold chills went over Fianna's body! She grasped Jamie's arm.

"That voice, the one who is speaking really low and hoarse. I've heard it before. Dear saints, Jamie, it's the man I overheard talking to Mr. Whyte about the prisoners!"

"Are you sure, girl?" Jamie whispered. "Which one is he?"

Carefully she raised up and peered through the broken wattle hole of a window.

"He's not talking now," she whispered. "I can see Eamon at the table. There is Conor, talking as usual. The voice was not him." She listened for seconds as several fellows made comments. "Wait! I hear him. Over by the hearth."

A man in an old suit and pampootie boots moved in front of the fire to get a straw to light his pipe. The glow from the burning peat reflected on his face as he leaned over. A thrill of fear and fury darted through Fianna!

It was Spencer George!

"Jamie, it is Major Spencer George. He always talks so loud and bossy that I didn't recognize his voice whispering to Mr. Whyte! He was on the train when we bogged down, but I didn't know who he was. It's a lot older he is and heavier, but the same arrogant, conceited man that I knew as a child. He saw the tinkers ride away with me, so he knew them! I smuggled letters across on the ferry from England, and he was with me the whole way, never knowing I had them. Then the newspapers came out exposing the assassination plot. When he came here and Conor told him that I was at the Whyte house to spy on them, he must have realized that I was working with the IRB, and I was the only one not searched at the dock. I'm sure he was the one who tried to drown me. Those boots, those shuffled footsteps! Oh, he'd want to kill me, sure!"

Fianna's desperate whispers flooded out, leaving Jamie stunned. When she moved aside, he leaned to the window. "Which one is he?"

"There by the hearth—the tall man in a brown suit and pampootie boots."

Chapter 21

"T he Cobbler! Him with his tales of the Peelers tormenting his family and how he hates the Anglos! Wait here, out of sight. I'm going to tell Eamon."

Through the hole in the wall, Fianna saw Jamie enter and lean over to whisper to Eamon. Instantly, the atmosphere in the room became electric! Everyone in the room could feel trouble in the air. Nan stopped fussing with some potatoes at the dresser and fixed her yellow-green eyes on the men.

Spencer, sitting in the corner now, tried to keep his casual attitude, but it was clear that he could feel a difference in the men around him. He rose up from his seat and stretched. "I have a need to go outside for a bit," he said in that hoarse, deliberate soft brogue, his shark-white smile showing behind his beard.

"I think we all had best go out." Eamon smiled easily. "We are about to leave right now to get on about our evening's work. Shall we go, lads?"

The men got to their feet, moving mechanically toward the doorway, all the time watching Eamon for signals.

Quickly, Fianna retrieved the tinker's horse from its tether in the scrub trees by the wall. She mounted it and, hair tucked tightly under the big hat, quietly joined the group in the dark. Jamie glanced at her disapprovingly, but he kept silent.

Somewhere in the dark, Jonathon waited. Fianna hoped he would go into the cave house after they left. Nan stood in the doorway, watching.

Jamie and Eamon kept close to the Cobbler as they rode out of the yard. The group followed the bohreen for a while and then headed off across the lea, leaping low hedges and stone fences. Fianna kept up with them easily.

They reached a stile, and Spencer pulled up his horse. "I believe my old horse has gone lame, boys. I'm thinking I'd best pass up tonight's pleasures. I'll hold you up."

"Not at all!" Eamon was too cheery. "Looks alright to me. Try him a bit longer, Cobbler. He'll be alright."

The other riders looked at Eamon. Now they saw which way the wind blew. They rode on, keeping a wary eye on the Cobbler.

They came to a road. Spencer's horse reared and began to head off down the path. Jamie caught up with him and grabbed the reins.

"Sorry, friend," the Cobbler jokingly apologized. "I told you this old horse has something wrong with him tonight. Got away from me."

"Too bad," the stable master's son said. "I've dealt with many an animal like that in Connaught. Used to work the stables there at Leaghanor in Mayo, d'ye see?"

Spencer said no more. The mention of Leaghanor seemed to make him more alert. He regained the reins and rode back to the group, with Jamie right behind.

After that the Fenians rode hard on toward their goal. Spencer George rode with them, silent.

At last Eamon pulled up and the riders clustered around him. "Here we are, boyos! A fine, dry barley field. Where are the torches?"

The field stretched out long up the grade in front of them. Something looked familiar to Fianna. Then, far across the bristling grain, she saw the lights of a Big House. Whytes!

"Thinks he will bring in soldiers and Orangemen to harvest his crops, does he—after driving all of his tenant farmers out in the road to starve," Eamon said. "Let's see him take in harvest after tonight!"

Greasy rags wrapped tightly around wooden clubs ignited quickly after the first one was lit with a match. Torches were passed around. When Conor came to hand one to the extra rider, he caught sight of Fianna's face in the fiery glow.

"By all the saints—!" he started to shout.

Fianna yanked the blazing club from his hand. "Get on with you!" she hissed.

He looked once more and then turned his horse and secured himself a torch.

Within seconds the entire half-mile edge of the barley field was afire! The men rode up and down the stone fence, reaching down and touching the fiery wands to the crackling dry grain. Eamon had calculated just right. There was a stiff breeze blowing across the field away from the firebrands. And, as it does, the fire made its own wind. It went roaring up the grade, devouring every stalk and blade and kernel. It was grand!

The Cobbler hung back, without a torch, pretending to have trouble controlling his mount. Fianna enjoyed her share of the arson, and then, seeing him apart from the rest, she rode over to him.

221

Everything around them was brilliant from the light of the flames. He had no trouble identifying the strange rider.

"You!" His voice was his own again—loud and brassy. "You little bitch! You made a fool of me on the boat! You were smuggling those letters yourself! I don't know why you didn't drown or how you got away from those tinkers, but I know you're going to die now before you can tell the RIC how I was tricked!"

He came at her on his horse, reaching for his pistol.

"I did it all!" She tossed off her hat, letting her hair blow in the wind. "And you tried to kill me!" she shouted over the roar of the flames. Out of her coat pocket came her pepperbox. "Now we will see who is going to die!"

A noise of horses came from up on the rise by the house. In the light of the fire, the Fenians saw a squad of dragoons racing down the track beside the barley field. Eamon shouted to his men. They turned their horses and ran off into the dark night.

Fianna turned her pistol to the spy, but it was too late. He kicked his horse and went flying up the hill through the thick red smoke toward the soldiers, waving his gun. Fianna could hear him shouting his identity and orders at the horsemen.

If he tells them...! If he identifies the Fenian men and Nan and all of it...! For a split second, she wanted to ride after him and kill him before the soldiers could hear his words. She knew she would die, but he had to be stopped!

Before she could do it, gunfire bursts exploded from the guns of the dragoons charging down the hill into the smoke. Spencer George dropped off the saddle and lay motionless on the ground, killed for a Fenian by British troops.

Chapter 22

After the glaring flames of the raging fire, the dark was blinding as Fianna turned her horse and headed into the night. Someone pulled in beside her.

"Fianna, keep riding. I'll be behind you!"

Without a pause, Fianna pushed her horse ahead. The fields and meadows opened up under a sliver of moon that hung over the horizon. She could hear Jamie's voice behind her, urging her on, faster! The crack of gunfire rang around them.

She heard a shout of pain! Looking back, she saw Jamie fall from his horse. The animal kept going on over the knoll.

Instantly, Fianna jumped off her horse, slapped his rear to send it on, and ran back to Jamie.

"Girl, get on with you! They'll be on us in a second!"

Ignoring his words, Fianna rolled him over into the hedge alongside the meadow. She pushed him back under the edge of the bristling bushes and squeezed up against him to hold him there, hiding herself in the black shadow.

The two held their breath as the dragoons came pounding up the incline. Leaping over the hedge, their hooves barely missed the pair skulking below. Then they were gone, following the wildly racing horses. Fianna didn't speak until she could hear the soldiers still riding hard on a distant lea.

"You're hurt, Jamie. Where?" she whispered.

"I've a burning pain in me side. Blast, it hurts, Fianna!"

Carefully, Fianna crawled to her knees and felt along his side. It was wet. Blood!

"Lie still, Jamie. I'm going to bind the wound with something and try to stop the bleeding. This wouldn't have happened if you hadn't waited for me."

"Sure, you would have done the same. We're a team." His words were forced between efforts to breathe.

"We are that," she agreed tenderly.

The horsemen were coming back, walking their mounts. They must have seen the riderless horses and decided the raiders were somewhere about. Fianna crushed herself against Jamie again under the hedge. She could hear them grumbling.

"They'd be long gone on foot by now."

"Could be running off in any direction."

"We'll have to wait until morning and see if we can find tracks."

"Well, we got one of them for sure. Laying up there on the road with a dozen bullets in him. Must have run at us to try to protect his stupid men. It will be interesting to see who he is."

It will indeed. Wait until you find you have killed your own informer. It's a grand, ironic way for him to go!

Waiting for the dragoons to go along back to the Whyte house and out of earshot, Fianna began to be frantic about Jamie. His breath was getting shallow. As soon as she could, she rolled out from under the bush and pulled him into the open.

"Jamie!" she whispered. "Jamie!"

No answer. He lay still. Placing her head against his thick chest, she could hear his heart beating. He wasn't dead, but he was unconscious. How long before he would lose too much blood and die? No, not Jamie!

How was she going to get him out of there? How would she get help? The horses were long gone. The farmhouses along the road, even if she found one near, were broken to rubble with no people anyplace near.

She leaned over her helpless friend and whimpered, "Jamie, Jamie!"

"Ah, that magic name."

Someone was standing beside her. When she looked up, all she could see was the figure of a man, his face unreadable in the moonlit shadow of his wide hat.

Neill McBride dropped to his knees beside Jamie. Nudging Fianna aside, he began feeling for Jamie's injury.

"Ah, good. It's only a flesh wound. The boy is lucky he is so stocky built. It didn't penetrate any organs."

"Neill!" Fianna was astonished. "What are you doing out here?"

"Apparently I'm looking after you and your sweetheart, as always," he said.

"Jamie is not my sweetheart," she announced angrily.

"Indeed?" He cast a quick look in her direction. "It appears otherwise."

"Never mind that. How are we going to get him away from here?"

Neill stood up and removed his short tweed jacket. Then he took off his white shirt, revealing lean but well-developed chest and arms. He began to rip the tail of the shirt into wide strips.

"First we've got to block the bleeding. Then we can move him."

Kneeling beside the unconscious boy, Neill packed folds of the cloth against Jamie's side where the bullet had gone through. With Fianna's help he lifted the limp body and tightly wrapped the strips around him. Fianna watched Neill working swiftly to bandage the badly bleeding wound on Jamie, her brotherly friend. Neill was shirtless, leaning over the boy, and she wished she could touch that lean body of his, run her hands over the smooth, rounded muscles as he lifted and worked to save Jamie.

How she loved the boyish red-haired young fellow, who was proving himself to be as compassionate as he was canny and loyal. Would she ever be able to make him understand about her affection for Jamie? She just had to!

Neill gave a soft, low whistle like a bird call. The sound of hooves stepping came from a cluster of trees not far away, and a horse moved across the grass to Neill.

"Bless that smithy. He can always find a good horse when it's needed," Neill said.

Jamie stirred and moaned.

"He's coming awake," Neill whispered. "Quiet now, boyo. We're going to put you on a horse and get you back to Nan's."

Neill put on what was left of his shirt and started to lift Jamie. The wounded boy became alert. He gritted his teeth to keep from groaning in pain as Neill and Fianna pushed him up onto the saddle.

Suddenly he went limp and Neill said, "Fianna, you're going to have to ride and hold him on."

Neill put his jacket back on and began leading the animal, but it was hard to keep Jamie on the back of the horse. His body leaned against Fianna, and her arms were around him, but he kept sliding, comatose. Sometimes Neill had to stop leading the horse and help her get Jamie steadied again.

At first they moved in silence, Neill leading the animal around hedges and through brooks and under bridges. On occasion it was necessary to toss aside the loose stones of a fencerow to make a path through for them. They were afraid that their voices would carry and be heard by the dragoons or police. Finally, once they were far enough from the Whyte plantation, Fianna ventured a question.

"Neill McBride, what were you doing out here in the night? Did you see the raid?"

"I did."

"And did you see Spencer George go riding up the hill to be shot down by his own army?"

"I saw that."

"He was the informer, Neill. I recognized him sitting so big and smug right in among the Fenians. He was the one who pushed me into the river and sent the Gypsies to kidnap me. He was the one who had Larkin and O'Dwyer captured and tortured in the Whytes' cellar. Did you know that?"

"I did not."

"The justice of it all," she murmured. Then, "Tell me now, how did you come to be out here?"

"Watching."

"Watching, is it?" Fianna rode for a while before she spoke again. "Jamie boy is slipping again, Neill. Will you help me?"

Neill stopped the horse and came to Fianna's side. He pushed Jamie back up onto a fairly secure seat. Fianna got another grip on the unconscious boy, and her hand chanced to touch Neill's. She let it lie there for a second, next to his fingers, which Jamie's blood still stained. *Dear Saint Brigid, how I love those hands. How I love the man.*

They started off again.

"So, it's watching you're doing, is it? Sure, it seems you do a lot of that. On the boat—"

"It's my job. Someone had to keep an eye on you in the crossing. You had important papers."

"Was that the only reason?"

"At the time, it was."

"And now?"

"Now I'm thinking we'd best attend to the business of getting your Jamie to a bed and bringing him around."

His words were crisp. Obviously he was angry at the affection she showed toward Jamie Rooney, her "love."

Fianna wanted to talk to Neill. She wanted to tell him that her very real love and concern for Jamie was a fellowship grown from years of close companionship. She wanted to explain that Fianna herself had realized the difference the first time Neill had kissed her in the hall of the hotel. The glorious embraces she shared with Neill in the blacksmith shop had confirmed the exciting magnetism that enveloped her.

And the more she knew of him—his loyalty to the Brotherhood, his competency and honor in time of jeopardy, as he was exhibiting right then—the more her romantic captivation was multiplied by admiration and pride. Remembering his tender sympathy for Eileen McCrory on the train, his determination as he held Fianna above the strangling dark water of the river—thinking of all that, overwhelming love filled her heart.

Could it be that it was because he was only the second unattached man she had ever met? Not likely. There was Robert Whyte and the other fellows on the train. There were dozens of good-looking young men fawning over her at the ball. Not one of them appealed to her.

She would tell Neill that Jamie was already very much in love with little Annie, the maid. But not right now. He would think that Fianna only turned to him after Jamie had found someone else. *How to tell him? How to make Neill McBride see the difference?*

"Why were you there when I fell into the river in Dublin?"

"Watching. I had a feeling that, once Major George learned that the story was out, he might put things together and realize it was you who smuggled the letters. He wouldn't want his superiors to know."

"You were there in the night to protect me. Oh, Neill—"

"It's my job," he said again.

Fianna knew better.

It took almost an hour for Neill to walk the horse to the hovel where the Fenians huddled, waiting. Just outside the door, Neill stopped.

"Listen to me, Fianna. I'll not be going inside."

She started to protest, but he hushed her. "No one in there knows me. And you're not to tell them, do you hear? As far as they will know, you took care of Jamie and brought him here by yourself. Will you do that now?"

Things started to fall in place in Fianna's memory. "I will," she said.

Neill disappeared into the dark stand of trees. Fianna gave a low call for help, and the Fenians first peered out the hole and then came tumbling out the door. They helped take Jamie down off the horse so Fianna could slip to the ground. With Eamon carefully holding his head and shoulders, Jamie was carried into the hovel and laid on the straw mattress of the cupboard bed.

"You're a grand girl," Eamon told Fianna. "Bringing him here that way. Looking at his wound, I believe he is going to be alright. I don't know how you did it by yourself."

"I will not believe that she did," Nan said, but the men did not take note of her statement.

"It had to be," Fianna answered. "Sure, I couldn't leave my Jamie out there to be found by the dragoons and shot or hanged."

"Well then, now we know that neither you nor Jamie were caught, so the soldiers don't know about us. But we have to worry about that filthy spy, the Cobbler. He knows every one of us."

"I think not." Fianna told them about the wry fate of the grand informer, Major Spencer George, brought down by the guns of his own men. "He must have warned Whyte about the raid. He had soldiers there waiting for you."

Relief flooded the room. The weary men gathered their hats and pipes and left in ones and twos, crowing joyfully over the success of their mission to cripple Whyte's power and lose his money. They went to their families, wherever they were, in bogs or stone huts or camped in a ditch, happy to have cast at least one stone for the independence of Ireland and her people.

As they left, Eamon spoke sharply. "John Conor, since you're loving to tell tales, you can go to the smithy and give him the report of this evening's work. He needs to know."

Without a word, Conor ducked his head, accepting the chastising that had begun while they waited in fear in the hovel. "I will that, Eamon. I will do it."

Eamon turned to Fianna, "I can't believe you did this all alone."

"Believe it."

Nan spoke up. "It was *himself* that helped you, wasn't it? He knows everything."

"Jamie is here, and he's hurt bad. That's all you need to know." Fianna closed the discussion, and Eamon slipped out into the wee hours before the dawn.

Nan walked over to a dark place behind the rough stone fireplace. "Jonathon Brehon, they're all gone now, and I'm thinking this boy here is needing you."

Quickly, from the shadows, Jonathon came hurrying on his short bowed legs into the candlelit room. He picked up the stool from its spot at the hearth and, placing it beside the cupboard bed where Jamie lay, he stood on it to reach the unconscious boy. With deft little fingers, he unwrapped the crude bandage and investigated the wound.

"He's bled a lot, but that's good. His body can make more blood, but likely it won't become infected. Nan, would you be having some clean cloth for a new bandage. This one is saturated. And is there any foxglove growing hereabout? I'm needing to make a poultice."

"There is foxglove," Nan said, bringing an old muslin apron from the dresser. "But will potato do until I can gather the weed come daylight?"

"For now, it will do. Thank you, kind lady."

Nan quickly peeled a fresh potato and brought him thin slices.

He completed the dressing of Jamie's side and said, "I wish we could get some food and water down him. He's going to need strength."

The rickety door to the hovel opened just then, and Neill McBride stepped inside. Nan's eyes grew wide.

"It's *himself*! I knew it was *him* that helped you."

With an affirmative nod in Nan's direction, Neill addressed Fianna, "How is your Jamie? Will he live?"

"He will," Jonathon interjected. "But I worry that he is unconscious. It may be the weakness from loss of blood, or it may be his young body is in shock from the pain. We really must bring him around soon."

Jonathon began to work over Jamie, trying to wake him up. He bathed the boy's face in cold water. He called his name loudly. He even pinched Jamie on the cheek. Still, Jamie lay motionless on the rough bed. Jonathon laid his large head against the boy's chest time and again to be sure his heart was beating and he was breathing.

As Neill stood beside the fire watching, Fianna bent over Jamie, calling his name. No response.

Finally, Fianna headed for the door. "I know someone who needs to be here now!"

"Where are you going?" Neill followed her outside into the early morning twilight.

"I'm going! Don't try to stop me." Fianna shoved her hair up under the old campaign hat and readied to mount Neill's horse.

"Here then," Neill said. "If you are determined to go, then I must go too. There is another horse tied in the grove of trees. Take that one."

They rode side by side across the meadows, past empty, broken-down farm cottages and sheep like black-faced cotton balls wandering in the fields. Fianna in her grubby, too-big clothes and Neill in his incongruous student's suit, his missing shirttail barely hidden by his short jacket.

"Is it the Whyte house you're going to?" Neill asked. "We can't go there, and sure, not together like this!"

"I must!" Fianna answered. "That is where Annie is. Jamie needs her!"

Neill said no more. He rode silently beside Fianna, frowning thoughtfully.

They mounted the last hill, the place where Jamie had left her to walk into danger in the Whyte mansion weeks before. From there they should see the plantation house. But instead of the elaborate red-brick mansion, what they saw were ugly blackened walls and smoke rolling from the remains of the Whytes' fine house.

Drawing the reins, Fianna and Neill stopped and stared.

"It must have been the flames from the barley field that set the house on fire," Neill surmised.

Fianna became frantic. "What of Annie? She could be hurt in the fire! Where is she? I must find her!"

"Annie? The little housemaid?"

"Jamie needs his Annie, and she should be with him when he is at death's door like this! How will I find her?"

"So that's it. I'm seeing your reasoning now, Fianna. I'll go. Robert Whyte thinks I am his friend. I'll find the family and make the excuse that I was out fishing and heard about the fire and came to help. I'll find Annie and, if possible, bring her to you. Wait here behind this hill."

Fianna waited, jittery and anxious. Watching Neill ride off across the knoll, she loved him all the more. It seemed that he understood now that Annie and Jamie belonged together. But did he know that Fianna had fallen in love with him—that her affection for Jamie had not transferred to Neill, but had sprung fresh and new, altogether different? Somehow, she must tell him and make him believe it.

In a surprisingly short time, Neill was back, riding double.

"Here's your lass!" he said with a grin. "Found her hiding under a little haystack away from the house. The Whytes are on their way to England. It's defeated, they are! But they were determined to take Annie with them. Good maids are hard to find. She had to run away!"

The girl's sandy hair was grayed with smoke. Her cheeks appeared too red, as if singed.

"Praise the saints!" Fianna rejoiced. "Did you tell her about Jamie? Let's go!"

Annie, perching sideways in front of Neill on his horse, clutched a handful of mane and hung on. "Hurry! Please hurry. Oh, my poor Jamie!"

In the early morning light, they were able to ride hard over the countryside and back to the cave hovel. As soon as Neill swung Annie down from the horse, she headed for the door.

"Jamie! Where is me Jamie?"

Once inside, Annie went directly to the crude bed where her sweetheart lay. Falling on his chest, she cried, "Jamie, me love, please don't die!"

Everyone watched with sympathy as the little housemaid yearned over her love. It was heartbreaking. Neill looked at Fianna. He saw empathy in her wide brown eyes.

Then Jamie moved! First his right arm tried to rise. With a moan of pain, he dropped it onto the mattress again. That side was wounded. His left arm rose up and encircled the girl's shoulders, and the pair of them clung together in a sweet embrace.

Nan and Jonathon smiled. Tears shimmered in Fianna's eyes. She hurried out of the house. Neill found her leaning against one of the young trees. She had shed the coarse, oversized jacket. He smiled at the network of rope around her waist and over her shoulders that held up the loose trousers.

"Does it hurt you so much to see your Jamie in love with someone else?" he asked gently.

"Not at all!" Fianna burst out. "Jamie has been my companion and protector almost all of my life. I will always love him like a brother. It makes me happy to see him and Annie together, so tender. She is a sweet little thing, and they will do well."

Then a shaft of sunlight broke through the morning cover of clouds, and Fianna realized what she looked like. Her white silk blouse was smeared with soot off the old jacket. Dirt and smoke made her face gray and grimy. The light turned her windblown, ragged auburn hair into copper strings.

She turned away from Neill and laid her forehead against the tree. "It's a mess I am, for sure," she moaned. "I wish you couldn't see me like this."

Neill McBride took her shoulder and turned her back around. "Fianna Fitzmichael, you are a valiant, brave lass. In my eyes, you're more beautiful now than ever before."

Chapter 23

His lips had just touched hers when they heard the sound of buggy wheels coming down the bohreen. The pair of them shrank into the cluster of trees and watched while a small two-seated conveyance pulled up before the hovel. A slim gentleman in a black suit alighted, bringing a bag with him.

"It's Marcus!" Fianna ran to him.

"Who is this thin, ragged boy in filthy clothing?" Marcus teased when Fianna rushed to hug him. "Why, by all the saints, it's my pet! Thank God!"

He hugged her tight. "Fianna, I've been nearly out of my mind. And from what the smithy tells me, I had a right to be. I blame myself. How could I have let you out of my sight in the crowd at the races? Bless all the saints for bringing you back to me alive!"

"Marcus, this is Neill McBride."

"Ah, indeed. We met before at the Clarence. And were you the one who found her?"

Neill shook his head and smiled. "I apologize, sir. The lass was one step ahead of me all the time, until Jamie's injury slowed her down."

"Jamie injured? How bad is it? Will he recover? That boy is like one of the family at Leaghanor."

An odd look of affirmation was in Neill's grin. So Fianna had told it true. Jamie was indeed like a brother.

"He will be fine now that we brought his Annie to him. Wait until you meet her, Marcus. She is a dear," Fianna said.

"My pet, you are a disgrace! The wire I received from the smithy said only, 'Come. Bring clothes.' By that, I gladly assumed you were alive, but I certainly wondered about the request for apparel! Now I see what he meant. Brandeen packed up what she thought might be needed. Here then."

He handed Fianna the carpetbag.

"Many things have happened these past two days," Marcus continued. "I received a wire from a certain Mr. Hinkley in London. He tells me that Horace Nugent suffered a stroke on learning that his letters were exposed. The grand MP will never be able to speak or care for himself again—he was paralyzed. Those two partners of his and a lot of others in the Parliament are loudly proclaiming innocence and forgery. Our little Rodney has asked Hinkley to take over control of all the family holdings."

"Mixed blessings," Fianna commented. "That abominable spy, Spencer George, was shot by his own soldiers last night. We're finally rid of him. And I can tell you this—Mr. Hinkley and Emily Nugent will not be too sorry to hear it."

"Indeed?"

Inside the dwelling, Marcus noted the miserable earthen walls and the muddy floor before he was introduced to Nan and Annie. It was then that Fianna noticed the change in the room. Gone were the shriveled and rotting apples and potatoes. The dresser was scrubbed. The table was clean, and the crockery beakers for tea were spotless. Nan's straggly hair was covered with a neatly tied kerchief. Her apron was clean. Dry rushes were strewn over the soggy floor to make walking more bearable in the cave.

Wisely, Fianna made no comment about the difference. She couldn't help but wonder what had brought about the change. Surely, Nan had neglected the hovel, which was truly not much different from the floorless, dark cottages that the farmers had always lived in, but her neglect had reflected hopelessness and loneliness. Had something given her hope—a reason to take hold and try to make the dreadful dark hole tolerable?

Jamie was awake, holding Annie's hand. Marcus told him in no uncertain words that the boy had done his service to the IRB for now and would be going back to Leaghanor as soon as he was able to travel.

"You and this pretty lass here may raise horses on one of the farmsteads. I will inform Father Tobin to prepare to announce the banns for your wedding. And your Da is that worried about you."

That big smile spread across Jamie's ruddy, freckled face. Annie's rosy cheeks, recently washed of the gray smoke, fairly glowed with relief and anticipation. Jamie would have his horse ranch and she would have Jamie.

Fianna introduced Jonathon to Marcus, as she had to so many others. "Jonathon, please meet my uncle, Marcus Maher, whom I have told you about. Marcus, this is Jonathon Brehon, a very wise and kind gentleman who saved me from the Gypsies. He is my hero and also something of a doctor. He is tending to Jamie's wounds."

Marcus leaned down, and the two learned sages respectfully shook hands.

"I am pleased to meet you, Mr. Maher," Jonathon said. "Aside from the wonderful recommendations of your loving niece, I believe that some years back I heard a bit of rumors about a certain Captain Moonlight. I'm sure you heard such rumors also."

Marcus's thin face broke into a knowing smile. It was obvious that he had a compatriot in the gray-haired gentleman who stood before him in a newly mended but very outmoded suit.

"Ah, indeed, I did hear some such things at one time. Now then, I'm hearing from the smithy that you protected Fianna by hiding her in your residence in the dungeon of an old castle. Mr. Brehon, I would be honored if you, too, would come to Leaghanor to live. We could use a good physician."

"The gentleman stays here!"

Everyone turned startled eyes on Nan. She stood by the hearth, broom in hand, yellow-green eyes staring belligerently at them all.

An embarrassed smile tugged at the corners of Jonathon's wide mouth. "The kind lady has invited me to stay here. We are both alone. I may be able to help a bit around the place. Besides," he said with a puckish twinkle in his old eyes, "every witch needs a leprechaun at the least."

So that's it! There was the reason for the tidying up in the miserable hovel. Fianna felt a surge of affection for the strange couple—Nan and Jonathon—lonely, odd characters, joining together to make life better for them both.

"So be it," Marcus said, smiling. "However, there is an unused cottage waiting for you both in Cullymor townland if you should decide to move out of this place."

"I'll not be moving from here yet," Nan said firmly. "Not until I can no longer be of use to the Fenians. I still have a debt to pay to the Anglos."

Marcus turned a questioning look at Jonathon.

"I find that I have the same inclination." Jonathon nodded his head. "A bit of inconvenience is well worth it if I can be of some use to the patriots. I want to stay here in the middle of it instead of hiding away from society."

"God bless you both!" Marcus was emphatic. "I am proud of you. Perhaps I can help in some way. Perhaps by sending some supplies or food to you—"

"Or ammunition," Nan interrupted.

"Or ammunition," Marcus amended his offer cheerfully. "Such items will be delivered to the smithy for you in just a few days. Now then."

Throughout all of the conversation, Marcus had been glancing at Neill McBride. The young man stood silently by the doorway. His expression reacted to all of the developments, but his eyes followed Fianna constantly. It was not hard to see where his interests lay.

"Fianna, it's shameful the way you look," Marcus scolded. "I'm thinking it's time you got yourself cleaned up."

She laughed and gave her best friend a grand, sooty hug. "Indeed, dear uncle. Nan, where is that holy well you told me about?"

"Just over the stile of the stone wall and out to the maybush, but you can't be washing—"

"Only my face and hands," Fianna said with a laugh. "That is allowed, isn't it?"

She picked up the carpetbag and slipped out the door. Finding the stile, Fianna climbed over it, and there it was—a pretty flowered maybush a little way out in the meadow.

Inside the cave, Marcus said, "Neill, without getting too close, would you go out and be watching in the direction Fianna has gone? I'm seriously troubled about all that she has gone through. I don't want to lose her again, do you see? I love that child."

"I will and gladly."

At the lovely artesian well that ran a tiny stream into a small depression in the earth, Fianna opened the carpetbag. The clothing fairly burst out of it, it was packed so tight. There were two shifts—one straight and simple muslin, the other mildly ruffled linen. A pair of soft leather slippers was a welcome sight. Fianna hadn't been out of her riding boots for three days.

A hairbrush lay in the bottom of the bag, and a lacy snood. The gown she pulled out was crisp cotton—yellow with tiny sprigs of printed flowers, narrow lace at the elbows, and a scooped neckline.

Brandeen had never failed to be sure that Fianna had nice things and good care after her mother died, and the thoughtfulness of the woman when she packed the bag was evidence of that. The bright-yellow gown would bring out the copper tones of Fianna's full, dark hair. Fianna must try to be more agreeable with Brandeen...maybe.

Stripping out of the coarse, dirty clothes down to her chemise and pantaloons, Fianna knelt by the well. Cupping her hands, she drank the fresh, cold water. Then she poured the sacred water over her face and arms. It felt so good. Perhaps the legends of healing power in holy wells were true.

As she smoothed away the soot and grime off her arms and throat, her weariness diminished. *Thank you, Saint Brigid. You know what I need and why, don't you?*

After she donned the soft garments, she sat beside the well, brushing her long auburn hair, smoothing the tangles that were left from bunching it up under the big hat. Slipping her locks into the white lace snood, she tied it on top of her head in a perky bow. She used the clear pool of water for a mirror. Her reflection was satisfactory.

Fianna stuffed her boots and once-white blouse and wrinkled skirt into the bag, and, swinging it in her hands, she rose to go across the meadow to Crazy Nan's hovel.

In the distance, she could see a figure sitting atop the stile.

As Fianna neared the stone fence, Neill saw a vision of a pretty girl in a flowing yellow gown crossing the rich green lea. Her dark hair caught the sunlight in smooth, shining copper tones. He stood down off the steps as she approached. He said nothing.

Fianna was silent too, but the expression in those large brown eyes told him what he wanted to know. He reached out and laid his hands on her shoulders, gently, tenderly drawing her close to him.

"Fianna Fitzmichael, I love you."

"And, sure, I love you. It was there the first time you kissed me. I was confused. I never felt that way before, not with Jamie. Neill McBride, I—"

Her words were lost in his kiss. He held her in his arms, touching her soft face, his lips caressing her closed eyelids, where the dark lashes shadowed her cheeks. Fianna clung to him, almost afraid to let him go. It was sweet, tender, sensitive.

She studied his face, that deceivingly youthful, disarming appearance. She loved the way the sun glinted on the thick waves of his red-gold hair, the curl of that surprising golden cowlick over his forehead, the sprinkling of freckles on his cheeks.

"I will love you forever, my lass—only please tell me, where did you hide those letters? You can take my word, I looked over your person very well, and I saw nothing that could have been a packet of papers. Where were they?"

A lilting laugh came from Fianna as she whispered the answer in his ear. His hazel eyes went wide.

"In your bustle!"

Acknowledgments

From the old Celtic crosses to the beauty of the fields set apart like patchwork quilts to the delightful Irish people, I have loved every minute of my study of Ireland.

With a history and culture so delightful and intriguing, how can I not thank Ireland for its enchantment and smoldering quest for freedom and Home Rule. That spirit for freedom burned brightly for the American people and helped to win and establish our liberty.

About the Author

Bettse Folsom/2009

Helen Walsh Folsom was born in Armourdale, Kansas, on a snowy early morning the day after All Hallows Eve, in the home of her great-grandmother, Lizzie Walsh Smith.

Helen knew she was part Irish, and she grew up delighting in both Irish and Scots-Irish music, dance, movies, theater, and characters.

When she left community-service work several years ago, Helen knew that there was one thing she wanted to do: research Irish history and write books. She studied, and the more exhaustively she studied the more enchanted she became with Ireland's legends and whimsical characters, as well as the isle's most prominent figure, Saint Patrick.

Helen found so many quirky and fun-filled little facts about Ireland, she wanted to share them. She published her first book, *St. Patrick's Secrets, 101 Little-Known Truths and Tales of Ireland* in 2002.

However, as charmed as she has been, Helen also understood the battle against injustices that the Irish people have had to endure. It is not surprising that her next book was *Ah, Those Irish Colleens!* published in 2003. It helped to explain the history of Ireland as seen from the women who affected it. This book was listed for several years on the bestseller list of the former Irish Books and Media.

Helen has visited Ireland and still remains enchanted with the country, its ancient history, and charismatic people. Many times she met friendly, down-to-earth people who loved her American heritage and were not too shy to inquire, "Are you spending your money?"

With her current book, *Fianna, The Dark Web of the Brotherhood*, Helen developed characters who, to her, represent the Irish people. Strong, intelligent, smart, and stubborn, but always with a flare of independence.

One of Helen's favorite limericks about the Irish is from G. K. Chesterton,

From the great Gales of Ireland, Are the men that God made mad, For all their wars are merry, And all their songs are sad.

Made in the USA
Charleston, SC
08 November 2012